ARALUEN AND ITS NEIGHBOURS

Frozen Sea

Northern Wastes

WESTERN OCEAN

Greystone Forest

SKANDIA

Hallasholm

Eastern Steppe

SONDERLAND

Stormwhite Sea

Skorghijl

TEUTLANDT

PICTA

Castle Araluen

Narrow Sea

La Rivage

Montsombre

ALPINA

ARALUEN

GALLICA

CELTICA

IBERION

TOSCANA

ASLAVA

ENDLESS OCEAN

The Constant Sea

Sea of Rostov

ARRIDA

BOOKS BY JOHN FLANAGAN

The *Ranger's Apprentice* series
Book One: *The Ruins of Gorlan*
Book Two: *The Burning Bridge*
Book Three: *The Icebound Land*
Book Four: *Oakleaf Bearers*
Book Five: *The Sorcerer in the North*
Book Six: *The Siege of Macindaw*
Book Seven: *Erak's Ransom*
Book Eight: *The Kings of Clonmel*
Book Nine: *Halt's Peril*
Book Ten: *The Emperor of Nihon-Ja*
Book Eleven: *The Lost Stories*
Book Twelve: *The Royal Ranger*

The *Ranger's Apprentice: The Early Years* series
Book One: *The Tournament at Gorlan*
Book Two: *The Battle of Hackham Heath*

The *Brotherband* series
Book One: *The Outcasts*
Book Two: *The Invaders*
Book Three: *The Hunters*
Book Four: *Slaves of Socorro*
Book Five: *Scorpion Mountain*
Book Six: *The Ghostfaces*

Discover more at **www.worldofjohnflanagan.com**

RANGER'S APPRENTICE: THE ICEBOUND LAND
A CORGI YEARLING BOOK 978 0 440 86740 1

Published in Great Britain by Corgi Yearling,
an imprint of Random House Children's Publishers UK
A Penguin Random House Company

Originally published in Australia by Random House Australia (Pty) Ltd

This edition published 2008

16

Copyright © John Flanagan, 2005
Cover design by Tony Sahara. Cover illustration © Shane Rebenschied

Penguin Random House is committed to a sustainable future for
our business, our readers and our planet. This book is made from
Forest Stewardship Council® certified paper.

Printed and bound in Great Britain by Clays Ltd, Elcograf S.p.A.

Corgi Yearling Books are published by Random House Children's Publishers UK,
61–63 Uxbridge Road, London W5 5SA

www.**randomhousechildrens**.co.uk
www.**totallyrandombooks**.co.uk
www.**randomhouse**.co.uk

Addresses for companies within The Random House Group Limited can be found at:
www.randomhouse.co.uk/offices.htm

THE RANDOM HOUSE GROUP Limited Reg. No. 954009

A CIP catalogue record for this book is available from the British Library.

RANGER'S APPRENTICE

THE ICEBOUND LAND

BOOK 3

JOHN FLANAGAN

CORGI YEARLING

To Penny, who set such a high standard

One

The wolfship was only a few hours from Cape Shelter when the massive storm hit them.

For three days, they had sailed north towards Skandia through a sea that was calm as a millpond — a fact appreciated by Will and Evanlyn.

'This isn't too bad,' Will said, as the narrow ship cut smoothly through the waters. He had heard grim tales of people becoming violently sick on board ships at sea. But he could see nothing to worry about in this gentle rocking motion.

Evanlyn nodded, a little doubtfully. She was by no means an experienced sailor but she had been to sea before.

'If this is as bad as it gets,' she said. She had noticed the worried looks that Erak, the ship's captain, was casting to the north, and the way he was urging *Wolfwind*'s rowers on to greater speed. For his part, Erak knew that this deceptively calm weather heralded a change for the worse

— much worse. Dimly, on the northern horizon, he could see the dark storm line forming. He knew that if they couldn't round Cape Shelter and get into the lee of the land mass in time, they would take the full force of the storm. For several minutes, he assessed speeds and distances, judging their progress against that of the onrushing clouds.

'We're not going to make it,' he said finally to Svengal. His second in command nodded agreement.

'Looks that way,' Svengal said philosophically. Erak was glancing keenly round the ship, making sure that there was no loose gear that needed to be secured. His eye lit on the two prisoners, huddled in the bow.

'Better tie those two to the mast,' he said. 'And we'll rig the sweep steering oar as well.'

Will and Evanlyn watched Svengal as he made his way towards them. He had a coil of light hemp in his hand.

'What now?' Will asked. 'They can't think we're going to try to escape.'

But Svengal had stopped by the mast, and was beckoning urgently to them. The two Araluans rose and moved uncertainly towards him. Will noticed that the ship's motion was becoming a little more pronounced and the wind was increasing. He staggered as he made his way to Svengal. Behind him, he heard Evanlyn mutter an unladylike swearword as she stumbled and barked her shin on a bollard.

Svengal drew his saxe knife and cut two lengths of cord from the coil.

'Tie yourselves to the mast,' he told them. 'We're in for the mother of all storms any minute.'

'You mean we could be blown overboard?' Evanlyn asked incredulously. Svengal noted that Will was tying himself to the mast with a neatly executed bowline knot. The girl was having some trouble, so Svengal took the rope, passed it around her waist and then secured her as well.

'Maybe,' he replied to her question. 'More likely washed overboard by the waves.'

He saw the boy's face go pale with fear.

'You're telling us that the waves actually . . . come on board?' Will said. Svengal darted a fierce, humourless grin at him.

'Oh yes indeed,' he said, and hurried back to assist Erak in the stern, where the captain was already rigging the massive sweep oar.

Will swallowed several times. He had assumed that a ship like this would ride over the waves like a gull. Now he was told that the waves were likely to come crashing on board. He wondered how they could possibly stay afloat if that were to happen.

'Oh God . . . what is that?' Evanlyn said softly, pointing to the north. The thin dark line that Erak had seen was now a roiling black mass only a quarter of a kilometre away, sweeping down on them faster than a horse could gallop. The two of them huddled close to the base of the mast, trying to wrap their arms all the way round the rough pine pole, scrabbling for a grip with their fingernails.

Then the sun was blotted out as the storm hit them.

The sheer force of the wind took Will's breath away. Literally. This wasn't a wind like any Will had ever known. This was a savage, living, primeval force that wrapped around him, deafening him, blinding him, punching the breath out of his lungs and preventing his taking another: smothering him as it tried to claw his grip loose. His eyes were shut tight as he struggled to breathe, holding desperately to the mast. Dimly, he heard Evanlyn scream and felt her begin to slip away from him. He grabbed blindly at her, caught her hand and dragged her back.

The first massive wave struck and the wolfship's bow canted up at a terrifying angle. They began to rise up the face of the wave, then the ship faltered and began to slide — *backwards and downwards*! Svengal and Erak screamed at the rowers. Their voices were plucked away by the wind but the crew, their backs to the storm, could see and understand their body language. They heaved on the oars, bending the oak shafts with their efforts, and the backwards slide slowly eased. The ship began to claw its way up the face of the wave, rising higher and higher, moving more and more slowly until Will was sure they must begin the terrible backwards sliding motion again.

Then the crest of the wave broke and thundered over them.

Tonnes of water crashed onto the wolfship, driving it down, rolling it far over to the right until it seemed that it would never recover. Will screamed in absolute animal terror, then had the scream cut off as freezing salt water hammered against him, breaking his grip on the mast, filling his mouth and lungs and hurling him along the deck until the fragile cord brought him to a stop, swirling this way and that until the mass of water passed over and around him. He was left flapping on the deck like a fish as the ship righted itself. Evanlyn was beside him and together they scrambled back to the mast, clinging on with renewed desperation.

Then the bow pitched forward and they went plummeting down the back of the wave into the trough, leaving their stomachs far behind and screaming with sheer terror once more.

The bow sliced into the trough of the wave, splitting the sea and hurling it high above them. Once again, water cascaded over the deck of the ship, but this time it lacked the full force of the breaking wave and the two young people managed to hold on. The water, waist deep, surged past them. Then the slender wolfship seemed to shake itself free of the massive weight.

In the rowing benches, the relief crew were already hard at work, baling water over the side with buckets. Erak and Svengal, in the most exposed part of the ship, were also tied in place, either side of the storm sweep. This was a massive steering oar, half as big again as one of the normal oars. It was used instead of the smaller steering board at times like these. The long oar gave the helmsman greater purchase, so he could assist the rowers in dragging the head of the ship around. Today, it took the strength of both men to manage it.

Deep in the trough between waves, the wind seemed to have lost some of its force. Will dashed the salt from his eyes, coughed and vomited sea water onto the deck. He met Evanlyn's terrified gaze. Weakly, he felt he should do something to reassure her. But there was nothing he could say or do. He couldn't believe that the ship could withstand another wave like that.

Yet another was already on the way. Even bigger than the first, it marched towards them across several hundred metres of the trough, rearing and massing itself high above them, higher than the walls of Castle Redmont. Will buried his face against the mast, felt Evanlyn doing the same as the ship began that awful, slow rise again.

Up and up they went, clawing at the face of the wave, the men heaving until their hearts might burst as they tried to drag *Wolfwind* up the wave against the combined force of wind and sea. This time, before the wave broke, Will felt the ship seem to lose the last moment of the battle. He opened his eyes in horror as she began to surge backwards to certain disaster. Then the crest curled over and smashed down upon them and again, he was sent spinning and scrabbling on the deck, fetching up against the rope that secured him, feeling something slam painfully into his mouth and realising that it was Evanlyn's elbow. Water thundered over him then the bow pitched down once more, and *Wolfwind* began another sliding, careering dive down the far side, rolling upright, shedding the sea water like a duck. This time, Will was too weak to scream. He moaned softly and crawled back to the mast. He looked at Evanlyn and shook his head. There was no way they could survive this, he thought. He could see the same fear in her eyes.

In the stern, Erak and Svengal braced themselves as *Wolfwind* slammed into the trough, sending sheets of water high either side of the bow, the whole fabric of the ship vibrating to the impact. She rolled, shook, righted herself again.

'She's taking it well,' Svengal shouted. Erak nodded

grimly. Terrifying as it might seem to Will and Evanlyn, the wolfship was designed to cope with massive seas like this. But even a wolfship had its limitations. And if they reached them, Erak knew, they would all be dead.

'That last one nearly had us,' he replied. It was only a last-minute surge by the rowers that had dragged the ship through the crest as she had been about to slide backwards into the trough.

'We're going to have to turn her and run before the storm,' he concluded and Svengal nodded agreement, staring ahead through eyes slitted against the wind and the salt spray.

'After this one,' he said. The next wave was a little smaller than the one that had nearly finished them. But 'smaller' was a relative term. The two Skandians tightened their grip on the sweep oar.

'Heave, damn you! Heave!' Erak roared at the rowers as the mountain of water reared high above them and *Wolfwind* began another slow, precarious climb.

'Oh no. Please, please, let it end,' Will moaned as he felt the bow cant upwards once more. The terror was physically exhausting. He just wanted it to stop. If necessary, he thought, let the ship go under. Let it all go. Make an end of it. Just make this mind-numbing terror stop. He could hear Evanlyn beside him, sobbing with fear. He placed an arm around her but he couldn't bring himself to do anything more to comfort her.

Up, up and up they went, then there was the familiar roar of the collapsing crest and the thunder of water crashing down upon them. Then the bow came through the crest, slamming against the back of the wave and plummeting down. Will tried to scream but his throat was raw and his energy exhausted. He managed only a low sob.

Wolfwind sliced into the sea at the base of the wave again. Erak bellowed instructions to the rowers. They would have a short time in the wind shadow of the next approaching wave, and that was the time to make their turn.

'To the steerboard side!' he bellowed, pointing his hand in the direction of the turn just in case his voice didn't carry to some of the forward rowers — although there was little fear of that.

The rowers set their feet against the wooden bracing boards. Those on the steerboard, or right-hand, side of the ship drew their oar handles back towards them. The left-hand side rowers pushed theirs forward. As the ship levelled, Erak roared out his order.

'Now!'

The oar blades dipped into the sea and, as one side pushed and the other pulled, Erak and Svengal threw their weight on the sweep. The long, narrow ship pivoted neatly, almost in one spot, bringing the stern around to the wind and sea.

'Now pull together!' Erak roared and the oarsmen went to it with a will. He had to keep the ship moving a little faster than the following sea or it would overwhelm them. He glanced once at the two young Araluan captives, huddled miserably by the mast, then forgot them as he went back to judging the ship's movements, keeping her stern to the following sea. Any error on his part and she'd broach sideways, and that would be the end of them. They were riding easier, he knew. But this was no time to be distracted.

To Will and Evanlyn, the ship was still plunging and rearing in a terrifying fashion, travelling through a vertical distance of as much as fifteen metres as she went from crest to trough. But now the movement was more controlled. They were going with the sea, not fighting it. Will sensed a slight easing in the motion. Spray and solid water still slammed over them at regular intervals but the terrifying, backsliding motion was a thing of the past. As the ship coped with each successive mountain of water sweeping under and around it, Will began to believe that they *might* have a slight chance of survival.

But it was a slim *might*. He still felt the same surge of bowel-gripping terror with every wave that overtook them. Each time, he felt that this could well be the last. He put both arms around Evanlyn, felt her arms go round his neck in return, her icy cheek pressed against his own. And so the two young people sought, and found, comfort and courage from each other. Evanlyn was whimpering with fear. And so was he, Will realised with some surprise — muttering meaningless words over and over, calling out to Halt, to Tug, to anyone who might listen and help. But as wave followed wave and *Wolfwind* survived, the blinding terror lessened and nervous exhaustion took its place and, eventually, he slept.

For seven more days, the ship was driven far to the south, out of the Narrow Sea and into the fringes of the Endless Ocean. And Will and Evanlyn huddled by the mast: sodden, exhausted, freezing. The numbing fear of disaster was always present in their minds but, gradually, they began to believe that they might survive.

On the eighth day, the sun broke through. It was weak and watery, to be sure, but it was the sun. The violent plunging motion ceased, and once again the ship rode smoothly across the face of the rollers.

Erak, his beard and hair rimed with salt, hauled tiredly on the sweep, bringing the ship round in a smooth curve to face north once more.

'Let's head for Cape Shelter,' he told his crew.

Two

Halt stood motionless against the massive trunk of an oak tree as the bandits swarmed out of the forest to surround the carriage.

He was in full view but nobody saw him. In part this was due to the fact that the robbers were totally intent on their prey, a wealthy merchant and his wife. For their part, they were equally distracted, staring with horror at the armed men who now surrounded their carriage in the clearing.

But in the main, it was due to the camouflage cloak that Halt wore, its cowl pulled up over his head to leave his face in shadow, and the fact that he stood absolutely stock-still. Like all Rangers, Halt knew the secret of merging into the background lay with the ability to remain unmoving, even when people seemed to be looking straight at him.

Believe you are unseen, went the Ranger saying, *and it will be so.*

A burly figure, clad entirely in black, now emerged from the trees and approached the carriage. Halt's eyes narrowed for a second, then he sighed silently. Another wild goose chase, he thought.

The figure bore a slight resemblance to Foldar, the man Halt had been pursuing since the end of the war with Morgarath. Foldar had been Morgarath's senior lieutenant. He had managed to escape capture when his leader died and his army of sub-human Wargals faded away.

But Foldar was no mindless beast. He was a thinking, planning human being — and a totally warped and evil one. The son of a noble Araluan family, he had murdered both his parents after an argument over a horse. He was barely a teenager at the time and he had escaped by fleeing into the Mountains of Rain and Night, where Morgarath recognised a kindred spirit and enlisted him. Now he was the sole surviving member of Morgarath's band and King Duncan had made his capture and imprisonment a number one priority for the Kingdom's armed forces.

The problem was, Foldar impersonators were springing up everywhere — usually in the form of everyday bandits like this one. They used the man's name and savage reputation to strike fear into their victims, making it easier to rob them. And as each one sprang up, Halt and his colleagues had to waste time tracking them down. He felt a slow burning of anger at the time he was wasting on these minor nuisances. Halt had other matters to attend to. He had a promise to keep and fools like this were preventing him doing so.

The fake Foldar had stopped by the carriage now. The black cloak with its high collar was somewhat similar to the one Foldar wore. But Foldar was a dandy and his cloak was immaculate black velvet and satin, whereas this was simple wool, badly dyed and patched in several places, with a collar of crudely tanned black leather.

The man's bonnet was unkempt and badly creased as well, while the black swan's feather that adorned it was bent in the middle, probably where some careless bandit had sat on it. Now the man spoke, and his attempt to imitate Foldar's lisping, sarcastic tones was spoiled by his thick rural accent and clumsy grammar.

'Step down from the carriage, good sor and mad'm,' he said, sweeping a clumsy bow. 'And fear not, good lady, the noble Foldar ne'er harms one as fair as thee art.' He attempted a sardonic, evil laugh. It came out more as a thin cackle.

The 'good lady' was anything but fair. She was middle aged, overweight and plain in the extreme. But that was no reason why she should be subjected to this sort of terror, Halt thought grimly. She held back, whimpering with fear at the sight of the black figure before her. 'Foldar' took a pace forward, his voice harsher, his tone more threatening.

'Get down, missus!' he shouted. 'Or I'll hand you your husband's ears!'

His right hand dropped to the hilt of a long dagger in his belt. The woman cried out and cowered further back into the carriage. Her husband, equally terrified and more than fond of his ears where they were, was trying to push her towards the carriage door.

Enough, Halt thought. Satisfied that no one was looking in his direction, he nocked an arrow, drew and sighted in one economical motion, and released.

'Foldar', real name Rupert Gubblestone, had a brief impression of something flashing past, just in front of his nose. Then there was an almighty jerk on the raised collar of his cloak and he found himself pinned against the carriage by a quivering black arrow that thudded into the wood. He gave a startled yelp, lost his balance and stumbled, saved from falling by his cloak, which now began to choke him where it fastened around his neck.

As the other bandits turned to see where the arrow had come from, Halt stepped away from the tree. Yet to the startled robbers, it seemed as if he had stepped *out* of the massive oak.

'King's Ranger!' Halt called. 'Drop your weapons.'

There were ten men, all armed. Not a single one thought to disobey the order. Knives, swords and cudgels clattered to the ground. They had just seen a first-hand example of a Ranger's black magic: the grim figure had stepped clean out of the living trunk of an oak tree. Even now, the strange cloak that he wore seemed to shimmer uncertainly against the background, making it difficult to focus on him. And if sorcery weren't enough to compel them, they could see a more practical reason — the massive longbow, with another black-shafted arrow already on the string.

'On the ground, belly down! All of you!' The words cut at them like a whip and they dropped to the ground. Halt pointed to one, a dirty-faced youth who couldn't have been more than fifteen.

'Not you!' he said and the boy hesitated, on his hands and knees. 'You take their belts and tie their hands behind them.'

The terrified boy nodded several times, then moved towards the first of his prone comrades. He stopped as Halt gave him a further warning.

'Tie them tight!' he said. 'If I find one loose knot, I'll . . .' He hesitated for a second, while he framed a suitable threat, then continued, 'I'll seal you up inside that oak tree over there.'

That should do it, he thought. He was aware of the effect that his unexplained appearance from the tree had on these uneducated country folk. It was a device he had used many times before. Now he saw the boy's face whiten with fear under the dirt and knew the threat was effective. He turned his attention to Gubblestone, who was plucking feebly at the thong securing his cloak as it continued to choke him. He was already red in the face, his eyes bulging.

They bulged further as Halt unsheathed his heavy saxe knife.

'Oh, relax,' said Halt irritably. He slashed quickly through the cord and Gubblestone, suddenly released, fell awkwardly to the ground. He seemed content to stay there, out of the reach of that gleaming knife. Halt glanced up at the occupants of the carriage. The relief on their faces was all too obvious.

'I think you can be on your way if you like,' he said pleasantly. 'These idiots won't bother you any further.'

The merchant, remembering guiltily how he had tried to shove his wife out of the carriage, tried to cover his discomfort by blustering.

'They deserve hanging, Ranger! Hanging, I say! They have terrified my poor wife and threatened my very person!'

Halt eyed the man impassively until the outburst was finished.

'Worse than that,' he said quietly, 'they've wasted my time.'

'The answer is no, Halt,' said Crowley. 'Just as it was the last time you asked.'

He could see the anger in every line of Halt's body as his old friend stood before him. Crowley hated what he had to do. But orders were orders and, as the Ranger Commandant, it was his job to enforce them. And Halt, like all Rangers, was bound to obey them.

'You don't need me!' Halt burst out. 'I'm wasting time hunting these imitation Foldars all over the Kingdom when I should be going after Will!'

'The King has made Foldar our number one priority,' Crowley reminded him. 'Sooner or later, we'll find the real one.'

Halt made a dismissive gesture. 'And you have forty-nine other Rangers to do the job!' he said. 'For God's sake, that should be enough.'

'King Duncan wants the other forty-nine. And he wants you. He trusts you and depends on you. You're the best we have.'

'I've done my share,' Halt replied quietly and Crowley knew how much it hurt the other man to say those words. He also knew that his best reply would be silence — silence that would force Halt further into the sort of rationalisation that Crowley knew he hated.

'The Kingdom owes that boy,' Halt said, with a little more certainty in his tone.

'The boy is a Ranger,' Crowley said coldly.

'An apprentice,' Halt corrected him and now Crowley stood, knocking his chair over with the violence of his movement.

'A Ranger apprentice assumes the same duties as a Ranger. We always have, Halt. For every Ranger, the rule is the same: Kingdom first. That's our oath. You took it. I took it. And so did Will.'

There was an angry silence between the two men, made all the uglier by the years they had lived as friends and comrades. Halt, Crowley realised, was possibly his closest friend in the world. Now here they were, trading bitter words and angry arguments. He reached behind him and straightened the fallen chair, then made a gesture of peace to Halt.

'Look,' he said in a milder tone, 'just help me clear up this Foldar business. Two months, maybe three, then you can go after Will, with my blessing.'

Halt's grizzled head was already shaking before he'd finished.

'In two months he could be dead. Or sold on as a slave and lost forever. I need to go now while the trail is still warm. I promised him,' he added after a pause, his voice thick with misery.

'No,' said Crowley, with a note of finality. Hearing it, Halt squared his shoulders.

'Then I'll see the King,' he said.

Crowley looked down at his desk.

'The King won't see you,' he said flatly. He looked up and saw the surprise and betrayal in Halt's eyes.

'He won't see me? He refuses me?' For over twenty years, Halt had been one of the King's closest confidants, with constant, unquestioned access to the royal chambers.

'He knows what you'll ask, Halt. He doesn't want to refuse you, so he refuses to see you.'

Now the surprise and betrayal were gone from Halt's eyes. In their place was anger. Bitter anger.

'Then I'll just have to change his mind,' he said quietly.

Three

As the wolfship rounded the point and reached the shelter of the bay, the heavy swell died away. Inside the small natural harbour, the tall, rocky headlands broke the force of both wind and swell so that the water was flat calm, its surface broken only by the spreading V of the wolfship's wake.

'Is this Skandia?' Evanlyn asked.

Will shrugged uncertainly. It certainly didn't look the way he had expected. There were only a few small, ramshackle huts on the shore, with no sign of a town. And no people.

'It doesn't seem big enough, does it?' he said.

Svengal, coiling a rope nearby, laughed at their ignorance.

'This isn't Skandia,' he told them. 'We're barely halfway to Skandia. This is Skorghijl.'

Seeing their puzzled looks, he explained further. 'We can't make the full crossing to Skandia now. That storm in the Narrow Sea delayed us so long that the Summer Gales have set in. We'll shelter here until they've blown out. That's what those huts are for.'

Will looked dubiously at the weathered timber huts. They looked grim and uncomfortable.

'How long will that take?' he asked and Svengal shrugged.

'Six weeks, two months. Who knows?' He moved off, the coil of rope over one shoulder, and the two young people were left to survey their new surroundings.

Skorghijl was a bleak and uninviting place of bare rock, steep granite cliffs and a small level beach where the sun and salt-whitened timber huts huddled. There was no tree or blade of green anywhere in sight. The rims of the cliffs were scattered with the white of snow and ice. The rest was rock and shale, granite black and dull grey. It was as if whatever gods the Skandians worshipped had removed all vestige of colour from this rocky little world.

Unconsciously, without the need to battle the constant backward set of the waves, the rowers slackened their pace. The ship glided across the bay to the shingle beach. Erak, at the tiller, kept her in the channel that ran deep right up to the water's edge, until the keel finally grated into the shingle and the wolfship was, for the first time in days, still.

Will and Evanlyn stood, their legs uncertain after days of constant movement.

The ship rang with the dull thuds of timber on timber as the oars were drawn inboard and stowed. Erak looped a leather thong over the tiller to secure it and prevent the rudder banging back and forth with the movement of the tide. He glanced briefly at the two prisoners.

'Go ashore if you like,' he told them. There was no need to restrain them or guard them in any way. Skorghijl was an island, barely two kilometres across at its widest point. Apart from this one perfect natural harbour that had made it a refuge for Skandians during the Summer Gales, Skorghijl's coast was an uninterrupted line of sheer cliffs, dropping into the sea.

Will and Evanlyn moved to the bow of the ship, passing the Skandians, who were unshipping barrels of water and ale and sacks of dried food from the sheltered spaces below the centre deck. Will climbed over the gunwale, hung full length for a few seconds then dropped to the shale below. Here, with the prow canted up as it had slid up the beach, there was a considerable drop to the stones. He turned to help Evanlyn, but she was already dropping after him.

They stood uncertainly.

'My God,' Evanlyn muttered, feeling herself sway as the solid land beneath her seemed to roll and pitch. She stumbled and fell to one knee.

Will was in no better state. Now that the constant movement had ceased, the dry land beneath them seemed to heave and lurch. He placed one hand against the timbers of the boat to stop himself from falling.

'What is it?' he asked her. He stared at the ground beneath his feet, expecting to see it forming and rolling into hummocks and hills. But it was flat and motionless. He felt the first traces of nausea gathering in the pit of his stomach.

'Look out down there!' a voice from above warned, and a sack of dried beef thudded onto the pebbles beside him. He looked up, swaying uncertainly, into the grinning eyes of one of the crew.

'Got the land-wobbles, have you?' he said, not unsympathetically. 'Should be all right again in a few hours' time.'

Will's head spun. Evanlyn had managed to regain her feet. She was still swaying, but at least she wasn't assailed by the same nausea that Will was feeling. She took his arm.

'Come on,' she said. 'There are some benches up there by those huts. We might be better off sitting down.'

And, lurching drunkenly, they stumbled through the shingle to the rough wooden benches and tables that were set outside the huts.

Will sank gratefully onto one, holding his head in his hands and resting his elbows on his knees for support. He groaned in misery as another wave of nausea swept over him. Evanlyn was in slightly better shape. She patted his shoulder.

'What's causing this?' she said in a small voice.

'It happens when you've been on board ship for a few days.' Jarl Erak had approached behind them. He had a sack of provisions slung over one shoulder and he swung it down to the ground outside the door of one of the huts, grunting slightly with the effort.

'For some reason,' he continued, 'your legs seem to think you're still on the deck of a ship. Nobody knows why. It'll only last a few hours and then you'll be fine.'

'I can't imagine ever feeling fine again,' Will groaned in a thick voice.

'You will be,' Erak told him. 'Get a fire going,' he said brusquely. He jerked a thumb towards a blackened circle of stones a few metres from the nearest hut. 'You'll feel better with a hot meal inside you.'

Will groaned at the mention of food. Nevertheless, he rose unsteadily from the bench and took the flint and steel that Erak held out to him. Then he and Evanlyn moved to the fireplace. Stacked beside it was a pile of sun and salt dried driftwood. Some of the planks were brittle enough to break with bare hands and Will began to stack the slivers into a pyramid in the middle of the circle of stones.

Evanlyn, for her part, gathered together bunches of dried moss to act as kindling, and within five minutes they had a small fire crackling, the flames licking eagerly at the heavier pieces of firewood they added now to the blaze.

'Just like old times,' Evanlyn murmured with a small grin. Will turned quickly to her, smiling in return. All too clearly, he could see Morgarath's bridge looming above them once more, with the fires they had set feeding voraciously on the tarred ropes and resin-laden pine beams. He sighed deeply. Given the chance to do it over, he still would have acted as he had. But he wished Evanlyn hadn't been involved. Wished she hadn't been captured with him.

Then, even as he wished it, he realised that she was the one bright spark in his life of misery now and that by wishing her away, he was wishing away the only small glow of happiness and normality in his days.

He felt a sense of confusion. In a moment of extreme surprise, he realised that, if she were not here with him, life would be barely worth living. He reached out and touched her hand lightly. She looked at him again and, this time, he was the first to smile.

'Would you do it again?' he asked her. 'You know, the bridge and everything?'

This time, she didn't smile back at him. She thought seriously for several seconds, then said:

'In a moment. You?'

He nodded. Then he sighed again, thinking of all that they had left behind.

Unnoticed by the two young people, Erak had seen the little exchange. He nodded to himself. It was good for each of them to have a friend, he thought. Life was going to be hard for them when they reached Hallasholm and Ragnak's court. They'd be sold as slaves and their life would be hard physical labour, with no respite and no release. One grindingly hard day after another, month in, month out, year after year. A person living that life would need a friend.

It would be going too far to say that Erak was fond of the two youngsters. But they had won his respect. The Skandians were a warrior race who valued bravery and valour in battle above all else, and both Will and Evanlyn had proved their courage when they'd destroyed Morgarath's bridge. The boy, he thought, was quite a scrapper. He'd dropped the Wargals like ninepins with that little bow of his. Erak had rarely seen faster, more accurate shooting. He guessed that was a result of the Ranger training.

And the girl had shown plenty of courage too, first of all making sure the fire had caught properly on the bridge, then, when Will finally went down, stunned by a rock hurled by one of the Skandians, she'd tried to grab the bow herself and keep shooting.

It was difficult not to feel sympathy for them. They were both so young, with so much that should have been ahead of them. He'd try to make things as easy as possible for them when they reached Hallasholm, Erak thought. But there wasn't a lot he'd be able to do. Then he shook himself angrily, breaking the introspective mood that had fallen over him.

'Getting damn maudlin!' he muttered to himself. He noticed that one of the rowers was trying to sneak a prime piece of pork from a provision sack nearby. He moved quietly behind the man and planted his foot violently in his backside, lifting him clean off the ground with the force of the kick.

'Keep your thieving hands to yourself!' he snarled. Then, ducking his head under the doorway lintel, he went into the dark, smoke-smelling hut to claim the best bunk for himself.

Four

The tavern was a dingy, mean, little place, low ceilinged, smoke filled and none too clean. But it was close to the river where the big ships docked as they brought goods for trade into the capital, and so it usually enjoyed good business.

Right now, though, business had dropped off, and the reason for the decline was sitting at one of the spill-stained bare tables, close to the fireplace. He glared up at the tavern keeper now, his eyes burning under the knotted brows, and banged the empty tankard on the rough pine planks of the table.

'It's empty again,' he said angrily. There was just the slightest slurring of his words to remind the tavern keeper that this would be the eighth or ninth time he'd refilled the tankard with the cheap, fiery brandy-spirit that was the stock in trade of dockside bars like this. A sale was a sale, he told himself doubtfully, but this customer looked like trouble waiting to happen and the tavern keeper wished fervently that he'd go and let it happen some place else.

His usual customers, with their uncanny instinct for trouble brewing, had mostly cleared out when the small man had arrived and begun drinking with such unswerving purpose. Only half a dozen had remained. One of them, a hulking stevedore, had looked over the smaller man and decided he was easy pickings. Small and drunken the customer might be, but the grey-green cloak and the double knife scabbard at his left hip marked him as a Ranger. And Rangers, as any sensible person could tell you, were not people to trifle with.

The stevedore learned that the hard way. The fight barely lasted a few seconds, leaving him stretched unconscious on the floor. His companions hastily departed for a friendlier, and safer, atmosphere. The Ranger watched them go and signalled for a refill. The innkeeper stepped over the stevedore, nervously topped up the Ranger's tankard, then retreated behind the relative safety of the bar.

Then the real trouble started.

'It has come to my attention,' the Ranger announced, enunciating his words with the careful precision of a man who knows he has drunk too much, 'that our good King Duncan, lord of this realm, is nothing but a poltroon.'

If the atmosphere in the bar before this had been antici-patory, it now became positively sizzling with tension. The eyes of the few remaining customers were locked on the small figure at the table. He gazed around, a grim little smile playing on his lips, just visible between the grizzled beard and the moustache.

'A poltroon. A coward. And a fool,' he said clearly.

Nobody moved. This was dangerous talk. For a normal citizen to abuse or insult the King in public like this would be a serious crime. For a Ranger, a sworn member of the Kingdom's special forces, it was close to treason. Nervous glances were exchanged. The few remaining customers wished they could leave quietly. But something in the Ranger's calm gaze told them this was no longer an option. They noticed now that the longbow he had leant against the wall behind him was already strung. And the quiver beside it was full of arrows. They all knew that the first person to try to go through the front door would be followed in rapid time by an arrow. And they all knew that Rangers, even drunk Rangers, rarely missed what they aimed at.

Yet to remain here while the Ranger berated and insulted the King was equally dangerous. Their silence might well be taken as acquiescence should anyone ever find out what was going on.

'I have it on good authority,' the Ranger continued, almost jovially now, 'that Good King Duncan is not the lawful occupant of the throne. I've heard it said that he is, in fact, the son of a drunken privy cleaner. Another rumour has it that he was the result of his father's fascination with a travelling hatcha-hatcha dancer. Take your pick. Either way, it is hardly the correct lineage for a king, is it?'

A small sigh of concern passed from someone's lips. This was becoming more and more dangerous by the moment. The tavern keeper shifted nervously behind the bar, saw a movement in the back room and moved to get a clearer view through the doorway. His wife, on her way into the tap room with a plate of pies for the bar, had stopped as she heard the Ranger's last statement. She stood white-faced, her eyes meeting her husband's in an unspoken question.

He glanced quickly at the Ranger, but the other man's attention was now focused on a wagoner who was trying to make himself inconspicuous at the far end of the bar.

'Don't you agree, sir . . . you in the yellow jerkin with most of yesterday's breakfast spilt upon it . . . that such a person doesn't deserve to be King of this fair land?' he asked. The wagoner mumbled and shifted in his seat, unwilling to make eye contact.

The tavern keeper jerked his head almost impercept-ibly towards the back entrance of the building. His wife looked away to it, then back to him, her eyebrows raised in a query. 'The Watch,' he mouthed carefully and saw understanding dawn in her eyes. Stepping quietly, and still out of the Ranger's line of sight, she crossed the back room and let herself out the rear door, closing it behind her as silently as she could manage.

For all her care, the latch made a slight click as it fell into place behind her. The Ranger's eyes snapped around to the tavern keeper, suspicious and questioning.

'What was that?' he demanded and the tavern keeper shrugged, rubbing damp palms nervously on his stained apron. He didn't try to speak. He knew his throat was far too dry to form words.

For a fleeting moment, he thought he saw a flash of satisfaction in the other man's expression, but he dismissed the thought as ridiculous.

As the minutes dragged by, the Ranger's insults and slanders of King Duncan grew more vivid and more outrageous. The landlord swallowed nervously. His wife had been gone ten minutes now. Surely she must have found a detachment of the Watch? Surely they should be arriving here any minute, to remove this dangerous man and stop this treasonous talk?

And, even as he framed the thought, the front door banged back on its hinges and a squad of five men, led by a corporal, forced their way into the dimly lit room. Each of them was armed with a long sword and a short, heavy-headed club hanging at his belt, and each wore a round buckler slung across his back.

The corporal appraised the room as his men fanned out behind him. His eyes narrowed as they made out the figure hunched at the table.

'What's going on here?' he demanded and the Ranger smiled. It was a smile that never reached his eyes, the tavern keeper noticed.

'We were talking politics,' he said, his words laden with sarcasm.

'Not what I heard,' the corporal replied, thin lipped. 'I heard you were talking treason.'

The Ranger's mouth formed an incredulous O and his eyebrows arched in mock surprise.

'Treason?' he repeated, then looked curiously around the room. 'Has someone here been telling tales out of school then? Is someone here a tell-tale tit, whose tongue should be . . . split!'

It happened so quickly that the tavern keeper barely had time to throw himself flat behind the bar. As the Ranger spat out the last word, he had somehow scooped up the longbow from behind him and nocked and fired an arrow. It slammed into the wall behind the spot where the tavern keeper had been standing a second before, and buried itself deep into the wood panel, quivering still with the force of its impact.

'That's enough . . .' the corporal began. He started to move forward but, incredibly, the Ranger had another arrow nocked already. The dully gleaming broadhead was aimed at the corporal's forehead, the bow was drawn and tensed. The corporal stopped, staring death in the face.

'Put it down,' he said. But his voice lacked authority and he knew it. It was one thing to keep dockside drunks and rowdies in line, another entirely to face a Ranger, a skilled fighter and a trained killer. Even a knight would think twice about such a confrontation. It was way beyond the capabilities of a simple corporal of the Watch.

Yet the corporal was no coward and he knew he had a duty to perform. He swallowed several times, then slowly, slowly, raised his hand to the Ranger.

'Put . . . down . . . the . . . bow,' he repeated. There was no answer. The arrow remained centred on his forehead, at eye level. Hesitantly, he took a pace forward.

'Don't.'

The word was flat and unequivocal. The corporal was sure he could hear his own heart beating, rattling like a kettledrum. He wondered if others in the room could hear it too. He took a deep breath. He'd taken an oath of loyalty to the King. He wasn't a noble or a knight, just an ordinary man. But his word meant as much to him as it did to any highborn officer. He'd been happy to wield his authority for years, dealing with drunks and minor criminals. Now the stakes were higher, much higher. Now was the time to return payment for those years of authority and respect.

He took another step.

The twang of the bow releasing was almost deafening in the tension-charged room. Instinctively, violently, the corporal flinched and staggered back a pace, expecting the burning agony of the arrow, then the blackness of certain death.

And realised what had happened: the bowstring had snapped.

The Ranger stared incredulously at the useless weapon in his hands. The tableau remained frozen for a full five seconds. Then the corporal and his men leapt forward, swinging the short, heavy clubs that they carried, swarming over the small grey and green clad figure.

As the Ranger went down under the rain of blows, no one noticed him drop the small blade he had used to sever the bowstring. But the tavern keeper did wonder how a man who had moved so quickly to defeat a stevedore twice his size now seemed to be so slow and vulnerable.

Five

On the barren, windswept island of Skorghijl, Will was running.

He had done five laps of the shingle beach. Now he turned towards the steep cliffs that reared above the tiny harbour. His legs burned with the effort as he forced himself to climb, the muscles in his thighs and calves protesting. The weeks of inactivity on the wolfship had taken their toll on his fitness and now he was determined to regain it, to harden his muscles and bring his body back to the fine-tuned edge that Halt had demanded of him.

He might not be able to practise his archery or knifework, but he could at least make sure his body was ready if the chance came to escape.

And Will was determined that such a chance would come.

He drove himself up the steep slope, the small stones and shale slipping and giving way under his feet. The higher he went, the more the wind plucked at his clothes until, finally, he reached the top of the cliff and was exposed to the full force of the north wind — the Summer Gales, as the Skandians called them. On the northern side of the island, the wind drove the waves against the unyielding black rock, sending fountains of spray high into the air. In the harbour behind him, the water was relatively calm, sheltered from the wind by the massive horseshoe of cliffs that surrounded it.

As he always did when he reached this point, he scanned the ocean for some sign of a ship. But as ever, there was nothing to see but the relentlessly marching waves.

He looked back into the harbour. The two large huts seemed ridiculously small from here. One was the dormitory where the Skandian crew slept. The other was the eating hall where they spent most of their time, arguing, gambling and drinking. To the side of the dormitory, built against one of the long side walls, was the lean-to that Erak had assigned to him and Evanlyn. It was a small space but at least they didn't have to share with the Skandians, and Will had rigged an old blanket across one end to provide Evanlyn with a little privacy.

She was sitting outside the lean-to now. Even from this distance, Will could see the dispirited slump in her shoulders and he frowned. Some days ago, he had suggested that she might like to join him in his attempt to keep fit. She had dismissed the idea out of hand. She seemed to have simply accepted their lot, he thought. She had given in and over the past few days, their exchanges had become increasingly waspish as he tried to boost her spirits and talked about the possibility of escape — for he already had an idea forming in that direction.

He was puzzled and hurt by her attitude. It was unlike the Evanlyn he remembered from the bridge — the brave, resolute partner who had run across the narrow beams of the bridge to help him without any thought for her personal safety, then tried to fight off the Skandians as they closed in on them.

This new Evanlyn was strangely dispirited. Her negative attitude surprised him. He would never have picked her as someone who would quit when the going got tough.

Maybe that's how girls were, he told himself. But he didn't believe it. He sensed there was something else, something she hadn't told him. Shrugging away the thoughts, he started down the cliff once more.

The downhill run was easier than uphill, but not by too much. The slippery, treacherous surface beneath his feet meant that he had to continually run faster and faster to maintain his balance, setting off miniature landslides as he went. Where the uphill course had burned his thigh muscles, now he felt it in his calves and ankles. He reached the bottom of the slope, breathing hard, and dropped to the shingle to do a series of rapid pushups.

His shoulders were burning after a few minutes but he kept at it, forcing himself past the point of pain, blinded by the perspiration that was running into his eyes until, eventually, he could continue no longer. Exhausted, he collapsed, his arms unable to bear his weight, and lay face down on the shingle, panting for breath.

He hadn't heard Evanlyn approaching as he was doing the pushups. Now he was startled by the sound of her voice.

'Will, it's a waste of time.'

Her voice didn't have the argumentative tone that had been so much in evidence in the last few days. She sounded almost conciliatory, he thought. With a slight groan of pain, he pushed himself up from the shingle, then rolled over and sat, dusting the wet sand from his hands.

He smiled at her and she smiled in return, then moved to sit beside him on the beach.

'What's a waste of time?' he asked. She made a vague gesture that included the beach where he had just been doing pushups and the cliff he had climbed and descended.

'All this running and exercising. And all this talk of escape.'

He frowned slightly. He didn't want to start an argument with her, so he was careful not to react too vehemently to her words. He tried to keep a reasonable, neutral tone.

'It's never a waste of time to stay in shape,' he said.

She nodded, conceding that point. 'Perhaps not. But escaping? From here? What chance would we have?'

He knew he would have to be careful now. If it seemed he was lecturing her, she might well retreat into her shell again. But he knew how important it was to keep hope alive in a situation like this and he wanted to impress that fact on her.

'I'll admit it doesn't look too promising,' he said. 'But you never know what tomorrow may bring. The important thing is to stay positive. We mustn't give up. Halt taught me that. Never give up because, if an opportunity arises, you have to be ready to take it. Don't give up, Evanlyn, please.'

She was shaking her head again but not in argument.

'You're missing my point. I haven't given up. I'm just saying this is a waste of time because it's not necessary. We don't need to escape. There's another way out of this.'

Will made a show of looking around, as if he might see this other way she was talking about.

'There is?' he said. 'I don't see it, I'm afraid.'

'We can be ransomed,' she said and he laughed out loud — not scornfully but in genuine amusement at her naivety.

'I very much doubt it. Who's going to ransom an apprentice Ranger and a lady's maid? I mean, I know Halt would if he could but he doesn't have the sort of money it would take. Who's going to pay out good money for us?'

She hesitated, then seemed to come to a decision.

'The King,' she said simply and Will looked at her as if she'd lost her senses. In fact, for a moment he wondered if she had. She certainly didn't seem to have too firm a grip on reality.

'The King?' he repeated. 'Why would the King take the slightest interest in us?'

'Because I'm his daughter.'

The smile faded from Will's face. He stared at her, not sure that he had heard her correctly. Then he recalled Gilan's words back in Celtica, when the young Ranger had warned him that there was something not quite right about Evanlyn.

'You're his . . .' he began, then stopped. It was too much to comprehend.

'His daughter. I'm so sorry, Will. I should have told you sooner. I was travelling incognito in Celtica when you found me,' she explained. 'It had become almost second nature not to tell people my real name. Then, after Gilan left us, I was going to tell you. But I realised if I did, you'd insist on getting me back to my father immediately.'

Will shook his head, trying to catch up with what he was hearing. He glanced round the tiny, cliff-bound harbour.

'Would that have been so bad?' he asked her, with a touch of bitterness. She smiled sadly at him.

'Think, Will. If you'd known who I was, we never would have followed the Wargals. We never would have found the bridge.'

'We never would have been captured,' Will put in, but she shook her head once more.

'Morgarath would have won,' she said simply.

He looked into her eyes then and realised she was right. There was a long moment of silence between them.

'So your name is . . .' He hesitated and she finished the sentence for him.

'Cassandra. Princess Cassandra.' Then she added, with a rueful smile, 'And I'm sorry if I've been behaving like a bit of a princess over the past few days. I've been feeling bad because I hadn't told you. I didn't mean to take it out on you.'

'No, no, that's all right,' he said vaguely. He was still overwhelmed by her news. Then a thought struck him. 'When are you going to tell Erak?'

'I don't think I should,' she replied. 'This sort of thing is best handled at the highest levels. Erak and his men are little more than pirates, after all. I don't know how they'd react. I think it's best if I remain as Evanlyn until we reach Skandia. Then I'll find a way to approach their ruler — what's his name?'

'Ragnak,' Will said, his mind racing. 'Oberjarl Ragnak.' Of course she was right, he thought. As Princess Cassandra of Araluen, she would be worth a small fortune to the Oberjarl. And since Skandians were essentially mercenaries, there was no doubt that she would be ransomed.

He, on the other hand, was a different matter. He realised she was talking again.

'Once I tell them who I am, I'll arrange for both of us to be ransomed. I'm sure my father will agree.'

And that was the problem, Will knew. Perhaps if she could appeal to her father in person, he might be swayed. But the matter would be in the hands of the Skandians. They would tell King Duncan that they had his daughter, and set a price for her ransom. Nobles and princesses might be ransomed – in fact, they often were in times of war. But people like warriors and Rangers were a different matter. The Skandians could well be reluctant to release a Ranger, even an apprentice Ranger, who might cause trouble for them in the future.

There was another side to it all, too. The message would take months, perhaps the best part of a year, to reach Araluen. Duncan's reply would take an equally long time to make the return trip. Then negotiations would begin. In all that time, Evanlyn would be kept safe and comfortable. She was a valuable property, after all. But who could say what might have happened to Will? He could be dead by the time any ransom was paid.

Evanlyn obviously hadn't thought that far ahead. She was continuing with her previous thought.

'So you see, Will, there's no point to all this running and climbing and trying to find a way to escape. You don't need to do it. And besides, Erak is getting suspicious. He's no fool and I've seen him watching you. Just relax and leave it all to me. I'll get us home.'

He opened his mouth, about to explain what he had been thinking. Then he shut it again. Suddenly, he knew that she wouldn't accept his point of view. She was strong-willed and determined — used to having her own way, he realised now. She was convinced that she could organise their return and nothing he said would change her mind. He smiled at her and nodded. But it was a thin parody of his normal smile.

In his heart, he knew he was going to have to find his own way home.

Six

Castle Araluen, the seat of King Duncan's rule, was a building of majestic beauty.

The tall, spire-topped towers and soaring buttresses had an almost lifelike grace to them that belied the strength and solidity of the castle. It was beautiful, surely enough, built in huge blocks of honey-coloured hardstone, but it was almost impregnable as well.

The many high towers gave the castle a sense of light and air and gracefulness. But they also provided the inhabitants with a score of positions from which to pour arrows, rocks and boiling oil on any attackers who might be unwise enough to assault the walls.

The throne room was the heart of the castle, situated inside a series of walls and portcullises and drawbridges, which, in the event of a prolonged siege, provided defenders with a succession of fall-back positions. Like everything else about the castle, the throne room was vast in scale, with a vaulted ceiling that towered high above, and a paved floor finished in black and dull pink marble squares.

The tall windows were glazed with stained glass that glowed brilliantly in the low angle sunshine of winter. The columns that added immense strength to the walls were grouped and fluted to heighten the illusion of lightness and space in the room. Duncan's throne, a simple affair carved from oak, surmounted with a carving of an oak leaf, dominated the northern wall. At the opposite end, wooden benches and tables were provided for the members of Duncan's cabinet. In between, the room was bare, with room for several hundred courtiers to stand. On ceremonial occasions, they would throng the area, their brightly coloured clothes and coats of arms catching the red, blue, gold and orange light that spilled through the stained glass windows, sending highlights sparkling from their polished armour and helmets.

Today, by Duncan's command, there were barely a dozen people present – the minimum number required by law to see justice dispensed. The King faced the task before him with little pleasure. And he wanted as few witnesses as possible present to see what he knew he would have to do.

He sat, frowning heavily, on the throne, facing straight ahead, his eyes locked on the towering double doors at the other end of the room. His massive broadsword, its pommel carved with the leopard's head that was Duncan's personal insignia, rested in its scabbard, leaning against the right-hand arm of the throne.

Lord Anthony of Spa, Duncan's Chamberlain for the past fifteen years, stood to one side of the throne and several steps below it. He looked meaningfully at the King now and cleared his throat apologetically to attract the monarch's attention.

Duncan's blue eyes swivelled to him, the eyebrows raised in an unspoken question, and the Chamberlain nodded.

'It's time, your majesty,' he said quietly.

Short and overweight, Lord Anthony was no warrior. He had no skill at arms at all and, as a consequence, his muscles were soft and untrained. His value was as an administrator. Largely due to his help, the Kingdom of Araluen had long been a prosperous and contented realm.

Duncan was a popular King, and a just one. Which wasn't to say that he wasn't a strong ruler, willing and committed to enforcing the laws of the realm — laws that had been laid down and maintained by his predecessors, going back six hundred years.

And there lay the reason for Duncan's frown and his heavy heart. Because today he would have to enforce one of those laws on a man who had been his friend and loyal servant. A man, in fact, to whom Duncan owed everything — a man who twice in the past two decades had been instrumental in saving Araluen from the dark threat of defeat and enslavement at the hands of a madman.

Lord Anthony shifted restlessly. Duncan saw the movement and waved one hand in a defeated gesture.

'Very well,' he said. 'Let's have done with this business.'

Anthony turned to face the throne room. The few people gathered there stirred at the movement, looking expectantly towards the doors. The Chamberlain's symbol of office was a long ebony staff, shod in steel. He raised it now and brought it down twice on the flagstone floors. The ringing crack of steel on stone echoed through the room, carrying clearly to the men who waited beyond the closed doors.

There was a slight pause, then the doors swung open, almost soundless on their well-oiled, perfectly balanced hinges. As they came to a stop, a small party of men entered, proceeding at ceremonial slow march pace to stand at the base of the wide steps leading up to the throne.

There were four men all told. Three of them wore the surcoats, mail and helmets of the King's Watch. The fourth was a small figure, clad in nondescript green and dull grey clothes. He was bareheaded and his hair was a pepper and salt grey, shaggy and badly cut. He marched between the two leading men of his guard, the third bringing up the rear directly behind him. The small man's face was matted with dried blood, Duncan saw, and there was an ugly bruise on his upper left cheek that all but closed the eye above it.

'Halt?' he said, before he could stop himself. 'Are you all right?'

Halt's gaze rose now to meet his. For a brief moment, Duncan thought he saw an unfathomable depth of sadness there. Then the moment was gone and there was nothing in those dark eyes but fierce resolve and a hint of mockery.

'I'm as well as can be expected, your majesty,' he said dryly. Lord Anthony reacted as if stung by a wasp.

'Hold your tongue, prisoner!' he snapped. At his words, the corporal standing beside Halt raised one hand to strike the prisoner. But before the blow could be launched, Duncan half rose from his throne.

'That's enough!' His voice cracked out in the near

empty room. The corporal lowered his hand, a little shamefaced. It occurred to Duncan that nobody present was enjoying this scene. Halt was too well known and too well respected a figure in the Kingdom. He hesitated, knowing what he must do next but hating to do it.

'Shall I read the charges, your majesty?' Lord Anthony asked. It was actually up to Duncan to tell him to do that. Instead, the King waved one hand in reluctant acquiescence.

'Yes, yes. Go ahead, if you must,' he muttered, then regretted it as Anthony looked at him, a wounded expression on his face. After all, Duncan realised, Anthony didn't want to do this either. Duncan shrugged apologetically.

'I'm sorry, Lord Anthony. Please read the charges.'

Anthony cleared his throat uncomfortably at that. It was bad enough that the King had abandoned the formal procedure. But infinitely more embarrassing to the Chamberlain was the fact that the King now saw fit to apologise to him.

'The prisoner Halt, a Ranger in your majesty's forces, carrying the King's commission and a bearer of the Silver Oakleaf, was heard to scandalise the King's personage, his birthright and his parentage, your majesty,' he said.

From the small knot of official witnesses, an almost inaudible sigh carried clearly to the two men on the throne platform. Duncan glanced up, looking for the source. It could have been Baron Arald, lord of Castle Redmont, and ruler of the fief Halt was commissioned to serve. Or possibly Crowley, Commandant of the Ranger Corps. The two men were Halt's oldest friends.

'Your majesty,' Anthony continued tentatively, 'I remind you that, as a serving officer of the King, such comments are in direct contravention of the prisoner's oath of loyalty and so constitute a charge of treasonous behaviour.'

Duncan looked to the Chamberlain with a pained expression. The law was very clear on the matter of treasonous behaviour. There were only two possible punishments.

'Oh, surely, Lord Anthony,' he said. 'A few angry words?'

Anthony's gaze was troubled now. He had hoped that the King wouldn't try to influence him in this matter.

'Your majesty, it's a contravention of the oath. It's not the words themselves that are the issue, but the fact that the prisoner broke his oath by saying them in public. The law is clear on the matter.' He looked at Halt and spread his hands in a helpless gesture.

A slight smile touched the Ranger's battered features. 'And you'd be breaking yours, Lord Anthony, by not informing the King so,' Halt said. This time, Anthony didn't order him to remain silent. Unhappily, he nodded his agreement. Halt was right. He had created an intolerable situation for everyone with his ridiculous drunken behaviour.

Duncan went to speak, hesitated, then started again.

'Halt, surely there must be some misunderstanding here?' he suggested, hoping that the Ranger could somehow find a way out of the charge. Halt shrugged.

'I can't deny the charges, your majesty,' he said evenly. 'I was heard to say some . . . unpleasant things about you.'

And there was the other horn of the dilemma: Halt had made his appalling comments in public, in front of at least half a dozen witnesses. As a man and a friend, Duncan could — and certainly would — be willing to forgive him. But as King, he must uphold the dignity of his office.

'But . . . why, Halt? Why do this to us all?'

It was the Ranger's turn to shrug now. His eyes dropped from the King's. He muttered something in a low voice that Duncan couldn't quite make out.

'What did you say?' he asked, wishing for some way out of the corner he found himself in. Halt's eyes came up to meet his again.

'Too much brandy spirit, your majesty,' he said in a louder tone. Then, forcing a humourless grin, he added, 'I never had much of a head for liquor. Perhaps you could add a charge of drunkenness as well, Lord Anthony?'

For once, Anthony's composure and sense of protocol was rattled.

'Please, Halt . . .' he began, about to plead with the Ranger not to make light of the proceedings. Then he recovered himself and turned to the King.

'Those are the charges, your majesty. Admitted to by the prisoner.'

For a long moment, Duncan sat, unspeaking. He stared at the small figure in front of him, trying to see through the defiant expression in those eyes to find the reason behind Halt's actions. He knew the Ranger was angry because he had been refused permission to try to rescue his apprentice. But Duncan truly believed that it was vital that Halt remain in Araluen until the situation with Foldar was resolved. With each day that passed, Morgarath's former lieutenant was becoming a greater danger, and Duncan wanted his best advisers around him to deal with the matter.

And Halt was one of the very best.

Duncan drummed his fingers on the wooden arm of the throne in frustration. It was unlike Halt not to be able to see the bigger picture. In all the years they had known each other, Halt had never put his own interests before those of the Kingdom. Now, seemingly out of spite and anger, he had allowed alcohol to cloud his thinking and his judgement. He had publicly insulted the King, in front of witnesses — an action that could not be ignored, nor passed off as a few angry words between friends. Duncan looked at his old friend and adviser. Halt's eyes were cast down now. Perhaps if he would plead for mercy, claim some leniency for his past services to the crown . . . anything.

'Halt?' Duncan began before he realised it. The Ranger's eyes came up to meet his and Duncan made a helpless little interrogatory gesture with his hands. But Halt's eyes hardened even as they met the King's and Duncan could tell that there would be no plea for mercy there. The greying head shook slightly in refusal and Duncan's heart sank even further. He tried one more time to bridge the gap that had grown between him and Halt. He forced a small, conciliatory smile to his face.

'After all, Halt,' he added in a reasonable tone, 'it's not as if I don't understand exactly how you feel. My own daughter is with your apprentice. Do you think I wouldn't like to simply leave the Kingdom to its own devices to go and rescue her?'

'There is a fairly major difference, your majesty. A king's daughter can expect to be treated a little better than a mere apprentice Ranger. She's a valuable hostage, after all.'

Duncan sat back a little in his chair. The bitterness in Halt's tone was like a slap in the face. Worse, the King realised, Halt was right. Once the Skandians knew Cassandra's identity, she would be well treated while she waited to be ransomed. Sadly, he realised that his attempt at reconciliation had only widened the rift between them.

Anthony broke the growing silence in the room.

'Unless the prisoner has anything to say in his own defence, he is adjudged guilty,' he warned Halt.

Halt's eyes remained on the King's, however, and once again there came that tiny negative movement of the head. Anthony hesitated, looking round the room at the other noblemen and officers gathered there, hoping that someone, anyone, might find something to say in Halt's defence. But of course, there was nothing. The Chamberlain saw Baron Arald's heavy-set shoulders slump in despair, saw the pain on Crowley's face as the Ranger Commandant looked away from the scene unfolding before them all.

'The prisoner is guilty, your majesty,' said Anthony. 'It remains for you to pass sentence.'

And this, Duncan knew, was the part of being King that they never prepared you for. There was the loyalty, the adulation, the power and the ceremony. There was luxury and fine foods and wines and the best clothes and horses and weapons.

And then there were the moments when one paid for all of those things. Moments like this, when the law must be upheld. When tradition must be preserved. When the dignity and power of the office must be protected even if, by so doing, he would destroy one of his most valued friends.

'The law sets down only two possible punishments for treason, your majesty,' Anthony was prompting again, knowing how Duncan was hating every minute of this.

'Yes. Yes. I know,' Duncan muttered angrily, but not soon enough to stop Anthony in his next statement.

'Death or banishment. Nothing less,' the Chamberlain intoned solemnly. And, as he said the words, Duncan felt a small thrill of hope in his chest.

'Those are the choices, Lord Anthony?' he asked mildly, wishing to be sure. Anthony nodded gravely.

'There are no others. Death or banishment only, your majesty.'

Slowly, Duncan stood, taking the sword in his right hand. He held it out in front of him, grasping the scabbard in his right hand below the intricately carved and inlaid crosspiece. He felt a warm glow of satisfaction. He had asked Anthony twice, to make sure. To make sure that the Chamberlain's exact words were heard by the witnesses in the throne room.

'Halt.' He spoke firmly, feeling every eye in the room upon him. 'Former King's Ranger to the Redmont Fief, I hereby, as lord of this realm of Araluen, declare you to be banished from all my lands and holdings.'

Again, there was that small intake of breath throughout the room, as the listeners felt the relief of knowing that the sentence was not to be death. Not, he realised, that any of those present would have expected it to be. But now came the part they weren't expecting.

'You are forbidden, under pain of death, to set foot in this Kingdom again ...' He hesitated, seeing now the sadness in Halt's eyes, the pain that the greying Ranger could no longer hide. Then he completed his statement:

'... for the period of one year from this day.'

Instantly, there was uproar in the throne room. Lord Anthony started forward, the shock evident on his face.

'Your Majesty! I must protest! You can't do this!'

Duncan kept his face solemn. Others in the room were not quite so controlled. Baron Arald's face, he saw, was creased in a broad smile, while Crowley was doing his best to hide a grin in the grey cowl of his Ranger's cloak. Duncan noted with a grim sense of satisfaction that, for the first time this morning, Halt was somewhat startled by the turn of events. But not nearly so much as the loudly protesting Lord Anthony. The King looked at the Chamberlain, his eyebrows raised in question.

'Can't, Lord Anthony?' he queried, with great dignity. Anthony hurriedly retracted the statement, realising that it was not his part to issue orders to the King.

'I mean, your majesty ... banishment is ... well, it's banishment,' he concluded lamely. Duncan nodded gravely.

'Quite so,' he replied. 'And, as you told me yourself, it's one of only two choices that I can make.'

'But, your majesty, banishment is ... it's total! It's for life!' Anthony protested. His face was red with embarrassment. He bore Halt no ill feeling. In fact, up until the

Ranger had been arrested for scandalising the King's reputation, Anthony had felt a distinct admiration for him. But it was his job, after all, to advise the King on matters of law and propriety.

'The law stipulates that specifically, does it?' Duncan asked now and Anthony shook his head and made a helpless gesture with his hands, very nearly losing his grip on his staff of office in the process.

'Well, not specifically, no. It doesn't need to. Banishment has always been for life. It's traditional!' he added, finding the words he was looking for.

'Exactly,' replied Duncan. 'And tradition is not law.'

'But . . .' Anthony began, then found himself wondering why he was protesting so much. Duncan had, after all, found a way to punish Halt, but at the same time to leaven that punishment with mercy.

The King saw the hesitation and took the initiative.

'The matter is settled. Banished, prisoner, for twelve months. You have forty-eight hours to leave the borders of Araluen.'

Duncan's gaze met Halt's one last time. The Ranger's head inclined slightly, in a mark of respect and gratitude to his King. Duncan sighed. He had no idea why Halt had forced this situation upon them all. Perhaps, sometime after the next year had passed, he might find out. Suddenly, he felt a welling up of distaste for the whole matter. He shoved the scabbarded sword through his belt.

'This matter is completed,' he told those assembled. 'This court is closed.'

He turned and left the throne room, exiting through

a small anteroom on the left. Anthony surveyed those assembled and shrugged his shoulders.

'The King has spoken,' he said, his tone suggesting how overwhelmed he was by the whole thing. 'The prisoner is banished for a twelvemonth. Escort, take him away.'

And so saying, he followed the King out of the throne room.

Seven

Evanlyn watched with growing irritation as Will completed another lap of the beach, then dropped to the ground and performed a rapid ten pushups.

She couldn't understand why he persisted with this ridiculous exercise programme. If it were simply a matter of keeping fit, she might have accepted it — after all, there was little enough to do on Skorghijl and it was one way of keeping busy. But she sensed it was tied to a deeper reason. In spite of their conversation some days earlier, she was sure he still had plans to escape.

'Stubborn, pig-headed idiot,' she muttered. It was just like a boy, she thought. He couldn't seem to accept that she, a girl, could take charge of things and arrange their return to Araluen. She frowned. It wasn't the way Will had behaved in Celtica. When they were planning the destruction of Morgarath's massive bridge, he seemed to welcome her input and ideas. She wondered why he had changed.

As she watched, Will moved down the beach to the water's edge, where Svengal was rowing the wolfship's skiff back to shore. The Skandian second in command was a keen fisherman. He took the skiff out most mornings, weather permitting, and the fresh cod and sea bass that he caught in Skorghijl harbour's deep, cold waters made a welcome change to their diet of salted meat and fish and stringy vegetables.

She watched with a small pang of jealousy as Will spoke to the Skandian. She didn't have Will's easy manner with people, she knew. He had an open, friendly attitude that made it easy for him to strike up a conversation with anyone he met. People seemed to instinctively like him. She, on the other hand, often felt awkward and ill at ease with strangers and they seemed to sense it. It didn't occur to her that this might be a result of her upbringing as a princess. And because she was in a mood to resent Will this morning, the sight of him helping Svengal haul the little skiff up past the high tide mark simply increased her annoyance.

She kicked angrily at a rock on the beach, swore when it turned out to be bigger and more solidly anchored than she had expected and limped off to the lean-to, where she would be spared the sight of Will and his new friend.

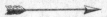

'Any luck?' Will asked, posing the question that every fisherman in history has been asked. Svengal jerked his head at the pile of fish in the bottom of the boat.

'Got one beauty there,' he said. There was a large cod among eight or nine smaller but still respectable fish. Will nodded, impressed.

'He's a beauty, all right,' he said. 'Need a hand cleaning them?'

The odds were that he would be told to clean the fish anyway. He and Evanlyn were tasked with all the house-keeping, cooking and serving duties. But he wanted to strike up a conversation with Svengal and this way, he thought, the Skandian might stay and chat while Will worked. Skandians were great chatters, he had noticed, particularly when someone else was busy.

'Help yourself,' the big Skandian said easily, tossing a small fish knife onto the pile of fish. He sat on the bulwark of the skiff as Will lifted the fish out and began the messy work of scaling, gutting and cleaning. Will had known Svengal would stay. He knew that the Skandian would want to carry the huge cod to the hut himself. Fishermen loved praise.

'Svengal,' Will said, concentrating on scaling a bass and making sure his voice sounded casual, 'why don't you go fishing at the same time each day?'

'The tide, boy,' Svengal replied. 'I like to fish the tide when it's rising. It brings the fish into the harbour, you see.'

'The tide? What's that?' Will asked. Svengal shook his head at the Araluan boy's ignorance of natural things.

'Haven't you noticed how the water in the harbour gets higher and then lower during the day?' he asked. When Will nodded, he went on, 'That's the tide. It comes in and it goes out. But each day, it happens a little later than the day before.'

Will frowned. 'But where does it go out to?' he asked. 'And where does it come from in the first place?'

Svengal scratched his beard thoughtfully. This wasn't something he had ever bothered to pursue. The tide was simply a fact of his life as a sailor. The why and where he left to other people.

'They say it's because of the Great Blue Whale,' he said, remembering the fable he had heard as a child. Seeing Will's incomprehension, he continued. 'I suppose you don't know what a whale is either?' He sighed at the boy's blank expression. 'A whale is a giant fish.'

'As big as the cod?' Will said, indicating the pride of Svengal's catch. The sea wolf laughed in genuine amusement.

'A good bit bigger than that, boy. Quite a bit.'

'As big as a walrus, then?' Will asked. There was a colony of the lumbering animals on the rocks at the southern end of the anchorage and he had learned the name from one of the crew. Svengal's grin widened even further.

'Even bigger. Normal whales are as big as houses. Huge things, they are. But the Great Blue Whale is something else again. He's as big as one of your castles. He breathes the water in and then spits it out through a hole in the top of his head.'

'I see,' Will said carefully. Some comment seemed to be necessary.

'So,' Svengal continued patiently, 'when he breathes in, the tide goes out. Then he spits it out again —'

'Through a hole in the top of his head?' Will said. He began to clean the cod. This all seemed far too fantastic — fish with holes in their heads that breathed water in and out. Svengal frowned at the interruption, and the note of disbelief he detected in Will's tone.

'Yes. Through a hole in the top of his head. When he does that, the tide comes back in again. He does it twice a day.'

'So why doesn't he do it at the same time every day?' Will asked and Svengal showed a further flash of annoyance. Truth be told, he had no idea. The legend hadn't covered this point.

'Because he's a whale, boy! And whales can't tell what time it is, can they?' Irritably, he grabbed the string of cleaned fish, making sure that he had the knife as well, and stalked off up the beach, leaving Will to wash the fish blood and scales off his hands.

Erak was sitting on a bench outside the eating hall as Svengal came up the beach.

'Nice cod,' he said and Svengal nodded briefly. Erak jerked a thumb in Will's direction and added, 'What was all that about?'

'What? Oh, the boy? We were just talking about the Great Blue Whale,' Svengal replied.

Erak rubbed his chin thoughtfully.

'Really? How did you get onto that subject?'

Svengal paused, thinking back on the conversation. Finally, he said, 'He just wanted to know about the tide, that was all.' He waited to see if Erak had anything further to say, then shrugged and went inside.

'Did he now?' Erak said to himself. The boy was going to need watching, he thought.

For the next few hours, he remained outside the hut, to all appearances dozing in the sun. But his eyes followed the apprentice Ranger wherever he went. Several hours later, he saw the boy tossing pieces of driftwood into the water, then watching them as the receding tide took them out to sea.

'Interesting,' the wolfship skipper muttered to himself. Then he noticed that Will was standing and peering under his hand at the harbour entrance. Erak followed the direction of his gaze and stood up in surprise.

Listing heavily to one side, lying low in the water and crabbing with an uneven complement of oars, a wolfship was dragging itself into the bay.

Eight

The grey-clad rider hunched miserably inside his cloak as he rode slowly through the misting rain that swept across the fields. The hooves of his two horses — one a saddle horse and the other serving as a lightly laden pack horse — clopped wetly in the puddles that had gathered in the undulations of the road.

Behind him as he reached a crest, the towers and spires of Castle Araluen soared into the grey sky. But Halt didn't look back at the magnificent sight. His gaze was set forward.

He heard the two riders following him long before they caught up. Abelard's ears twitched at the sound of the drumming hoof beats and Halt knew his small horse had recognised the other two as Ranger horses. Still he didn't look back. He knew who the two riders would be. And he knew why they were coming. He felt a small shaft of disappointment. He had hoped that, in the confusion and sorrow over his banishment, Crowley had forgotten the one small item that Halt would now have to surrender.

Sighing and accepting the inevitable, he touched Abelard's reins lightly. The highly trained Ranger horse responded instantly, coming to a halt. Behind them, the pack horse did the same. The hoof beats grew closer and he sat, staring dully ahead, as Crowley and Gilan reined in beside him.

The four horses nickered gently in greeting to each other. The three men were a little more reserved. There was an unpleasant silence between them, finally broken by Crowley.

'Well, Halt, you got away early. We had to ride hard to catch up to you,' he said, striving for a false heartiness that concealed his misery at the way events had turned out. Halt glanced incuriously at the two other horses. Steam rose gently from them in the cold damp air.

'I can see that,' he replied calmly. He tried to ignore the anguish on Gilan's young face. He knew that his former apprentice would be suffering deeply because of his inexplicable actions and he hardened his heart to shut the young Ranger's sorrow out.

Now Crowley lost his heartiness as well. His face grew serious and troubled.

'Halt, there is one thing you may have forgotten. I'm sorry to have to insist but . . .' He hesitated. Halt tried to play the scene out to the bitter end, assuming a puzzled expression.

'I have forty-eight hours to leave the Kingdom,' he replied. 'The time started from dawn this morning. I'll make it clear of the border by then. There's no need for you to escort me.'

Crowley shook his head. Out of the corner of his eye, Halt saw Gilan drop his gaze to the road. This was simply causing pain to all of them. He knew what Crowley had come for. He reached inside his cloak to the silver chain around his throat.

'I had rather hoped you might forget,' he said, trying to make his voice light. But there was a catch in his throat that belied the effort. Sadly, Crowley shook his head.

'You know you can't keep the Oakleaf, Halt. As a person under banishment, you're automatically expelled from the Corps as well.'

Halt nodded. He felt the sting of tears behind his eyes as he unclasped the chain and passed the small silver amulet to the Ranger Commandant. The metal was still warm from contact with his body. His vision blurred as he saw it coiled in Crowley's palm. Such a small piece of bright metal, he thought, and yet it meant so much to him. He had worn the Oakleaf, with the intense pride that all Rangers felt, for the greater part of his life. And now, it was no longer his.

'I'm sorry, Halt,' Crowley said miserably. Halt lifted one shoulder in a shrug.

'It's a small matter,' he said.

Again, a silence fell between them. Crowley's eyes looked into his, trying to penetrate the veil that Halt held in place there. A veil of uncaring, unfeeling acceptance of the situation. It was a sham, but it was a superbly maintained one. Finally the Commandant leaned towards him in the saddle, gripping Halt's forearm tightly.

'Why, Halt? Why did you do it?' he asked fiercely. Again, that infuriating shrug of the shoulders.

'As I said,' Halt replied, 'too much brandy spirit. You know I could never hold my liquor, Crowley.'

He actually managed a smile at that. It felt ghastly on his face, like a death's head grin. Crowley released his arm and sat back, shaking his head in disappointment.

'Godspeed, Halt,' he said finally, in a voice that broke with emotion. Then, with an uncharacteristically rough jerk of his reins, Crowley wheeled his horse's head and galloped away, back along the road to Castle Araluen.

Halt watched him go, the mottled Ranger cloak soon almost lost in the misting rain. Then he turned to his former apprentice. He smiled sadly, and this time the smile and the sadness were genuine.

'Goodbye, Gilan. I'm glad you came to farewell me.'

But the younger Ranger shook his head defiantly.

'I'm not here to farewell you,' he said roughly. 'I'm coming with you.' Halt raised one eyebrow. It was an expression so familiar to Gilan that it tore at his heart to see it.

'Into banishment?' Halt asked the younger man and again Gilan shook his head.

'I know what you're up to,' he replied. He jerked his head at the pack horse standing patiently behind Abelard. 'You have Tug with you. You're going after Will, aren't you?'

For a moment, Halt was tempted to deny it. But the days of pretence were getting too much for him. He knew it would be a relief, just this once, to admit his reasons.

'I have to, Gilan,' he said quietly. 'I promised him. And this was the only way I could be released from service.'

'By getting yourself banished?' Gilan's voice rose in an incredulous note. 'Did it occur to you that Duncan could have had you executed?'

Halt shrugged. But this time, it wasn't a mocking gesture. This time it was simply a gesture of resignation.

'I didn't think he would. I had to take the chance.'

Gilan shook his head sadly. 'Well, banished or not,' he said, 'I'm coming with you.'

Halt looked away then. He took a deep breath, let it out. He was tempted, he had to admit. He was heading for a long, hard, dangerous road where Gilan's company would be welcome and his sword might well be useful. But there was another call upon Gilan's service and Halt, already burdened by the knowledge that he had betrayed his own duty, couldn't allow the younger man to do the same.

'Gilan, you can't,' he said simply. Gilan drew breath to reply and he held up a hand to stop him. 'Look, I asked for a release so that I could go after Will,' he said, 'and they told me I was needed here.'

He paused and Gilan nodded his understanding.

'Well, I judge that need to be less. But it's my judgement only and I could be wrong. This situation with Foldar is dangerous, very dangerous. And it needs to be nipped in the bud. He needs to be stalked and tracked down and ambushed. And frankly, I can't think of a Ranger more suited to that job than you.'

'Other than yourself,' Gilan countered and Halt acknowledged the fact with a slight inclination of his head. It wasn't ego talking. It was an honest assessment of the truth.

'That may be true,' he said. 'But it bears out my point.

If we both go missing, Crowley will have to find someone else to do the job.'

'I don't care,' Gilan replied stubbornly, twisting the reins in his hand into a tight little knot, then releasing them again. Halt smiled gently at him.

'I do, Gilan. I know how it feels to break the faith like this. It's a deep, bitter hurt, believe me. And I won't allow you to inflict it on yourself.'

'But Halt,' Gilan said miserably and the grizzled, smaller man could see that tears weren't far from his eyes, 'I was responsible for leaving Will. I deserted him in Celtica! If I had stayed with him, he would never have been captured by the Skandians!'

Halt shook his head. His voice was gentler now as he consoled the young man.

'You can't blame yourself for that,' he told him. 'What you did at the time was right. Blame me, rather, for recruiting a boy with the honour and courage to act as he did. And for training him so that there would never be any doubt that he would act that way.'

He paused, to see if his words were having any effect. Gilan was wavering, he knew. Halt added the final touch.

'Don't you see, Gilan, it's because I know that you are here that I can desert my post like this. Because I know you can cover for me. But if you refuse to do so, I can't go myself.'

And at that, Gilan's shoulders slumped in submission. His eyes fell once more and he muttered throatily, 'All right, Halt. But find him. Find him and bring him back, banished or not.'

Halt smiled at him and leant across to grip his shoulder.

'It's only a year,' he said. 'We'll be back before you know it. Goodbye, Gilan.'

'Godspeed, Halt,' the Ranger said in a breaking voice. His vision was obscured by tears and he heard the dull clopping of hooves on the wet road as Abelard and Tug paced out towards the coast.

The wind was in Halt's face as he rode on his way and it drove the light rain against him. It formed into small drops on his weather-beaten features, drops that rolled down his cheeks.

Strangely, some of them tasted of salt.

Nine

The wolfship was in bad shape. She crabbed awkwardly towards the shingle beach, where the crew of Erak's ship were spilling out of their hut to watch. She was listing heavily, and she sat a good deal lower in the water than she should. The guard rail on the downward side of the list was barely ten centimetres from the water.

'It's Slagor's ship!' one of the Skandians on the beach called, recognising the wolfshead crest on the up-curving bowsprit.

'What's he doing here?' another asked. 'He was safe back in Skandia when we left for Araluen.'

Will had hurried around from the rocks where he had been tossing driftwood into the water. He saw Evanlyn making her way down from the lean-to and he joined her. Her former annoyance was forgotten at this new turn of events.

'Where did the ship come from?' she asked and Will shrugged.

'I have no idea. I was out on the rocks and I just looked up and there she was.'

The ship was close in now. The crewmen looked haggard and exhausted, Will noticed. Now he could see gaps between several of the planks forming the hull, and the ragged stump where the mast had shattered and gone overboard. The Skandians standing around them noted these facts, and commented on them.

'Slagor!' Erak called across the calm water. 'Where the devil did you spring from?'

The burly man at the stern, controlling the ship's steering oar, waved a hand in greeting. He was plainly exhausted, and glad to make harbour.

One of the crew now stood in the bow of the ship and tossed a heavy line to Erak's men waiting on the beach. In a few seconds, a dozen of them had tailed onto the rope and begun to haul the wolfship in the last few metres. Gratefully, the rowers slumped back on their benches, without the energy to ship their oars. The heavy, carved-oak sweeps trailed in the water, bumping dully against the ship's sides as they pivoted back in the oar locks.

The keel grated against the shingle and the ship came to a halt. Sitting lower in the water than *Wolfwind*, it wouldn't ride as far up the slope of the beach. The bow struck and stuck fast.

The men on board began to disembark, hauling themselves over the bulwarks at the bow and dropping to the beach. The rowing crew staggered up onto dry land and stretched themselves out with groans of weariness, dropping onto the coarse stones and sand and lying as if dead. One of the last to come ashore was Slagor, the captain.

He dropped tiredly to the beach. His beard and hair were matted and rimed white with salt. His eyes were red and haunted looking. He and Erak faced each other. Oddly, they didn't greet each other with the normal grasped forearms. Will realised that there must be little love between the two men.

'What are you doing here at this time of year?' Erak asked the other skipper.

Slagor shook his head disgustedly. 'We're damned lucky to be here. We were two days out of Hallasholm when the storm hit us. Waves as big as castles there were, and the wind was straight from the pole. The mast went in the first hour and we couldn't cut it loose. Lost two men trying to clear it. Then the butt end kept slamming into the ship's waterline and before we got rid of it, it had driven a hole in the planks. We had one compartment flooded before we knew what was happening, and leaks in the other three.'

The wolfships, in spite of the fact that they looked like open boats, were actually highly seaworthy vessels. This was in no small part due to the design that divided the hulls into four separate, watertight compartments beneath the main deck and between the two lower galleries where the rowers sat. It was the buoyancy of these compartments that kept the ships afloat even when they were swamped by the huge waves that coursed across the Stormwhite Sea.

Will glanced at Erak now. He saw the heavily built Jarl was frowning at Slagor's words.

'What were you doing at sea in the first place?' Erak asked. 'This is no time to try to cross the Stormwhite.'

Slagor took a wooden beaker of brandy-spirit offered by one of Erak's men. Around the small harbour, the crew of Erak's ship were bringing drinks to their exhausted countrymen and, in some cases, tending to injuries obviously sustained as their ship had tossed and heaved in the storm. Slagor made no gesture of thanks and Erak frowned slightly. Again, Will was conscious of a feeling of animosity between the two captains. Even Slagor's manner was belligerent as he described their misfortune, as if he were somehow defensive about the whole matter. Now he drank half the brandy in one long gulp and wiped the back of his hand across his mouth before answering.

'Weather had cleared back in Hallasholm,' he said shortly. 'I thought we had a break long enough to get across the storm zone.'

Erak's eyes widened in disbelief.

'At this time of year?' he asked. 'Are you mad?'

'Thought we could make it,' Slagor repeated stubbornly and Will saw Erak's eyes narrow. The burly Jarl lowered his voice so that it didn't carry to the other crewmen. Only Will and Evanlyn heard him.

'Damn you, Slagor,' he said bitterly. 'You were trying to get a jump on the raiding season.'

Slagor faced the other captain angrily. 'And if I was? It was my decision to make as captain. No one else's, Erak.'

'And your decision cost two men their lives,' Erak pointed out. 'Two men who were sworn to abide by your decisions, no matter how foolhardy those decisions might be. Any man with more than five minutes' experience would know that this is too early to make the crossing!'

'There was a lull!' the other man shot back and Erak snorted in disgust.

'A lull! There are always lulls! They last a day or two. But that's not long enough to make the crossing and you know it. Damn you for your greed Slagor!'

Slagor drew himself up. 'You've no right to judge me, Erak. A captain is master of his own ship and you know it. Like you, I'm free to choose when and where I go,' he said. His voice was louder than Erak's and Will sensed he was blustering.

'I'll note you chose not to join us in the war we've just been fighting,' Erak replied, scorn in his voice. 'You were content to sit at home for that, then try to sneak out and get the easy pickings before other captains were ready to leave.'

'My choice,' Slagor repeated, 'and a wise one, as it's turned out.' His voice became a sneer. 'I notice you didn't exactly have a great deal of success in your invasion, did you, Jarl Erak?'

Erak stepped closer. His eyes blazed a warning at the other man.

'Watch your tone, you sneak thief. I left good friends behind me there.'

'And more than friends, as I've heard,' replied Slagor, emboldened now. 'You'll get scant thanks from Ragnak for leaving his son behind as well.'

Erak stepped back, his jaw dropping. 'Gronel was taken in the battle?'

Slagor shook his head now, smiling at the other man's loss of poise. 'Not taken. Killed, I heard, at the Thorntree battle. Some of the ships managed to make it back to Skandia before the storms set in.'

Will glanced up quickly at that. *Wolfwind,* Erak's ship,

had been the last to leave the Araluan coast. The crew were still waiting for Erak's return when the survivors of Horth's ill-fated expedition had straggled back to the ships, bringing news of the failure and then sailing away. Will had later heard *Wolfwind*'s crew talking about the Thorntree battle. Two Rangers, one short and grizzled, the other young and tall, had led the King's forces that decimated the Skandian army as they had marched to outflank Duncan's main force. Somehow, Will knew in his heart that they had been Halt and Gilan.

Erak shook his head sadly. 'Gronel was a good man,' he said. 'We'll feel his loss sorely.'

'His father is feeling it. He's sworn a Vallasvow against Duncan.'

'That can't be right,' Erak said, frowning in disbelief. 'A Vallasvow is only to be taken against treachery or murder.'

Slagor shrugged. 'He's the Oberjarl. He can do as he likes, I'd say. Now for pity's sake, do you have any food on this godforsaken island? Our stores are ruined by sea water.'

Erak, still distracted by the news he'd just heard, became aware of Will and Evanlyn's presence. He jerked his head towards the huts.

'Get a fire going,' he told them. 'These men need hot food.'

He was angry that Slagor had to remind him of his duty in this matter. He may not have liked the other captain, but his men deserved help and attention after all they had been through. He shoved Will roughly towards the hut. The boy staggered, then began to run, Evanlyn close behind him.

Will had a nasty feeling in the pit of his stomach. He had no idea what a Vallasvow might be but he knew one thing. Keeping Evanlyn's identity a secret had suddenly become a matter of life and death.

Ten

The road neared the ocean, and the woods on either side gradually moved closer and closer, as fertile, tilled fields gave way to denser forest country.

It was the sort of country where peaceful travellers might well become fearful of bandits, as the thick trees close to the roadside gave ample cover for an ambush. Halt, however, had no such fears. In fact, his mood was so dark that he might well have welcomed an attempt by bandits to rob him of his few belongings.

His heavy saxe knife and throwing knife were easy to hand under his cloak, and he carried his longbow strung, resting across the pommel of his saddle, in Ranger fashion. One corner of his cloak, specially made for the purpose, folded back from his shoulder, leaving the feathered ends of the two dozen arrows in his quiver within quick, unimpeded reach. It was said that each Ranger carried the lives of twenty-four men in his quiver, such was their uncanny, deadly accuracy with the longbow.

Aside from these obvious weapons, and his own finely honed instinct for danger, Halt had two other, not so obvious, advantages over any potential attacker. The two Ranger horses, Tug and Abelard, were trained to give quiet warning of the presence of any strangers that they sensed. And now, as Halt rode, Abelard's ears twitched several times and he and Tug both tossed their heads and snorted.

Halt reached forward and patted his horse's neck gently.

'Good boys,' he said softly to the two stocky little horses, and their ears twitched in recognition of his words. To any observer, the cloaked rider was merely quietening his mount – a perfectly normal turn of events. In fact, his senses were heightened and his mind was racing. He spoke again, one word.

'Where?'

Abelard's head angled slightly to the left, pointing towards a copse of trees closer to the road than the rest, some fifty metres further on. Halt glanced quickly over his shoulder and noted that Tug, trotting quietly behind him, was looking in the same direction. Both horses had sensed the presence of strangers, or perhaps a stranger, in the trees. Now Halt spoke again.

'Release.'

And the two horses, knowing that their warning had been taken and the direction noted, turned their heads back from the direction they had indicated. It was this sort of specialised skill that gave Rangers their uncanny capacity for survival and for anticipating trouble.

Still apparently totally unaware of the presence of anyone in the trees, Halt rode forward at the same relaxed pace. He smiled grimly to himself as he considered the fact that the horses could only tell him that someone was there. They could not foretell that person's intentions, or whether or not he was an enemy.

That would be supernatural power indeed, he thought to himself.

He was forty metres from the trees now. There were half a dozen of them — bushy and surrounded by heavy undergrowth. They afforded perfect cover for an ambush. Or, he reasoned, for someone who simply wanted shelter from the soft rain that had fallen for the past ten hours or so. From beneath the cowl of his hood, shaded and invisible to any observer, Halt's eyes darted and searched the thick cover. Abelard, closer now to the potential danger, let go a deep-throated grumbling sound. It was barely audible, and was felt by his rider more as a rumbling vibration in his horse's barrel chest than anything else. Halt nudged him with one knee.

'I know,' he said softly, knowing the shadow of his cowl would hide any movement of his lips.

This was close enough, he decided. His bow gave him the advantage as long as he stayed at a distance. He tweaked the reins gently and Abelard halted, Tug taking one more pace before he too came to a stop.

With an easy, fluid motion, Halt reached for an arrow from his quiver and nocked it to the string of his bow. He made no attempt to draw the bow. Years of constant practice made him capable of drawing, aiming, firing and hitting in the blink of an eye.

'I'd like to see you in the open,' he called, in a carrying voice. There was a moment's hesitation, then a heavy-set mounted figure spurred forward from the trees, coming to a halt on clear ground at the verge of the road.

A warrior, Halt saw, noting the dull gleam of chain mail at his arms and around his neck. He wore a cloak as well, to keep the rain off. A simple, conical steel helmet was slung to his saddle bow and a round, unblazoned buckler was slung at his back. Halt could see no sign of a sword or other weapon, but he reasoned that any such would most likely be worn on the man's left side, the side furthest away from him. It was safe to assume that the rider would be carrying a weapon of some kind. After all, there was no point in wearing half armour and going weaponless.

There was something familiar about the figure, however. A moment more and Halt recognised the rider. He relaxed, replacing the arrow in his quiver with the same smooth, practised movement.

He urged Abelard forward and rode to greet the other rider.

'What are you doing here?' he asked, already having a pretty good idea what the answer was going to be.

'I'm coming with you,' said Horace, confirming what Halt had suspected. 'You're going to find Will and I want to join you.'

'I see,' Halt said, drawing rein as he came alongside the youth. Horace was a tall boy and his battlehorse stood several hands higher than Abelard. The Ranger found himself having to look up at the young face. It was set in determined lines, he noted.

'And what do you think your apprentice master will have to say about that when he finds out?' he asked.

'Sir Rodney?' Horace shrugged. 'He knows already. I told him I was leaving.'

Halt inclined his head in some surprise. He'd expected that Horace would have simply run away in his attempt to join him. But the apprentice warrior was a straightforward type, not given to guile or subterfuge. It was not in Horace's character to simply run off, he realised.

'And how did he greet this momentous news?'

Horace frowned, not understanding.

'Pardon?' he asked uncertainly and Halt sighed quietly.

'What did he say when you told him? I assume he gave you a good clout over the ear?' Rodney wasn't known for his tolerance of disobedient apprentices. He had a quick temper and the boys in Battleschool often felt the full force of it.

'No,' Horace answered stolidly. 'He said to give you a message.'

Halt shook his head in wonder. 'And the message was?' he prompted, and noted that Horace shifted uncomfortably in his saddle before answering.

'He said, "Good luck to you",' the boy replied finally. 'And he said to tell you that I came with his approval — unofficial, of course.'

'Of course,' Halt replied, successfully masking the surprise he felt at this unexpected gesture of support from the Battleschool commander. 'He could hardly give you official approval to go running off with a banished criminal, could he?'

Horace thought about that and nodded. 'I suppose not,' he replied. 'So you'll let me come with you?'

Halt shook his head. 'Of course I won't,' he said briskly. 'I don't have time to look after you where I'm going.'

The boy's face flushed with anger at Halt's dismissive tone.

'Sir Rodney also said to tell you that you could possibly use a sword to guard your back on your travels,' he said. Halt regarded the tall boy carefully as he spoke.

'Those were his exact words?' he asked, and Horace shook his head.

'Not exactly.'

'Then tell me exactly what he said,' Halt demanded.

Horace took a deep breath, 'His exact words were, "You could use a good sword to guard your back".'

Halt hid a smile.

'Meaning who?' he challenged. Horace sat his horse, flushing furiously, and didn't answer. It was the best reply he could have made. Halt was watching him closely. He didn't take Rodney's recommendation lightly and he knew the boy had courage to spare. He'd proven that when he'd challenged Morgarath to single combat at the Plains of Uthal.

But there was the chance that he might have become boastful and overconfident — that too much adulation and praise had turned his head. If that were the case, however, he would have answered Halt's sarcastic challenge immediately. The fact that he hadn't, but merely sat in front of him, face set in determined lines, said a lot about the boy's character. Strange how they turn out, Halt thought. He remembered Horace as somewhat of a bully when he'd been younger. Obviously, Battleschool discipline and a few years' maturity had wrought some interesting changes.

He considered the boy again. Truth be told, it would be handy to have a companion along. He'd refused Gilan because he knew the other Ranger was needed here in Araluen. But Horace was a different matter. His Craftmaster had given permission – unofficially. He was a more than capable swordsman. He was loyal and he was dependable.

And besides, Halt had to admit that, since Will had been taken prisoner, he'd missed having someone younger around him. He'd missed the excitement and the eagerness that came with young people. And, God help him, he'd even missed the endless questions that came with them as well.

He realised now that Horace was regarding him anxiously. The boy had been waiting for a decision and so far had received nothing more than Halt's sardonic challenge as to the identity of the 'good sword' suggested by Sir Rodney. He sighed heavily and let a savage frown crease his brow.

'I suppose you'll bombard me with questions day and night?' he said. Horace's shoulders slumped at the tone of voice then, suddenly, he understood the meaning of the words. His face shone and his shoulders lifted again.

'You mean you'll take me?' he said, excitement cracking his voice into a higher register than he intended. Halt looked down and adjusted a strap on his saddle bag that required no adjustment at all. It wouldn't do to let the boy see the slight smile that was creasing his weathered face.

'It seems I have to,' he said reluctantly. 'You can hardly go back to Sir Rodney now you've run away, can you?'

'No, I can't! I mean . . . that's wonderful! Thanks, Halt! You won't regret it, I promise! It's just that I sort of promised myself that I'd find Will and help rescue him.' The boy was fairly babbling in his pleasure at being accepted. Halt nudged Abelard with his knee and began to ride on, Tug following easily. Horace urged his battlehorse to fall into step with Halt, and continued his flow of gratitude.

'I knew you'd go after him, Halt. I knew that's why you pretended to be angry with King Duncan! Nobody at Redmont could believe it when we heard what had happened but I knew it was so you could go and rescue Will from the Skandians —'

'Enough!' Halt finally said, holding up a hand to ward off the flow of words, and Horace stopped in mid-sentence, bowing his head apologetically.

'Yes. Of course. Sorry. Not another word,' he said.

Halt nodded thankfully. 'I should think not.'

Chastened, Horace rode in silence beside his new master as they headed towards the east coast. They had gone another hundred metres when he finally could stand it no more.

'Where will we find a ship?' he asked. 'Will we sail directly to Skandia after the raiders? Can we cross the sea at this time of year?'

Halt turned in the saddle and cast a baleful eye on the young man.

'I see it's started already,' he said heavily. But inside, his heart felt lighter than it had for weeks.

Eleven

The unexpected arrival of Slagor's vessel, *Wolf Fang*, made life even more unpleasant on Skorghijl.

The crowded living conditions were now worse than ever, with two crews crammed into the space designed for one. And with the crowding came fighting. Skandians weren't used to long hours of inactivity, so they filled their time with drinking and gambling — an almost certain recipe for trouble. When the members of one crew were involved, the disagreements that arose were usually settled quickly and forgotten. But the separate loyalties of the two crews inflamed the situation so that arguments flared, tempers were lost and, at times, weapons were drawn before Erak could intervene.

It was noticeable, Will thought, that Slagor never raised his voice to quell the fights. The more he saw of *Wolf Fang*'s captain, the more he realised that the man had little real authority and commanded minimal respect from the other

Skandians. Even his own crew worked for pay, not out of any sense of loyalty.

The work for Will and Evanlyn had doubled, of course. There was twice as much cooking, serving and cleaning to be done now. And twice as many Skandians to demand that they take care of any other job that needed doing. But at least they had retained their living space. The lean-to was too cramped for any of the massive Skandians to even consider co-opting it for their own use. That was one compensation for having been captured by giants, Will thought.

But it was more than just the fighting and the extra work that had made life miserable for Will and Evanlyn. The news of the mysterious Vallasvow taken by Ragnak had been devastating for the princess. Her life was now at risk and the slightest mistake, the slightest incautious word, from either of them could mean her death. She pleaded with Will to be careful, to continue to treat her as an equal, as he always had before she told him her real identity. The least sign of deference on his part, the smallest gesture of respect, might well raise suspicions and spell the end for her.

Naturally, Will assured her that he would guard her secret. He schooled himself never to think of her as Cassandra, but always to use the name Evanlyn, even in his thoughts. But the more he tried to avoid the name, the more it seemed to want to spring unbidden to his tongue. He lived in constant fear that he would inadvertently betray her.

The bad feeling between them, borne out of boredom and frustration as much as anything, had melted away in the face of this new and very real danger. They were allies and friends again, and their resolve to help and support each other regained the strength and conviction that they had enjoyed in their brief time in Celtica.

Of course, Evanlyn's plan for ransom was now totally destroyed. She could hardly reveal herself to a man who had sworn to kill every member of her family. That realisation, coupled with her own natural resentment at being forced to do menial, unpleasant work, made her life on Skorghijl miserable. The one bright spot in her life was Will — always cheerful, always optimistic, always encouraging. She noticed how he unobtrusively took the worst, messiest jobs for himself whenever possible and she was grateful for it. Thinking back on the way she had treated him a few days earlier, she felt ashamed. But when she tried to apologise — and she was straightforward enough to admit that she had been in the wrong — he dismissed it with a laugh.

'We're all a little cabin crazy,' he said. 'The sooner we get away, the better.'

He still planned to escape, and she realised she must accompany him. She knew he had something in mind, but he was still working on his plan and so far he hadn't told her the details.

For now, the evening meal was over and there was a massive sack full of wooden platters, spoons and mugs to clean in the sea water and fine gravel at the water's edge. Sighing, she bent to pick them up. She was exhausted and the thought of crouching ankle-deep in the cold water while she scrubbed at the grease was almost too much to bear.

'I'll do those,' Will said quietly. He glanced around to make sure none of the Skandians were watching, then took the heavy sack from her.

'No,' she protested. 'It's not fair . . .' But he held up a hand to stop her.

'There's something I want to check anyway. This will be good cover,' he said. 'Besides, you've had a bad couple of days. Go and get some rest.' He grinned. 'If it makes you feel any better, there'll be plenty of washing up to do tomorrow. And the next day. You can do it all while I skive off.'

She gave him a tired smile and touched his hand in gratitude. The thought of just stretching out on her hard bunk and doing nothing was almost too good to be true.

'Thanks,' she said simply. His grin widened and she knew he was genuinely glad that relations between them were back to normal.

'At least our hosts are enthusiastic eaters,' he said cheerfully. 'They don't leave too much on the plates.'

He slung the sack and its clattering contents over his shoulder and headed for the beach. Smiling to herself, Evanlyn stooped and entered the lean-to.

Jarl Erak emerged from the noisy, smoke-filled mess hut and took a deep breath of the cold sea air. Life on the island was getting him down, particularly with Slagor not pulling his weight in maintaining discipline. The man was a useless drunk, Erak thought angrily. And he was no warrior — it was common knowledge that he selected only lightly defended targets for his raids and never took part in the fighting. Erak had just been forced to intervene between one of his own men and one of *Wolf Fang*'s crew of criminals. Slagor's man had been using a set of loaded dice and, when challenged, he had drawn his saxe knife on the other Skandian.

Erak had stepped in and knocked the *Wolf Fang* crewman senseless with one massive fist. Then, in order to show an even-handed approach, he was forced to knock his own man out as well.

Even-handedness, Skandian style, he thought wearily. A left hook and a right cross.

He heard the scrunch of feet in the gravel of the beach and looked up to see a dark figure heading towards the water's edge. He frowned thoughtfully. It was the Araluan boy.

Stealthily, he began to follow the boy. He heard the clatter of plates and mugs being spilled on the beach, then the sound of scrubbing. Maybe he was just doing the washing up, he thought. Maybe not. Stepping carefully, he worked his way a little closer.

Erak's concept of stealth didn't quite match Ranger standards. Will was scrubbing the platters when he heard the massively built Skandian approaching. Either that, he thought, or a walrus was beaching itself on the shingle.

Turning to look up, he recognised the bulky form of Erak, made even larger in the darkness by the bearskin cloak he wore against the biting cold of the wind. Uncertainly, Will began to rise from his crouched position, but the Jarl waved him back.

'Keep on with your work,' he said gruffly. Will continued to scrub, watching the Skandian leader out of the corner of his eye as he gazed across the anchorage and sniffed at the storm-borne air.

'Stinks in there,' Erak muttered finally.

'Too many people in too small a space,' Will ventured, eyes down and scrubbing at the plate. Erak interested him. He was a hard man and a pitiless fighter. But he was not actually cruel. Sometimes, in a gruff way, he could seem almost friendly.

Erak, in turn, studied Will. What was he up to? He was probably trying to figure out a way to escape, Erak thought. That's what he'd be doing in the boy's place. The apprentice Ranger was smart and resourceful. He was also determined. Erak had seen the way he stuck to his gruelling exercise programme, out running on the beach in fair weather or foul.

Once again he felt that sense of regard for the apprentice Ranger – and the girl. She'd shown plenty of grit, too.

The thought of the girl made him frown. Sooner or later, there'd be trouble in that quarter. Particularly with Slagor and his men. The crew of *Wolf Fang* were a sorry lot – jailbirds and minor criminals for the most part. Good crew wouldn't sign with Slagor.

Well, he thought philosophically, if it happened, he'd have to bang a few heads together. He wasn't going to have his authority challenged by a rabble like Slagor's men. The two slaves were Erak's property. They'd be his only profit from this disastrous trip to Araluen and if anyone tried to damage either one, they'd answer to him. As he had the thought, he tried to tell himself that he was only protecting his investment. But he wasn't sure it was entirely true.

'Jarl Erak?' the boy said in the darkness, uncertainty in his tone as he wondered whether he should ask questions of the Skandian leader. Erak grunted. The sound was noncommittal but Will took it as permission to continue.

'What was the Vallasvow Jarl Slagor spoke of?' he asked, trying to sound casual. Erak frowned at the title.

'Slagor's no jarl,' he corrected the boy. 'He's merely a skirl, a captain of a wolfship.'

'I'm sorry,' Will said humbly. The last thing he wanted to do was make Erak angry. Obviously, by referring to Slagor as his equal, Will had risked that. He hesitated, but Erak's annoyance seemed to have abated, so he asked again.

'And the Vallasvow?' he prompted.

Erak belched quietly and leaned to one side so he could scratch his backside. He was sure that Slagor's crew had brought fleas with them into the hut. It was the one discomfort they had not had to bear so far. Cold, damp, smoke and smell. But now they could add fleas. He wished, not for the first time, that Slagor's wolfship had gone down in the gales on the Stormwhite Sea.

'It's a vow,' he said, unhelpfully, 'that Ragnak took. Not that he had any cause to,' he added. 'You don't provoke the Vallas lightly. Not if you have any sense.'

'The Vallas?' Will asked. 'Who are they?'

Erak looked at the dark form crouched beneath him. He shook his head in wonderment. How ignorant these Araluans were!

'Never heard of the Vallas? What do they teach you in that damp little island of yours?' he asked. Will, wisely, said nothing in reply. There were a few moments' silence, then Erak continued.

'The Vallas, boy, are the three gods of vengeance. They take the form of a shark, a bear and a vulture.'

He paused, to see if that had sunk in. Will felt that this time, some comment was required.

'I see,' he said uncertainly. Erak snorted in derision.

'I'm sure you don't. Nobody in their right mind ever wants to see the Vallas. Nobody in their right mind ever chooses to swear to them either.'

Will thought about what the Skandian had said. 'So a Vallasvow is a vow of vengeance then?' he asked and Erak nodded grimly.

'Total vengeance,' he replied. 'It's when you hate so badly that you swear to be avenged, not just upon the person who has wronged you, but on every member of his family as well.'

'Every member?' said Will. For a moment, Erak wondered if there was something behind this line of questioning. But he couldn't see how information like this could help in an escape attempt so he continued.

'Every last one,' he told him. 'It's a death vow, of course, and it's unbreakable. Once it's made, if the person making the vow should ever recant, the Vallas will take him and his own family instead of the original victims. They're not the sort of gods you really want any business with, believe me.'

Again, a small silence. Will wondered if he had continued far enough with his questions, and decided he could try for a little more leeway.

'Then if they're so terrible, why would Ragnak . . .?' he began, but Erak cut him off.

'Because he's mad!' he snapped. 'I told you, only a

madman would swear to the Vallas! Ragnak has never been too stable, now the loss of his son has obviously tipped him over the edge.'

Erak made a gesture of disgust. He seemed to tire of the subject of Ragnak and the fearful Vallas.

'Just be thankful you're not of Duncan's family, boy. Or Ragnak's, for that matter.' He turned back to where the firelight showed through a dozen cracks and chinks in the hut walls, casting strange, elongated patterns of light onto the wet shingle.

'Now get back to your work,' he said angrily, and strode back towards the heat and smell of the hut.

Will watched him, idly sluicing the last of the plates in the cold sea water.

'We really have to get out of here,' he said softly to himself.

Twelve

There was so much to see and hear, Horace didn't know which way to turn his head first.

All around him, the port city of La Rivage seethed with life. The docks were crowded with ships: simple fishing smacks and two-masted traders moored side by side and creating a forest of masts and halyards that seemed to stretch as far as the eye could see. His ears buzzed with the shriek of gulls as they fought each other for the scraps hurled into the harbour by fishermen cleaning their catch. The ships, large and small, rose and fell and rocked with the slight swell inside the harbour, never actually still for a moment. Underlying the gulls' shrill voices was the constant creaking and groaning of hundreds of wickerwork fenders protecting the hulls from their neighbours.

His nostrils filled with the smell of smoke and the aroma of food cooking — but a different aroma to the plain, country fare prepared at Castle Redmont. Here, there was something extra to the smell: something exotic and exciting and foreign.

Which was only to be expected, he thought, as he was setting foot in a truly foreign country for the first time in his young life. He'd travelled to Celtica, of course, but that didn't count. It was really just an extension of Araluen. This was so different. Around him, voices were raised in anger or amusement, calling to each other, insulting each other, laughing with each other. And not a word of the outlandish tongue could he understand.

He stood by the quay where they had landed, holding the bridles of the three horses while Halt paid off the master of the tubby little freighter that had transported them across the Narrow Sea — along with a reeking cargo of hides bound for the tanneries here in Gallica. After four days in close proximity to the stiff piles of animal skin, Horace found himself wondering if he could ever wear anything made of leather again.

A hand tugged at his belt and he turned, startled.

A bent and withered old crone was smiling at him, showing her toothless gums and holding her hand out.

Her clothes were rags and her head was bound in a bandanna that might have once been colourful but was now so dirty that it was impossible to be sure. She said something in the local language and all he could do was shrug. He had no money anyway and obviously the woman was a beggar.

Her obsequious smile faded to a dark scowl and she spat a phrase at him. Even without any knowledge of the language, he knew it wasn't a compliment. Then she turned and hobbled away, making a strange, criss-cross gesture in the air between them. Horace shook his head helplessly.

A peal of laughter distracted him and he turned to see a trio of young girls, perhaps a few years older than himself, who had witnessed the exchange between him and the old lady. He gaped. He couldn't help himself. The girls, all of them extremely attractive, it seemed to him, were dressed in outfits that could only be described as excessively skimpy. One wore a skirt so short that it ended well above her knees.

Now the girls gestured at him again, aping his open-mouthed stare. Hastily, he snapped his mouth shut and they laughed all the louder. One of them called something to him, beckoning him. He couldn't understand a word she said and, feeling ignorant and foreign, he realised his cheeks were flushing deep red.

All of which set the girls to laughing even louder. They raised their hands to their own cheeks, mimicking his blushing, and chattering to each other in their own strange tongue.

'You seem to be making friends already,' Halt said behind him and he turned, guiltily. The Ranger — Horace could never think of Halt as anything else — was regarding him and the three girls with a hint of amusement in his eyes.

'You speak this language, Halt?' he asked. Strangely, he realised, he wasn't surprised by the fact. He had always assumed that Rangers had a wide variety of arcane skills at their disposal and, so far, events had proved him to be right. His companion nodded.

'Enough to get by,' he replied evenly and Horace gestured, as inconspicuously as he could manage, to the three girls.

'What are they saying?' he asked. The Ranger assumed the blank expression that Horace was beginning to know so well.

'Perhaps it's better that you don't know,' he replied eventually. Horace nodded, not really understanding, but not wishing to look sillier than he felt.

'Perhaps so,' he agreed. Halt was swinging easily up into Abelard's saddle and Horace followed suit, mounting Kicker, his battlehorse. The movement drew an admiring chorus of exclamations from the girls. He felt the flush mounting to his cheeks once again. Halt looked at him with something that might have been pity, mixed with a little amusement. Shaking his head, he led the way down the crowded, narrow waterfront street, away from the quay.

Mounted, Horace felt the usual surge of confidence that came from being on horseback. And with it came a feeling of equality with these squabbling, hurrying foreigners. Now, it seemed to him, nobody was rushing to make fun of him, or beg from him or spit insults at him. There was a natural deference from people on foot for mounted and armed men. It had always been that way in Araluen, but here in Gallica there seemed to be an extra edge to it. People here moved with greater alacrity to clear a path for the two horsemen and the sturdy little pack horse that followed them.

It occurred to him that perhaps the rule of law in Gallica was not quite so even-handed as in his home country. In Araluen, people on foot deferred to mounted men as a matter of commonsense. Here they seemed apprehensive, even fearful. He was about to ask Halt about the difference, and had actually drawn breath to ask the question, when he stopped himself. Halt was constantly chiding him for his questions and he was determined to curb his curiosity. He decided he would ask Halt about his suspicions when they stopped for the noon meal.

Pleased with his resolution, he nodded to himself. Then another thought occurred and, before he could stop himself, he had begun the prelude to yet another question.

'Halt?' he said diffidently. He heard a deep sigh from the short, slightly built man riding beside him. Mentally, he kicked himself.

'I thought you must be coming down with some illness for a moment there,' Halt said, straight faced. 'It must be two or three minutes since you've asked me a question.'

Committed now, Horace continued.

'One of those girls,' he began, and immediately felt the Ranger's eyes on him. 'She was wearing a very short skirt.'

There was the slightest pause.

'Yes?' Halt prompted, not sure where this conversation was leading. Horace shrugged uncomfortably. The memory of the girl, and her shapely legs, was causing his cheeks to burn with embarrassment again.

'Well,' he said uncertainly, 'I just wondered if that was normal over here, that's all.'

Halt considered the serious young face beside him. He cleared his throat several times.

'I believe that sometimes Gallican girls take jobs as couriers,' he said.

Horace frowned slightly. 'Couriers?'

'Couriers. They carry messages from one person to another. Or from one business to another, in the towns and cities.' Halt checked to see if Horace seemed to be believing him so far. There seemed no reason to think otherwise, so he added: 'Urgent messages.'

'Urgent messages,' Horace repeated, still not seeing the connection. But he seemed inclined to believe what Halt was saying, so the older man continued.

'And I suppose for a really urgent message, one would have to run.'

Now he saw a glimmer of understanding in the boy's eyes. Horace nodded several times as he made the connection.

'So, the short skirts . . . they'd be to help them run more easily?' he suggested. Halt nodded in his turn.

'It would certainly be a more sensible form of dress than long skirts, if you wanted to do a lot of running.' He shot a quick look at Horace to see if his gentle teasing was not being turned back on himself — to see if, in fact, the boy realised Halt was talking nonsense and was simply leading him on. Horace's face, however, was open and believing.

'I suppose so,' Horace replied finally, then added, in a softer voice, 'They certainly look a lot better that way, too.'

Again, Halt shot him a look. But Horace seemed to be content with the answer. For a moment, Halt regretted his deception, feeling a slight pang of guilt. Horace was, after all, totally trusting and it was so easy to tease him like this. Then the Ranger looked at those clear blue eyes and the contented, honest face of the warrior apprentice and any sense of regret was stifled. Horace had plenty of time to learn about the seamier side of life, he thought. He could retain his innocence for a little while longer.

They left La Rivage by its northern gate and headed into the farm country surrounding it. Horace's curiosity remained as strong as ever, and he peered from side to side as the road took them past fields and crops and farmhouses. The countryside was different to Araluen. There were more varieties of trees and, as a result, there were more shades of green. Some of the crops were unfamiliar, too: large, broad leaves on stalks that stood as high as a man's head were left to dry and seemingly to wither on the stalk before they were gathered. In several places, Horace saw those same leaves hanging in large, open-ended sheds, drying out even more. He wondered what sort of crop it might be. But, as before, he decided to ration his questions.

There was another difference, more subtle. For some time, Horace wasn't even aware that it was there at all. Then he realised what it was. There was a general air of unkemptness about the fields and the crops. They were tended, obviously, and some of the fields were ploughed. But they seemed to lack the loving, fastidious care that one saw in fields and crops at home. One could sense a lack of attention from the farmers, and in some crops weeds were clearly visible.

Halt sighed. 'It's the land that suffers when men fight,' he said softly. Horace glanced at him. It was unusual for the grizzled Ranger to break the silence himself.

'Who's fighting?' he asked, his interest piqued.

Halt scratched at his beard. 'The Gallicans. There's no strong central law here. There are dozens of minor nobles and barons — warlords if you like. They're constantly raiding each other and fighting among themselves. That's why the fields are so sloppily tended. Half the farmers have been conscripted to one army or another.'

Horace looked around the fields that bounded the road on either side. There was no sign of battle here. Only neglect. A thought struck him.

'Is that why people seemed a little . . . nervous of us?' he asked and Halt nodded approvingly at him.

'You picked that, did you? Good boy. There may be hope for you yet. Yes,' he continued, answering Horace's question, 'armed and mounted men in this country are seen as a potential threat — not as peace keepers.'

In Araluen, the farm workers looked to the soldiers to protect them and their fields from the threat of potential invaders. Here Horace realised, the soldiers themselves were the threat.

'The country is in absolute turmoil,' Halt continued. 'King Henri is weak and has no real power. So the barons fight and squabble and kill each other. Mind you, that's no great loss. But it gets damned unfair when they kill the poor innocent farm folk as well — simply because they get in the way. It could be something of a problem for us, but we'll just have to . . . oh, damn.'

The last two words were said quietly, but were no less heartfelt for that fact. Horace, following Halt's gaze, looked ahead along the road.

They were coming down a small hill, with the road bounded on either side by close-growing trees. At the foot of the hill, a small stream ran through the fields and between the trees, crossed by a stone bridge. It was a peaceful scene, normal enough, and quite pretty in its own way.

But it wasn't the trees, nor the bridge, nor the stream that had drawn the quiet expletive from Halt's lips. It was the armoured, mounted warrior who sat his horse in the middle of the road, barring their way.

Thirteen

Evanlyn felt Will's light touch on her shoulder. She gave a small start of surprise. Even though she had been lying awake, she hadn't heard him approaching.

'It's all right,' she said quietly. 'I'm awake.'

'The moon's down,' Will replied, equally softly. 'It's time to go.'

She tossed back the blankets and sat up. She was fully dressed, apart from her boots. She reached for them and began to pull them on. Will handed her a bundle of rags he had cut from his blanket.

'Tie these around your feet,' he told her. 'They'll muffle the sound on the shingle.' She saw that he had swathed his own feet in large bundles of cloth and she hurried to do the same.

Through the thin wall between the lean-to and the dormitory, they could hear the sound of men snoring and muttering in their sleep. One of the Skandians broke out in a fit of coughing and Will and Evanlyn froze, waiting to see if he had woken anyone. After a few minutes, the dormitory settled down again. Evanlyn finished tying the cloth bundles around her feet and stood, following Will to the door.

He had greased the hinges on the lean-to door with fat from the cooking pot. Holding his breath, he eased the door open, letting go a sigh of relief when it swung silently. With no moon, the beach was a dark expanse and the water a black sheet, dimly reflecting the starlight. The weather had been moderating over the past few days. The night was clear and the wind had dropped considerably. But they could still hear the dull thunder of waves crashing against the outer face of the island.

Evanlyn could just make out the dark bulk of the two wolfships drawn up on the beach. To one side was a smaller shape: the skiff, left there by Svengal after his latest fishing trip. That was where they were heading.

Patiently, Will pointed out the route he had selected. They had gone over it all earlier in the night but he wanted to make sure she remembered. Unseen movement was almost second nature to him but he knew that Evanlyn would be nervous once she was in the open. She would want to reach the ships quickly.

And speed meant noise and a greater chance of being heard or seen. He put his mouth very close to her ear and spoke in the lightest of whispers.

'Take it easy. The benches first. Then the rocks. Then the ships. Wait for me there.'

She nodded. He could see her swallowing nervously and he sensed that her breathing was speeding up. He squeezed her shoulder gently.

'Calm down. And remember, if anyone does come out, freeze. Wherever you are.'

That was the key to it all in uncertain light like this. A watcher might miss seeing a person standing perfectly still. But the slightest movement would draw the eye instantly.

Again, she nodded. He patted her shoulder gently.

'Off you go,' he said. She took another deep breath, then stepped out into the open.

She felt horribly exposed as she moved towards the shelter of the benches and the table, ten metres away from the huts. The dim starlight now seemed as bright as day and she forced herself to move slowly, placing her feet deliberately, fighting the temptation to rush for cover.

The cloth padding on her feet did a good job muffling the sound of her footsteps. But even so, the crunching of the shingle seemed deafening to her. Four more paces . . . three . . . two . . . one.

Heart pounding, pulse racing, she sank gratefully into the shadow of the rough table and benches. There was a small cluster of rocks halfway down the beach. That was her next goal. She hesitated, wanting to stay in the comforting shadow provided by the table. But she knew if she didn't go soon, she might never have the courage to move. She stepped out resolutely, one foot after the other, wincing at the muted scrunching of the stones underfoot. This part of the journey took her directly in front of the door to the dormitory. If any of the Skandians came out, she must be seen.

She reached the shelter of the rocks and felt the welcome protection of the shadows wrap around her once again. The hardest part of the trip was over now. She took a few seconds to let her pulse settle, then moved off towards the ships. Now that she was nearly there, she wanted desperately to run. But she fought the temptation and moved slowly and smoothly into the darkness beside *Wolf Fang*.

Utterly exhausted, she sank to the damp stones, leaning against the ship's planking. Now she watched as Will followed in her footsteps.

There were scattered clouds scudding across the sky, sending a series of darker shadows rippling over the beach. Will matched his movement to the rhythm of the wind and clouds and moved, sure-footed, along the track Evanlyn had just followed. She caught her breath in surprise as he seemed to disappear after the first few metres, melding into the pattern of moving light and shade and becoming part of the overall picture. She saw him again, briefly, at the benches and then at the rocks. Then he seemed to rise out of the ground a few metres from her. She shook her head in amazement. No wonder people thought Rangers were magicians, she reflected. Unaware of her reaction, Will grinned quickly at her and moved close so they could talk.

'All right?' he asked in a lowered tone and, when she nodded, 'Are you sure you want to go through with this?'

This time, there was no hesitation. 'I'm sure,' she said firmly. He gripped her shoulder again in a gesture of encouragement.

'Good for you.' Will glanced around. They were far enough from the huts now that there was little chance of their voices being overheard and the wind, although not as boisterous as it had been, provided plenty of cover as well.

He felt Evanlyn could use some encouragement so he pointed to the skiff.

'Remember, this thing is small. It's not like the wolfships. It'll ride over the big waves, not crash through them. So we're safe as houses.'

He wasn't sure about the last two statements but they seemed logical to him. He'd watched the gulls and penguins around the island riding the massive waves and it seemed that the smaller you were, the safer you were.

He was carrying a large wine skin, stolen from the provisions cabinet. He'd emptied the wine out and refilled the skin with water. It didn't taste too good, but it would keep them alive. Besides, he thought philosophically, the worse it tasted, the longer it would last them. He placed it carefully in the bottom of the skiff and took a few minutes to check that oars, rudder and the small mast and sail were all safely stowed. The incoming tide was lapping about a third of the way up the skiff now and he knew that was as high as it was going to come. In a few minutes, it would start to go out. And he and Evanlyn would go with it. Vaguely, he knew that the coast of Teutlandt was some-where to the south of them. Or perhaps they might sight a ship now that the Summer Gales seemed to be moderating. He didn't dwell on the future too much. He simply knew that he could not remain a prisoner. If it came to it, he would rather die trying to be free.

'Can't sit here all night,' he said. 'Take the other side and let's get this boat in the water. Lift first, then push.'

Taking hold of the gunwales on either side, they heaved and strained together. At first, it stuck fast in the shingle. But once they lifted and broke the hold, it began to slide more easily. Then, it was afloat, and the two of them clambered aboard. Will gave one last shove with his foot and the skiff drifted out from the beach. Will felt a moment of triumph, then he realised he didn't have time to congratulate himself. Evanlyn, white-faced and tense, was clinging to the gunwales either side of her as the boat rocked in the small waves.

'So far so good,' she said. But her voice betrayed the nervousness she was feeling. Clumsily, he settled the oars in the rowlocks. He'd watched Svengal do it a dozen times. But now he found that watching and doing were two different matters and, for the first time, he had a twinge of doubt. Maybe he'd taken on more than he could handle. He tried a clumsy stroke with the oars, stabbing at the water and heaving. He missed on the left hand side, crabbing the boat around and nearly falling onto the floorboards.

'Slowly,' Evanlyn advised him and he tried again, with greater care. This time, he felt a welcome surge of movement through the boat. He recalled that he'd seen Svengal twisting the oars at the end of each stroke to prevent the blades grabbing in the water. When he did the same, the action was easier. With more confidence, he took a few more strokes and the boat moved more smoothly. The tide was taking effect now and, when Evanlyn looked back at the beach, she felt a lurch of fear to see how far they had come.

Will noticed her reaction.

'It'll move faster as we get out into the middle,' he told her, between strokes. 'We're just on the edge of the tide run.'

'Will!' she cried out in an alarmed voice. 'There's water in the boat!'

The wrappings round her feet had prevented her feeling the water so far. But now it had soaked through and when she looked down, she could see water surging back and forth over the floorboards.

'It's just spray,' he said carelessly. 'We'll bale her out once we're clear of the harbour.'

'It's not spray!' she replied, her voice cracking. 'The boat is leaking! Look!'

He looked down and his heart leapt into his mouth. She was right. There were several centimetres of water above the floorboards of the skiff, and the level seemed to be rising.

'Oh my god!' he said. 'Start baling, quickly!'

There was a small bucket in the stern and she seized it and began frantically scooping water over the side. But the level was slowly gaining on her and Will could feel the boat responding more sluggishly as more and more water rushed in.

'Go back! Go back!' Evanlyn yelled at him. All thought of secrecy was abandoned now. Will nodded, too busy to talk, and heaved desperately on one oar, swinging the boat round to head for the beach. Now he had to fight against the tide run and panic made him clumsy. He missed a stroke and overbalanced again, nearly losing an oar over the side. His mouth was dry with fear as he grabbed at the oar, catching it at the last minute. Evanlyn, scooping frantically at the water in the boat, realised that she was spilling as much water back in as she was throwing overboard. She fought down the sick feeling of panic and forced herself to bale more calmly. That was better, she thought. But the water was still gaining on her.

Luckily, Will had the good sense to move the boat sideways, back to the edge of the tide run, where the outflow was not as fierce. Free of the grip of the main current, the boat began to make better headway. But it was still settling deeper into the water, and the deeper it settled, the faster the inflow of water became. And the more difficult the boat became to row.

'Keep rowing! Row like hell!' Evanlyn encouraged him. He grunted, heaving desperately on the oars, dragging the sluggish boat slowly back to shore. They nearly made it. They were three metres from the beach when the little boat finally went under. The sea poured over the gunwales and it sank beneath them. As they floundered in the waist-deep water, staggering with exhaustion, Will realised that, free of their weight, the skiff was floating again, just below the surface. He took hold and guided it back into the shallows, Evanlyn following him.

'Trying to kill yourselves?' said a grim voice. They looked up to see Erak standing by the water's edge. Several of his crew stood behind him, broad grins on their faces.

'Jarl Erak . . .' Will began, then stopped. There was nothing to say. Erak was turning a small object over in his hands. He tossed it to Will.

'Maybe you forgot this?' he said, his voice ominous. Will studied the object. It was a small cylinder of wood, perhaps six centimetres long and two across. He stared at it, uncomprehending.

'It's what we simple sailors call a bung,' Erak explained sarcastically. 'It stops water coming into the boat. Usually it's a good idea to make sure it's in place.'

Will's shoulders slumped. He was soaked, exhausted and shaking from the gut-gripping fear of the past ten minutes. Most of all, he felt a massive sense of despondency at their failure. A cork! Their plan was in ruins because of a damned cork! Then a massive hand grabbed the front of his shirt and he was hauled off his feet, his face centimetres from Erak's angry features.

'Don't ever take me for a fool, boy!' the Skandian snarled at him. 'You try anything like this again and I'll flog the skin off you!' He turned to include Evanlyn in the threat. 'Both of you!'

He waited until he was sure his warning had hit home, then hurled Will away from him. The apprentice Ranger sprawled on the hard stones of the beach, utterly defeated.

'Now get back to the hut!' Erak told them.

Fourteen

'Wouldn't you know it?' Halt said softly, in a disgusted tone.

Ahead of them, a humpbacked stone bridge reared over a small stream. Sitting his horse between the two travellers and the bridge was a knight in full armour.

Halt reached back over his shoulder and took an arrow from the quiver there, laying it on the bowstring without even looking to see what he was doing.

'What is it, Halt?' Horace asked.

'It's the sort of tomfoolery these Gallicans go on with when I'm in a hurry to be on my way,' he muttered, shaking his head in annoyance. 'This idiot is going to demand tribute from us to allow us to cross his precious bridge.'

Even as he spoke, the armoured man pushed up his visor with the back of his right hand. It was a clumsy movement, made even more so by the fact that he was holding a heavy, three-metre lance in that hand. He nearly lost his grip on the lance, managing to bang it against the side of his helmet in the process, an action that caused a dull clanging sound to carry to the two travellers.

'Arretez là mes seigneurs, avant de passer ce pont-ci!' he called, in a rather high-pitched voice. Horace didn't understand the words, but the tone was unmistakably supercilious.

'What did he say?' Horace wanted to know, but Halt merely shook his head at the knight.

'Let him speak our tongue if he wants to talk to us,' he said angrily, then, in a louder voice, he called: 'Araluans!'

Even at the distance they stood from the other man, Horace made out the shrug of disdain at the mention of their nationality. Then the knight spoke again, his thick accent making the words barely more recognisable than when he had been speaking Gallican.

'You, ma sewers, mah not croess ma brudge wuthut you pah meh a trebute,' he called. Horace frowned now.

'What?' he asked Halt and the Ranger turned to him.

'Barbaric, isn't it? He said, "You , my sirs" — that's us, of course — "may not cross my bridge without you pay me a tribute".'

'A tribute?' Horace asked.

'It's a form of highway robbery,' Halt explained. 'If there were any real law in this idiotic country, people like our friend there would never get away with this. As it is, they can do as they like. Knights set themselves up at bridges or crossroads and demand that people pay tribute to pass. If they can't pay tribute, they can choose to fight them. Since most travellers aren't equipped to fight a fully armoured knight, they pay the tribute.'

Horace sat back on his horse, studying the mounted man. He was trotting his horse back and forth across the road now, in a display that was doubtless intended to discourage them from resistance. His kite-shaped shield was emblazoned with a crude rendition of a stag's head. He wore full mail armour, covered by a blue surcoat that also bore the stag's head symbol. He had metal gauntlets, greaves on his shins, and a pot-shaped helmet with a sliding visor, currently open. The face under the visor was thin, with a prominent, pointed nose. A wide moustache extended past the sides of the visor opening. Horace could only assume that the knight crammed its ends inside when he lowered the visor.

'So what will we do?' he asked.

'Well, I suppose I'll have to shoot the silly idiot,' Halt replied in a resigned sort of voice. 'I'll be damned if I'll pay tribute to every jumped-up bandit who thinks the world owes him a free living. It could be a damn nuisance, though.'

'Why's that?' Horace asked. 'If he goes around asking for a fight, who's going to care if he gets killed? He deserves it.'

Halt laid the bow, arrow nocked and ready, down across his saddle.

'It's to do with what these idiots call chivalry,' he explained. 'If he were to be killed or wounded by another knight in knightly combat, that would be quite excusable. Regrettable perhaps, but excusable. On the other hand, if I put an arrow through his empty head, that would be considered cheating. He's sure to have friends or relatives in the area. These morons usually travel in packs. And if

I kill him they'll want to come after us. It's a damned nuisance, as I said.'

Sighing, he began to raise the bow.

Horace glanced once more at the imperious figure ahead of them. The man seemed totally oblivious to the fact that he was a few seconds away from a very messy end. Obviously, he'd had little to do with Rangers and was given confidence by the fact that he wore full armour. He seemed to have no idea that Halt could put an arrow through the closed visor of his helmet if he chose. The open visor was almost too easy a mark for someone of Halt's skill.

'Would you like me to take care of it?' Horace finally offered, a little hesitantly. Halt, his bow halfway up to the ready position, reacted with surprise.

'You?' he said.

Horace nodded. 'I'm not a full knight yet, I know, but I think I could handle him all right. And as long as his friends think he was knocked over by another knight, nobody will come after us, will they?'

'Sirrahs!' the man shouted now, impatiently, 'yer murst enswer mah demond!' Horace cocked an eyebrow at Halt.

'We must answer his demand. Are you sure you're not taking on too much?' the Ranger said. 'After all, he is a fully qualified knight.'

'Well . . . yes,' said Horace awkwardly. He didn't want Halt to think he was boasting. 'But he's not actually very good, is he?'

'Isn't he?' Halt asked sarcastically, and to his surprise the boy shook his head.

'No. Not really. Look at how he sits his horse. He's got

dreadful balance. And he's already holding his lance too tightly, see? And then there's his shield. He's got it slung way too low to cover a sudden Juliette, hasn't he?'

Halt's eyebrows raised. 'And what might a Juliette be?'

Horace didn't seem to notice the note of sarcasm in the Ranger's voice. He explained stolidly: 'It's a sudden change of target with the lance. You begin by aiming for the shield at chest height, then at the last moment you raise the tip to the helmet.' He paused, then added, with a slight tone of apology, 'I don't know why it's called a Juliette. It just is.'

There was a long silence between them. The boy wasn't boasting, Halt could see. He really seemed to know what he was talking about. The Ranger scratched his cheek thoughtfully. It might be useful to see how good Horace really was, he thought. If things got awkward for him, Halt could always revert to Plan A and simply shoot the loud-mouthed guardian of the bridge. There was one more small problem, however.

'Not that you'll be able to carry out any "Juliettes", of course. You don't appear to have a lance.'

Horace nodded agreement. 'Yes. I'll have to use the first pass to get rid of his. Shouldn't be too big a problem.'

'Sirrahs!' called the knight. 'Yer merst enswer!'

'Oh, shut up,' Halt muttered in his general direction. 'So it shouldn't be a problem, should it?'

Horace pursed his lips and shook his head decisively. 'Well, look at him, Halt. He's nearly dropped it three times while we've been sitting here. A child could take it from him.'

At that, Halt had to grin. Here was Horace, barely more than a boy, declaring that a child could take the lance away from the knight who blocked their way. Then Halt remembered what he'd been doing when he was Horace's age and recalled how Horace had battled with Morgarath, a far more dangerous opponent than the ludicrous figure by the bridge. He appraised the boy once more and saw nothing but determination and quiet confidence there.

'You actually do know what you're talking about, don't you?' he said. And even though it was phrased as a question, it was more a statement of fact. Again, Horace nodded.

'I don't know how, Halt. I just have a feeling for things like this. Sir Rodney told me I was a natural.'

Gilan had told Halt much the same thing after the combat at the Plains of Uthal. Abruptly, Halt came to a decision.

'All right,' he said. 'Let's try it your way.'

He turned to the impatient knight and called to him in a loud voice.

'Sirrah, my companion chooses to engage you in knightly combat!' he said. The horseman stiffened, sitting upright in his saddle. Halt noticed that he nearly lost his balance at this unexpected piece of news.

'Knightly cermbat?' he replied. 'Yewer cermpenion ers no knight!'

Halt nodded hugely, making sure the man could see the gesture.

'Oh yes he is!' he called back. 'He is Sir Horace of the Order of the Feuille du Chêne.' He paused and muttered to himself, 'Or should that have been Crêpe du Chêne? Never mind.'

'What did you tell him?' Horace asked, slinging his

buckler round from where it hung at his back and settling it on his left arm.

'I said you were Sir Horace of the Order of the Oakleaf,' Halt told him, then added uncertainly, 'At least, I think that's what I told him. I may have said you were of the Order of the Oak Pancake.'

Horace looked at him, a slight hint of disappointment in his eyes. He took the rules of chivalry very seriously and he knew he was not yet entitled to use the title 'Sir Horace'.

'Was that totally necessary?' he asked and the Ranger nodded.

'Oh yes. He won't fight just anybody, you know. Has to be a knight. I don't think he noticed you had any armour,' he added, as Horace settled his conical helmet firmly on his head. He had already pulled up the cowl of chain mail that had been folded back on his shoulders, under the cloak. Now he unfastened the cloak and looked to find somewhere to leave it. Halt held out a hand for it.

'Allow me,' he said, taking the garment and draping it across his own saddle. Horace noticed that, as he did so, Halt took care to keep his longbow clear of the cloak. The apprentice nodded at the weapon.

'You won't need that,' he said.

'I've heard that before,' Halt replied, then he looked up as the guardian of the bridge called again.

'Yewer freund hes no lence,' he said, gesturing with his own three-metre length of ash, surmounted by an iron point.

'Sir Horace proposes that you do combat with the sword,' Halt replied and the knight shook his head violently.

'No! No! Ah wull use my lence!'

Halt raised one eyebrow in Horace's direction. 'It seems chivalry is all very well,' he said quietly, 'but if it involves giving up a three-metre advantage, forget it.'

Horace merely shrugged. 'It's not a problem,' he said calmly. Then, as a thought struck him, he asked: 'Halt, do I have to actually kill him? I mean, I can handle him without going that far.'

Halt considered the question.

'Well, it's not obligatory,' he told the apprentice. 'But don't take any chances with him. After all, it'd serve him right if someone did kill him. He might not be so keen to extort tribute from passers-by after that.'

It was Horace's turn to raise a pained eyebrow at the Ranger this time. Halt shrugged.

'Well, you know what I mean,' he said. 'Just make sure you're okay before you let him off too lightly.'

'Seigneur!' the knight cried, setting his lance under his arm and clapping his spurs into his horse's flanks. 'En garde! Ah am cerming to slay yew!'

There was a quick hiss of steel on leather as Horace drew his long sword from its scabbard and wheeled Kicker to face his charging opponent.

'I won't be a minute,' he told Halt, then Kicker bounded away, reaching full stride in the space of a few metres.

Fifteen

Following the failed escape attempt, Will and Evanlyn were forbidden to move more than fifty metres from the huts. There was no more running, no more exercising. Erak managed to find a new range of tasks for the two captives to undertake, from re-weaving the rope mattresses in the dormitory to re-sealing the lower planks along *Wolfwind*'s hull with tar and pieces of frayed rope. It was hot, unpleasant work but Evanlyn and Will accepted it philosophically.

Confined in this fashion, they couldn't help noticing the growing tension between the two groups of Skandians. Slagor and his men, bored and seeking distraction, had called loudly for the two Araluans to be flogged. Slagor, licking his wet lips, had even offered to carry out the task himself.

Erak, very bluntly, told Slagor to mind his own business. He was becoming increasingly weary of the sneering, bragging manner in which Slagor conducted himself, and of the sly way his men cheated and taunted the crew of

Wolfwind at every opportunity. Slagor was a coward and a bully and when Erak compared him to the two captives, he was surprised to find that he had more in common with Will and Evanlyn than with his countryman. He held no grudge against them for their attempted escape. He would have tried the same thing in their place. Now to have Slagor baying after their hides for his own warped amusement somehow brought Erak closer to them.

As for Slagor's men, it was Erak's firm opinion that they were a collective waste of Skorghijl's fresh air.

The situation exploded one night during the evening meal. Will was placing platters and several carving knives on one table. Evanlyn was ladling soup from a large pot at the other, where Erak and Slagor sat with their senior crewmen. As she leaned between Slagor and his first mate, the skirl suddenly lurched back in his chair, throwing his arms wide as he laughed at a comment from one of his men. His hand jolted against the full ladle, spilling hot soup onto his bare forearm.

Slagor bellowed in pain and grabbed Evanlyn by the wrist, dragging her forward, twisting her arm cruelly so that she was bent awkwardly over the table. The soup pot and ladle clattered to the floor.

'Damn you, girl! You've scalded me! Look at this, you lazy Araluan swine!' He shook his dripping arm close to her face, holding her with his other hand. Evanlyn could hear his breath rasping in his nostrils and she was uncomfortably aware of the unwashed smell of him.

'I'm sorry,' she said hurriedly, wincing against the pain as he twisted her arm further. 'But you knocked against the ladle.'

'My fault, was it? I'll teach you to speak back to a skirl!'

His face was dark with rage as he reached for the short three-thonged whip that he carried at his belt. He called it his Encourager and claimed that he used it on lazy rowers — a claim disbelieved by those who knew him. It was common knowledge that he wouldn't have the nerve to strike a burly oarsman.

A young girl, however, was a different matter. Especially now that he was drunk and angry.

The room went silent. Outside, the ever-present wind moaned against the timbers of the hut. Inside, the scene seemed to be frozen for a moment, in the smoky, uncertain light of the fire and the oil lamps around the room.

Erak, sitting opposite Slagor, cursed to himself. On the far side of the room, Will quietly set down the pile of platters. His gaze, like everyone else's, was riveted on Slagor, on the unhealthy flush of alcohol on his face and in his eyes, and the way his tongue kept darting out between his crooked, stained teeth to moisten his thick lips. Unnoticed, the apprentice Ranger retained one of the knives — a heavy, double-edged knife that was used to carve portions of salt pork for the table. Around twenty centimetres in length, it was not unlike a small saxe knife, a knife he was more than familiar with, after his hours of training with Halt.

Now, finally, Erak spoke. His voice was pitched low and his tone was reasonable. That alone made his own crew sit up and take notice. When Erak blustered and yelled, he was usually joking. When he was quiet and intense, they knew, he was at his most dangerous.

'Let her go, Slagor,' he said.

Slagor scowled at him, furious at his order, and the confident tone of command behind it.

'She scalded me!' he shouted. 'She did it on purpose and she's going to be punished!'

Erak reached for his drinking cup and took a deep draught of ale. When he spoke again, he affected a sense of weariness and boredom with the skirl.

'I'll tell you once more. Let her go. She's my slave.'

'Slaves need discipline,' said Slagor, darting a quick glance around the room. 'We've all seen that you're not willing to do it, so it's time someone did it for you!'

Sensing his distraction, Evanlyn tried to twist out of his grip. But he felt her move and held her easily. Several of *Wolf Fang*'s crew, those who were most drunk, chorused agreement with his words.

Erak hesitated. He could simply lean over and knock Slagor senseless. He could do it without even leaving his seat. But that wouldn't be enough. Everyone in the room knew he could best Slagor in a fight and doing so would prove nothing. He was sick and tired of the man and he wanted him humiliated and shamed. Slagor deserved no less and Erak knew how to accomplish it.

He sighed now, as if tired of the whole business, and leaned forward across the table, speaking slowly, as he might to a less than intelligent being. Which, he reflected, was a pretty good summation of Slagor's mental capacities.

'Slagor, I've had a hard campaign and these two are my only profit. I won't have you responsible for the death of one of them.'

Slagor smiled cruelly. 'You've gone soft on these two, Erak. I'm doing you a favour. And besides, a good whipping won't kill her. It'll just make her more obedient in future.'

'I wasn't talking about the girl,' Erak said evenly. 'I meant the boy there.'

He nodded across the room to where Will stood in the flickering shadows. Slagor followed his gaze, as did the others.

'The boy?' He frowned, uncomprehending. 'I have no intention of harming him.'

Erak nodded several times. 'I know that,' he replied. 'But if you touch the girl with that whip of yours, odds are he'll kill you. And then I'm going to have to kill him to punish him. And I'm afraid I'm not prepared to lose so much profit. So let her go.'

Some of the other Skandians were already laughing at Erak's speech, delivered in such a matter-of-fact tone. Even Slagor's men joined in.

Slagor's brows darkened and drew together with rage. He hated being the butt of Erak's jokes and he, and most of the others, thought Erak was merely belittling him by pretending that the undersized Araluan boy could possibly best him in a fight.

'You've lost your wits, Erak,' he sneered now. 'The boy is about as dangerous as a field mouse. I could break him in half with one hand.'

He gestured with his free hand, the one that wasn't locked around Evanlyn's upper arm.

Erak smiled at him. There was no trace of humour in the smile.

'He could kill you before you took a pace towards him,' he said.

There was a calm certainty to his voice that said he wasn't joking. The room sensed it and went very quiet. Slagor sensed it too. He frowned, trying to work his way through this. The alcohol had confused his thinking. There was an element here he was missing. He started to speak, but Erak held up a hand to stop him.

'I suppose we can't actually have him kill you to prove it,' he said, sounding reluctant about the fact. He glanced around the room and his eyes lit on a small brandy cask, half empty, at the far end of the table. He gestured towards it.

'Shove that cask over here, Svengal,' he asked. His second in command put one hand against the small cask and sent it sliding along the rough table to his captain. Erak examined it critically.

'That's about the size of your thick head, Slagor,' he said, with a thin smile. Then he picked up his own belt knife from the table and quickly gouged two white patches out of the dark wood of the keg.

'And let's say they're your eyes.'

He pushed the keg across the table, setting it beside Slagor, almost touching his elbow. A murmur of anticipation went through the men in the room as they watched, wondering where this was leading. Only Svengal and Horak, who had served with Erak at the bridge, had some slight inkling of what their Jarl was on about. They knew the boy was an apprentice Ranger. They had seen, at first hand, that he was an adversary to be respected. But he had no bow here and they hadn't seen what Erak had: the knife that Will was holding concealed against his right arm.

'So, boy,' Erak continued, 'those eyes are a little close

together, but then so are Slagor's.' There was a ripple of amusement from the Skandians and Erak now addressed them directly. 'Let's all watch them carefully and see if anything appears between them, shall we?'

And as he said that, he pretended to peer closely at the keg on the table. It was almost inevitable that everyone else in the room should follow his example. Will hesitated a second, but he sensed that he could trust Erak. The message the Skandian leader was sending him was absolutely clear. Quickly, he drew back his arm in an overhand throw and sent the knife spinning across the room.

There was a brief flash as the spinning blade caught the red glare of the oil lamps and the fire. Then, with a loud 'thwock!' the razor-sharp blade slammed into the wood — not quite in the centre of the gap between the two gouged out patches. The keg actually slid backwards a good ten centimetres under the impact.

Slagor let out a startled cry and jerked away. Inadvertently, he released Evanlyn's arm from his grasp. The girl stepped quickly away from him, then, as Erak jerked his head urgently in the direction of the door, she ran from the room, unnoticed in the confusion.

There was a moment of startled outcry, then Erak's men began to laugh, and to applaud the excellent marksmanship. Even Slagor's men joined in eventually, as the skirl sat glowering at those around him. He wasn't popular. His men only followed him because he was wealthy enough to provide a ship for raiding parties. Now, several of them mimicked the raucous yelp he had let out when the knife thudded into the keg.

Erak rose from the bench and moved round the table, speaking as he went.

'So you see, Slagor, if the boy here had aimed for the wrong wooden head, you would surely be dead right now and I would have to kill him in punishment.'

He stopped, close to Will, smiling at Slagor as the skirl half crouched on the bench, waiting for what was to come next.

'As it is,' Erak continued, 'I simply have to reprimand him for frightening someone as important as you.'

And before Will saw the blow coming, Erak sent a backhanded fist crashing against the side of the boy's head, knocking him senseless to the floor. He glanced at Svengal and gestured to the unconscious figure on the rough wooden floor of the hut.

'Throw this disrespectful whelp into his hutch,' he ordered. Then, turning his back on the room, he stalked out into the night.

Outside, in the clean cold air, he looked up. The sky was clear. The wind was still blowing, but now it had moderated and shifted to the east. The Summer Gales were finished.

'It's time we got out of here,' he said to the stars.

Sixteen

The battle, if you could call it that, lasted no more than a few seconds.

The two mounted warriors spurred towards each other, the hooves of their battlehorses thundering on the unsealed surface of the road, clods of dirt spinning in the air behind them and dust rising in a plume to mark their passage.

The Gallic knight had his lance extended. Halt could now see the fault that Horace had picked in the other man's technique. Held too tightly at this early stage, the lance point swayed and wavered with the horse's movement. A lighter, more flexible hold on the weapon might have kept its point centred on its target. As it was, the lance dipped and rose and wobbled with every stride of the horse.

Horace, on the other hand, rode easily, his sword resting on his shoulder, content to conserve his strength until the time for action came.

They approached each other shield to shield, as was normal. Halt half expected to see Horace repeat the manoeuvre he'd used against Morgarath, and spin his horse to the other side at the last moment. However, the apprentice kept on, maintaining the line of attack. When he was barely ten metres away, the sword arced down from its rest position, the point describing a circle in the air, then, as the lance tip came towards Horace's shield, the sword, still circling, caught the lance neatly and flicked it up and over the boy's head.

It looked deceptively easy, but Halt realised as he watched that the boy was truly a natural weapons master. The Gallic knight, braced for the expected impact of his lance on Horace's shield, suddenly found himself heaving his body forward against no resistance at all. He swayed, feeling himself toppling from the saddle. In a desperate attempt at self-preservation, he grabbed at his saddle pommel.

It was bad luck that he chose to do so with his right hand, which was also trying to maintain control of the unwieldy lance. Twisted upwards by Horace's circling sword point, it was now describing a giant arc of its own. He couldn't manage his balance and the lance at the same time and a muffled curse came from inside the helmet as he was forced to let the lance drop.

Enraged, he groped blindly for the hilt of his own sword, trying to drag it clear of its scabbard for the second pass.

Unfortunately for him, there was to be only one pass.

Halt shook his head in silent admiration as Horace, the lance taken out of play, instantly hauled Kicker to a rearing, spinning stop, using his knees and his shield hand on the reins to wheel the horse on its hind legs before the Gallic knight had gone past him.

The sword, still describing those easy circles that kept his wrist fluid and light, now arced round once more and slammed into the back of the other man's helmet with a loud, ringing clang.

Halt winced, imagining what it must sound like from inside the steel pot. It was too much to expect that a single blow might shear through the tough metal. It would take a series of heavy strokes to accomplish that. But it put a severe dent in the helmet, and the concussion of the blow went straight through the steel to the skull of the knight wearing it.

Unseen by the two Araluans, his eyes glazed out of focus, went slightly crossed, then snapped back again.

Then, very slowly, he toppled sideways out of the saddle, crashed onto the dust of the road and lay there, unmoving. His horse continued galloping for a few more metres. Then, realising that nobody was urging it on any longer, it slowed to a walk, lowered its head and began cropping the long grass by the roadside.

Horace trotted his horse back slowly, stopping level with the point where the Gallic knight lay sprawled on the road.

'I told you he wasn't very good,' he said, quite seriously, to Halt.

The Ranger, who prided himself on his normal taciturn manner, couldn't prevent a wide grin breaking out across his face.

'Well, perhaps he's not,' he told the earnest young man before him. 'But you certainly looked reasonably efficient there.'

Horace shrugged. 'It's what I'm trained for,' he replied simply.

Halt realised that the boy just didn't have a boastful bone in his body. Battleschool had certainly had a good effect on him. He gestured to the knight, now beginning to regain consciousness. The man's arms and legs made weak, unco-ordinated little movements, giving him the appearance of a half-dead crab.

'It's what he's supposed to be trained for too,' he replied, then added, 'Well done, young Horace.'

The boy flushed with pleasure at Halt's praise. He knew the Ranger wasn't one to hand out idle compliments.

'So what do we do with him now?' he asked, indicating his fallen foe with the tip of his sword. Halt slipped quickly down from the saddle and moved towards the man.

'Let me take care of that,' he said. 'It'll be my pleasure.'

He grabbed hold of the fallen man by one arm and dragged him into a sitting position. The dazed knight mumbled inside the helmet and, now that he had time to notice such details, Horace could see that the ends of the moustache protruded from either side of the closed visor.

'Thank yew, sirrah,' the knight mumbled incoherently as Halt dragged him to a more or less upright sitting position. His feet scrabbled on the road as he tried to stand, but Halt shoved him back down, none too gently.

'None of that, thank you,' the Ranger said. He reached under the man's chin and Horace realised that he had the smaller of his two knives in his hand. For a moment, the horrified boy was convinced that Halt meant to cut the man's throat. Then, with a deft stroke, Halt severed the leather chin strap holding the helmet on the other man's head. Once the strap was cut, Halt dragged the helmet off and tossed it into the bushes at the roadside. The knight let out a small mew of pain as his moustache ends tugged free of the still-closed visor.

Horace sheathed his sword, finally sure that there was no further threat from the knight. For his part, the vanquished warrior peered owlishly at Halt and at the figure towering over them both on horseback. His eyes still wouldn't focus.

'We shell continue the cermbet ern foot,' he declared shakily. Halt slapped him heartily on the back, setting his eyes spinning once more.

'The hell you will. You're beaten, my friend. Toppled fair and square. Sir Horace, knight of the Order du Feuille du Chêne, has agreed to spare your life.'

'Oh . . . thenk you,' said the unsteady one, making a vague, saluting gesture in Horace's direction.

'However,' Halt went on, allowing a grim tone of amusement to creep into this voice, 'under the rules of chivalry, your arms, armour, horse and other belongings are forfeit to Sir Horace.'

'They are?' Horace asked, a little incredulously.

Halt nodded.

'They are.'

The knight tried once more to stand but, as before, Halt held him down.

'But sirrah . . .' he protested weakly. 'My erms and ermour? Surely not?'

'Surely so,' Halt replied. The other man's face, already shaken and pale, now looked even paler as he realised the full import of what the grey-cloaked stranger was saying.

'Halt,' Horace interrupted, 'won't he be a little helpless without his weapons — and his horse?'

'Yes, he certainly will,' was the satisfied reply. 'Which will make it a great deal harder for him to prey on innocent travellers who want to cross this bridge.'

Realisation dawned on Horace. 'Oh,' he said thoughtfully. 'I see.'

'Exactly,' Halt said, looking meaningfully at him. 'You've done a good day's work here, Horace. Mind you,' he added, 'it took you barely two minutes to do it. But you'll keep this predator out of business and make the road a little bit safer for the locals. And of course, we will now have a quite expensive suit of chain mail, a sword, a shield and a pretty good-looking horse to sell in the next village we come to.'

'You're sure that's in the rules?' Horace asked and Halt smiled broadly at him.

'Oh yes. It's all fair and above board. He knew it. He simply should have looked more carefully when he challenged us. Now, my beauty,' he said to the crestfallen knight sitting at his feet, 'let's have that mail shirt off you.'

Grudgingly, the dazed knight began to comply. Halt beamed at his young companion.

'I'm starting to enjoy Gallica a lot more than I expected,' he said.

Seventeen

Two days later, *Wolfwind* left Skorghijl harbour and turned north-east for Skandia. Slagor and his men remained behind, facing the task of making temporary repairs to their ship, before limping back to their home port. The ship was too badly damaged to continue west for the raiding season. Slagor's decision to leave port early was proving to be a costly one.

The wind, which for weeks had blown out of the north, now shifted to the west, allowing the Skandians to set the big mainsail. *Wolfwind* surged easily over the grey sea, her wake stretching behind her. The motion was exhilarating and liberating as the kilometres reeled off under her keel and the spirits of the crew lifted as they came closer to their homeland.

Only Will and Evanlyn failed to share in the general lightening of mood. Skorghijl had been a miserable place, barren and unfriendly. But at least the months there had postponed the time when they might be separated. They knew they were to be sold as slaves in Hallasholm and there was every chance they would go to different masters.

Will had tried once to cheer Evanlyn about their possible separation.

'They say Hallasholm isn't a big place,' he said, 'so even if we are split up, we may still be able to see each other. After all, they can't expect us to work twenty-four hours a day, seven days a week.'

Evanlyn hadn't replied. Her experience of Skandians so far told her that was exactly what they would expect.

Erak noticed their silence and the melancholy mood that had settled upon them and felt a twinge of sympathy. He wondered if there weren't some way he could make sure they stayed together.

Of course, he could always keep them as slaves himself, he reasoned. But he had no real need for personal slaves. As a war leader of the Skandians, he lived in the officers' barracks, where his needs were tended by orderlies. If he kept the two Araluans as his own, he'd have to pay to feed and clothe them. And he'd have to be responsible for them as well. He discarded the idea with an irritated shake of his head.

'To hell with them,' he muttered fiercely, driving them from his mind and concentrating on keeping the ship perfectly on course, frowning fiercely as he watched the Pole stone needle floating in its gimballed bowl by the steering blade.

On the twelfth day of the crossing, they made a landfall with the Skandian coast — exactly where Erak had predicted they would fetch up. From the admiring glances the men cast at the Jarl, Will could tell that this was a considerable feat.

Throughout the following days, they edged closer to the shore, until Will and Evanlyn could make out more detail. High cliffs and snow-covered mountains seemed to be the dominant features of Skandia.

'He's caught Loka's current perfectly,' Svengal told them as he prepared to climb to the lookout position on the mast's cross tree. The cheerful second in command had developed a certain fondness for Will and Evanlyn. He knew their lives would be hard and pitiless as slaves, and he tried to compensate with a few friendly words whenever possible. Unfortunately, his next comment, meant in a kindly fashion, was little comfort to either Will or Evanlyn.

'Ah well,' he said, seizing hold of a halyard to haul himself to the top of the mast, 'we should reach home in two or three hours.'

As it turned out, he was mistaken. The wolfship, finally under oars again, ghosted through the thick fog that shrouded the Hallasholm harbour mouth barely an hour and a quarter later. Will and Evanlyn stood silently in the waist of the ship as the town of Hallasholm loomed out of the fog.

It was not a large place. Nestled at the foot of towering pine-clad mountains, Hallasholm consisted of perhaps fifty buildings — all of them single storey and all, apparently, built from pine logs and roofed with a mixture of thatch and turf.

The buildings huddled round the edge of the harbour, where a dozen or more wolfships were moored at jetties or drawn up on the land, canted on their sides as men worked on the hulls, fighting a never-ending battle against the attacks of the marine parasites that constantly ate away at the wooden planks. Smoke curled up from most of the chimneys and the cold air was redolent with the heady smell of burning pine logs.

The principal building, Ragnak's Great Hall, was built from the same logs as the rest of the houses in the town. But it was larger, longer and wider, and with a pitched roof that let it tower above its neighbours. It stood in the centre of the town, dominating the scene, surrounded by a dry ditch and a stockade — more pine logs, Will noticed. Pine was obviously the most common building material available in Skandia. A long, wide road led up to the gateway in the stockade from the main quay.

Gazing at the town across the glass-smooth water of the harbour, Will thought that, in another time and under other conditions, he would probably find the neatly ordered houses, with the massive, snow-covered mountains towering behind them, to be quite beautiful.

Right now, however, he could see nothing to recommend their new home to him. As the two young people watched, light snow began to drift down around them.

'I should think it's going to be cold here,' Will said quietly.

He felt Evanlyn's chilled hand creep into his. He squeezed it gently, hoping to give her a sense of encouragement. A sense that was totally foreign to the way he himself was feeling at the moment.

Eighteen

'I told you that symbol on your shield would make travelling easier,' Halt remarked to Horace.

They sat at ease in their saddles, Halt with one leg cocked up over the pommel, as they watched the Gallic knight who had been barring passage to a crossroads ahead of them set his spurs to his horse and gallop away towards the safety of a nearby town. Horace glanced down at the green oakleaf device that Halt had painted on his formally plain shield.

'You know,' he said, with a hint of disapproval in his tone, 'I'm not actually entitled to any coat of arms until I have been formerly knighted.' Horace's training under Sir Rodney had been quite strict and he felt sometimes that Halt didn't pay enough notice to the etiquette of chivalrous behaviour. The bearded Ranger glanced sidelong at him and shrugged.

'For that matter,' he remarked, 'you're not entitled to contest any of these knights until you've been properly knighted either. But I haven't noticed that stopping you.'

Since their first encounter at the bridge, the two travellers had been stopped on half a dozen occasions by freebooting knights guarding crossroads, bridges and narrow valleys. All of them had been dispatched with almost contemptuous ease by the muscular young apprentice. Halt was highly impressed by the young man's skill and natural ability. One after another, Horace had sent the roadside guardians toppling from their saddles, at first with a few deftly placed strokes from his sword and, more recently, as he had captured a good, stout lance with a balance and a feel that he liked, in a thundering charge that unseated his opponent and sent him flying metres behind his galloping horse. By now, the two travellers had amassed a considerable store of armour and weapons, which they carried strapped to the saddles of the horses they had captured. At the next sizeable town they came to, Halt planned to sell horses, arms and armour.

For all his admiration of Horace's skill, and despite the fact that he felt a grim satisfaction at seeing the bullying vultures put out of business, Halt resented the continual delays it caused in their journey. Even without them, he and Horace would be hard put to reach the distant border with Skandia before the first winter blizzards made it impassable. Accordingly, five nights previously, as they camped in the half-ruined barn of a deserted farm property, he had rummaged through the piles of old rusting tools and rotting sacks until he unearthed a small pot of green paint and an old, dried-out brush. Using these, he had sketched a green oakleaf design onto Horace's shield. The result had been as he expected. The reputation of

Sir Horace of the Order of the Oakleaf had gone before them. Now, more often than not, as the brigand knights had seen them approaching, they had turned and fled at the sight of the device on Horace's shield.

'I can't say I'm sorry to see him go,' Horace remarked, gently nudging Kicker forward towards the now deserted crossroads. 'My shoulder's not totally healed yet.'

His previous opponent had been considerably more skilful than the general run of highway warriors. Undaunted by the oakleaf device on the shield, and obviously not bothered by Horace's reputation, he had joined combat eagerly. The fight had lasted several minutes and, during the course of their combat, a blow from his mace had glanced off the top rim of Horace's shield and deflected onto his upper arm.

Fortunately, the shield had taken a good deal of the force of the blow, or Horace's arm would, in all likelihood, have been broken. As it was, there was severe bruising and his arm and shoulder were still not as free-moving as he would have liked.

Barely half a second after the mace had done its damage, Horace's backhanded sword stroke had clanged sickeningly into the front of the other man's helmet, leaving a severe dent and sending the knight sprawling unconscious and heavily concussed on the forest floor.

Now, he was relieved that he hadn't had to fight since.

'We'll spend a night in town,' Halt said. 'We may be able to get some herbs and I'll make a poultice for that arm of yours.' He'd noticed the boy was favouring the arm. Even though Horace hadn't complained, it was obviously causing him considerable pain.

'I'd like that,' Horace said. 'A night in a real bed would be a pleasant change after sleeping on the ground for so long.'

Halt snorted derisively. 'Battleschool evidently isn't what it used to be,' he replied. 'It's a fine thing when an old man like me can sleep comfortably in the open while a young boy gets all stiff and rheumatic over it.'

Horace shrugged. 'Be that as it may,' he replied, 'I'll still be glad to sleep in a bed tonight.'

Actually, Halt felt the same way. But he wasn't going to let Horace know that.

'Perhaps we should hurry,' he said, 'and get you into a nice comfortable bed before your joints seize up altogether.'

And he urged Abelard into a slow canter. Behind him, Tug instantly increased his own pace to match. Horace, caught by surprise, and hampered by the captured horses he was leading, was a little slower to keep up.

The string of battlehorses, laden with armour and weapons, raised quite a bit of interest in the town as they rode through the streets. Horace noticed again how people scurried to clear the way in front of his battlehorse as he rode. He noticed the furtive glances cast his way and more than once he heard the phrase 'Chevalier du chêne' whispered as he passed people by. He glanced curiously at Halt.

'What's that they're saying about chains?' he asked. Halt gestured towards the oakleaf symbol on the shield hanging at Horace's saddle bow.

'Not chain,' he told the young warrior, 'They're saying "chêne". That's their word for oak. They're talking about you: the knight of the oak. Apparently your fame has spread.'

Horace frowned. He wasn't sure if he was pleased about that or not.

'Let's hope it doesn't cause any trouble,' he said uncertainly. Halt merely shrugged.

'In a small town like this? It's hardly likely. More the opposite, I'd expect.'

For it was a small town, barely more than a village, in fact. The single main street was narrow, with hardly room for their two horses to move abreast. People on foot had to press back out of the way, stepping into the side streets to let the horsemen pass — then remaining in that position as the small string of battlehorses clopped quietly along behind them.

The street itself was unpaved, a mere dusty track that would quickly turn to thick gluey mud in the event of any rain. The houses were small, mostly single storey affairs, which seemed to have been built on something less than the normal scale.

'Keep your eyes open for an inn,' Halt said quietly.

Travelling with a notorious companion was a novel experience for Halt. In Araluen, he was accustomed to the suspicion and sometimes fear which greeted the appearance of a member of the Ranger Corps. The mottled cloaks with their deep cowls were a familiar sight to people in the Kingdom. Here in Gallica, he was quite pleased to notice, the Ranger uniform, along with the distinctive weaponry of longbow and double knives, seemed to evoke little or no interest.

Horace was a different matter entirely. His reputation had obviously gone before them and people eyed him with the same edge of suspicion and uncertainty that Halt had become used to over the years. The situation pleased Halt quite well. In the event of any trouble, it would give him and Horace a decided edge if people had already decided that the main danger came from the strapping young man in armour.

The fact of the matter was that the grizzled older man in the nondescript cloak was a far more dangerous potential enemy.

'Up ahead there,' Horace said, rousing Halt from his musing. He followed the direction of the boy's pointing finger and there was a building, larger than the others, with a second storey leaning precariously out over the street, rather uncertainly supported by uneven oak beams that jutted out at first floor level. A weathered signboard swung gently in the breeze, with a crude depiction of a wine glass and a platter of food marked on it in peeling paint.

'Don't get your hopes too high about a nice soft bed for the night,' Halt warned the apprentice. 'We may well have slept softer in the forest.' He didn't add that they would almost certainly have slept cleaner.

As it turned out, he had done the inn an injustice. It was small and the walls weren't quite true to the perpendicular. The ceiling was low and uneven and the stairs seemed to lean to one side as they made their way up to inspect the room they had been offered.

But at least the place was clean and the bedroom had a large, glazed window, which had been flung wide open to let in the fresh afternoon breeze. The smell of freshly ploughed fields carried to them as they looked out over the higgledy-piggledy mass of steeply pitched roofs in the town.

The innkeeper and his wife were both elderly people, but at least they seemed welcoming and friendly to their two guests — particularly after they had seen the store of arms and armour piled on the riderless horses lined up outside the inn. The young knight was obviously a man of property, they decided. And a person of considerable importance as well, judging by the way he left all dealings to his manservant, the rather surly fellow in a grey and green cloak. It suited the innkeeper's sense of snobbery to assume that people of noble birth didn't deign to interest themselves in such commercial matters as the price of a room for the night.

Having ascertained that there was no market within the town where they might be able to convert their captured booty into money, Halt allowed the inn's stable boy to bed their horses down for the night. All except Abelard and Tug, of course. He saw to them personally, and he was pleased to note that Horace did the same for Kicker.

Once the horses were settled, the two companions returned to their room. Supper wouldn't be ready for an hour or two, the innkeeper's wife had told them.

'We'll use the time to take a look at that arm of yours,' Halt told Horace. The younger man sank gratefully onto the bed and sighed contentedly. Contrary to Halt's expectations, the beds were soft and comfortable, with thick, clean blankets and crisp white sheets. At a gesture from Halt, the apprentice stood up and pulled his mail shirt and tunic over his head, grunting slightly with pain as he had to raise his arm above shoulder height to do it.

The bruising had spread across the entire upper arm, creating a patchwork of discoloured flesh that ran from dark blue-black to an ugly yellow around the edges. Halt probed the bruised area critically, feeling to make sure there were no broken bones.

'Ow!' said Horace, as the Ranger's fingers probed and poked around the bruise.

'Did that hurt?' Halt asked, and Horace looked at him with exasperation.

'Of course it did,' he said sharply. 'That's why I said "ow!" '

'Hmmmm,' Halt muttered thoughtfully, and, seizing the arm, he turned it this way and that, while Horace gritted his teeth against the pain. Finally able to contain his annoyance no longer, he stepped back away from Halt's grasp.

'Are you actually hoping to accomplish anything there?' he asked in a peevish tone of voice. 'Or are you just having fun causing me pain?'

'I'm trying to help,' Halt said mildly. He reached for the arm once more but Horace backed away.

'Keep your hands off,' he said. 'You're just poking and prodding. I can't see how that's supposed to help.'

'I'm just trying to make sure there's nothing broken,' Halt explained. But Horace shook his head at the Ranger.

'Nothing's broken. I've got some bruising, that's all.'

Halt made a helpless gesture of resignation. He opened his mouth to speak, planning to reassure Horace that he was really trying to help, when matters were taken out of his hands — literally.

There was a brief knock at the door then, before the sound had died, the door was flung open and the innkeeper's wife bustled in with an armful of fresh pillows for the beds. She smiled at the two of them, then her gaze lit upon Horace's arm and the smile died, replaced instantly by a look of motherly concern.

She let go a torrent of Gallican that neither of them understood, and moved quickly to Horace's side, dumping the pillows on his bed. He watched her suspiciously as she reached out to touch the injured arm. She stopped, pursed her lips and met his gaze with a reassuring look. Satisfied, he allowed her to examine the injury.

She did so gently, with a light, almost imperceptible touch. Horace, submitting to her ministrations, looked meaningfully at Halt. The Ranger scowled and sat on the bed to watch. Finally, the woman stepped back and, taking Horace's arm, led him to sit on the edge of the bed. She turned to address the two of them, pointing to the discoloured arm.

'No breaking bones,' she said uncertainly. Halt nodded.

'I thought as much,' he replied and Horace sniffed disdainfully. The woman nodded once or twice, then continued, choosing her words carefully. Her command of the Araluan tongue was inexact, to say the least.

'Bruisings,' she said, 'Bad bruisings. Need . . .' She hesitated, seeking the word, then found it. 'Herbs . . .' She made a rubbing gesture with her two hands, miming the act of rubbing herbs together to form a poultice. 'Break herbs . . . put here.' She touched the injured arm once more. Halt nodded agreement.

'Good,' he told her. 'Please go right ahead.' He looked up at Horace. 'We're in luck here,' he said. 'She seems to know her business.'

'You mean I'm in luck,' Horace said stiffly. 'If I'd been left to your tender mercies, I probably wouldn't have an arm by now.'

The woman, hearing the tone of the voice but not understanding the words, hurried to reassure him, making crooning sounds and touching the bruise with a feather-soft hand.

'Two days . . . three . . . no more bruisings. No more pain,' she reassured him and he smiled at her.

'Thank you, madame,' he said, in the sort of courtly tone he imagined a gallant young knight should use. 'I shall be forever in your debt.'

She smiled at him and, in mime again, indicated that she was going to fetch her stock of herbs and medicines. Horace rose and executed a clumsy bow as she left the room, giggling to herself.

'Oh puh-lease,' said Halt, rolling his eyes to heaven.

Nineteen

The heat in Ragnak's dining hall was intense.

The large number of people present, and the huge, open fire that stretched almost the full width of one end of the room, combined to keep the temperature uncomfortably warm, in spite of the deep snow that lay on the ground outside.

It was an enormous room, long and low-ceilinged, with two tables stretching the length of the room and a third, Ragnak's head table, placed across the others at the end opposite the fire. The walls were bare pine logs, roughly trimmed and caulked, where their uneven shape left a gap, with a mixture of mud and clay that set hard as rock.

More pine logs slanted up at angles to support the roof, a tightly woven layer of rushes and thatch that was almost a metre thick in places. There was no interior lining. Lighter slats of rough timber were fastened across the roof beams to support the thatch.

The noise, with nearly one hundred and fifty drunken Skandians eating, laughing and shouting at each other, was deafening. Erak looked around him and smiled.

It was good to be home again.

He accepted another tankard of ale from Borsa, Ragnak's hilfmann. While Ragnak was the Oberjarl, or senior jarl of all Skandians, the hilfmann was an administrator who took care of the day-to-day running of the nation. He made sure that crops were planted, taxes paid, raids sent out on time and Ragnak's share of all raiding booty — a quarter of everything won — was paid promptly and reckoned fairly by the wolfship commanders.

'Bad business all round, Erak,' he said. They were discussing the ill-fated expedition to Araluen. 'We should never get involved in a long-running war. It's not our game at all. We're cut out for quick raids. Get in, grab the booty and get out again with the tide. That's our way. Always has been.'

Erak nodded. He'd thought the same thing when Ragnak had assigned him to the expedition. But the Oberjarl hadn't been in any mood to listen to his advice.

'Still, Morgarath paid us upfront,' the hilfmann continued. Erak's eyebrows raised at that.

'He did?' It was the first he'd heard of it. He'd assumed that he and his men were fighting simply for whatever booty they could find, and the expedition had been a definite failure in that regard. But his companion nodded emphatically.

'Oh yes indeed. Ragnak's no fool when it comes to money. He charged Morgarath for your services, and those of all your men. You'll all be paid your share.'

At least, thought Erak, he and his men would have something to show for the past few months. But Borsa was still shaking his head over the Araluan campaign.

'You know our biggest problem?' he said, and before Erak could respond, he continued. 'We don't have our own generals or tacticians. Skandians fight as individuals. And in that sense, we're the best in the world. But when we hire out as mercenaries, we don't have our own planners to lead us. So we're forced to rely on fools like Morgarath.'

Erak nodded agreement. 'When we were in Araluen, I said that his plans were too involved, too clever by half.'

Borsa jabbed a thick forefinger at him. Erak was surprised by the man's vehemence.

'And you're right! We could use a few people like those Araluan Rangers,' he added.

'Are you serious?' Erak said. 'Why do we need them?'

'Not them literally. I mean people like them. People who are trained in planning and tactics — with the ability to see the big picture and use our troops to best effect.'

Erak had to agree the other man had a point. But the mention of Rangers had led his mind to the matter of Will and Evanlyn. Now he saw a way to solve the problem of dealing with them.

'Could you use a couple of new slaves around the Great Hall?' he asked casually. Borsa nodded immediately.

'We can always use extras,' he said. 'Got someone in mind, have you?'

'A boy and a girl,' Erak told him. He thought it best not to mention that Will was an apprentice Ranger. 'Both strong. Healthy and intelligent. We captured them on the Celtic border. I was going to sell them so I could pay my crew something for the whole mess. But now, if you say we'll be paid anyway, I'd be happy to give them to you.'

Borsa nodded gratefully. 'I can certainly use them,' he replied. 'Send them over tomorrow.'

'Done!' said Erak cheerfully. He felt a nagging weight had been removed from his mind. 'Now where's that ale jug got to?'

While Erak was deciding their fate, Will and Evanlyn had been kept locked in a hut by the quayside, close to the point where *Wolfwind* was moored. The following morning, they were roused by a Skandian from Borsa's staff, who led them to the Great Hall. There, the Hilfmann looked them over, studying them critically. The girl was attractive, he thought, but she didn't look as if she'd done a lot of heavy work in her life. The boy, on the other hand, was well muscled and fit, if a little on the small side.

'The girl can go to the dining hall and kitchen,' he told his assistant. 'Put the boy in the yard.'

Twenty

An hour after sunset, Halt and Horace left their room and went downstairs to the taproom of the inn for supper.

The innkeeper's wife had prepared a huge pot of savoury stew. It hung, simmering, in the enormous fireplace that dominated one side of the room. A serving girl brought them large wooden bowls of the steaming food, along with curious, long loaves of bread, shaped in a style Horace had never seen before. They were very long, and narrow, so they looked like thick sticks rather than loaves. But they were crusty on the outside and delight-fully light and airy on the inside. And, the apprentice soon discovered, they were an ideal tool for mopping up the delicious gravy of the stew.

Halt had accepted a large beaker of red wine with his meal. Horace had settled for water. Now, having enjoyed a large serving of a delicious berry pie, they sat over mugs of an excellent coffee.

Horace spooned a large helping of honey into his cup, watched with a frown by the Ranger.

'Killing the taste of good coffee,' Halt muttered at him. Horace merely grinned. He was getting used to his companion's mock severity by now.

'It's a habit I learned from your apprentice,' he told him, and for a moment they were both silent, thinking of Will, wondering what had become of him and Evanlyn, hoping they were both safe and well.

Halt finally roused them from their thoughtful mood by nodding his head towards the small group of townspeople seated by the fire. He and Horace had taken a table at the back of the room. It was always Halt's way to do this, keeping his back to a solid wall and sitting where he could observe the rest of the room and, at the same time, remain relatively inconspicuous himself.

While they were eating, the room had gradually filled with townspeople, either coming to eat or to enjoy a few jugs of wine or beer before heading to their own homes. Now, the Ranger had noticed, one of the room's inhabitants had produced a set of pipes from inside his pack, and another was fiddling with the tuning pegs of a gourd-shaped, eight-stringed instrument.

'Looks like the entertainment's about to start,' he told Horace.

And as they spoke, the other people in the room began pulling their chairs closer to the fire and calling for refills from the innkeeper and his serving assistants.

The piper began playing a lament, and the string instrument quickly took up a counterpoint, playing rapid, vibrating strokes to form a continuous, high treble background to the soaring, swooping melody. The pipes themselves filled the room with a wild and plaintive sound, a voice that reached deep into the soul and brought thoughts of friends long gone and times past to the forefront of the listeners' minds.

As the notes echoed round the warm room, Halt found himself remembering the long summer days in the forest surrounding Castle Redmont, and a small, busy figure who asked endless questions and brought a new feeling of energy and interest to life. In his mind's eye, he could see Will's face — hair tousled by the cowl of his cloak, brown eyes alight and filled with an irrepressible sense of fun. He remembered him as he cared for Tug, remembered the pride the boy had shown at the prospect of having a horse of his own and the special bond that had formed between the two of them.

Perhaps it was because Halt could feel the years encroaching on him as the grey hairs in his beard became more the norm than the exception. But Will had brought a sense of youth and fun and vitality to his life, a sense that was a welcome contrast to the dark and dangerous paths that a Ranger was often required to tread.

He remembered, too, the pride he had felt when Horace had told him of the way Will took it upon himself to follow the Wargal forces in Celtica, and how the boy had stood alone against the Wargals and Skandians as Evanlyn had worked to make sure the fire took hold of the bridge. There was more to Will than just an irrepressible spirit. There was courage and ingenuity and loyalty. The boy would have made a truly great Ranger, Halt thought, then abruptly realised that he had thought of Will as if such an eventuality were no longer possible. His eyes moistened with tears and he shifted uncomfortably. It was a long time since Halt had shown any outward sign of emotion. Then, he shrugged. Will was worth at least a few tears from a grizzled old wreck like himself, he thought, and made no move to wipe them away. He glanced sideways at Horace to see if the boy had noticed, but Horace was entranced by the music, leaning forward on the bench they shared, his lips slightly parted, one finger beating time unconsciously on the rough table top. It was as well, Halt thought, smiling ruefully to himself. It wouldn't do for the boy to see him dissolving into tears at the first sound of sad music. Rangers, particularly treasonous ex-Rangers who had insulted the King, were supposed to be made of sterner stuff.

The music finally ended, to a roar of applause from the people in the room. Halt and Horace joined in enthusiastically and Halt used the moment to covertly dash a hand across his eyes and wipe away the traces of moisture there.

He noticed that the performers were being rewarded by the audience with coins tossed into the hat that had been artfully left, upturned, on the floor beside them. He shoved a couple of coins towards Horace and nodded towards the players.

'Give them these,' he said. 'They've earned it.'

Horace nodded wholehearted agreement and rose to cross the room, ducking his head under the heavy beams that supported the ceiling. He tossed the coins into the cap, the last in the room to do so. The piper looked up, saw an unfamiliar face and nodded his thanks. Then he began to pump the bellows on his pipes with his elbow again, and once more, the haunting voice of the pipes swelled up and began to fill the room.

Horace hesitated, loath to move now that another song had begun. He glanced back to where Halt sat in the shadows, shrugged and settled onto a table top at the edge of the small crowd surrounding the performers.

There was a different tone to this piece. There was a subtle note of triumph in the melody, augmented by the bold major chords struck by the stringed instrument, which came more to the fore for this piece. Indeed, before too long, the brittle, rippling notes of the gourd-shaped instrument had wrested the lead from the pipes and set toes tapping and hands beating time throughout the room. A delighted smile broke out on Horace's face and, as the door to the street opened and a gust of wind swept round the room, he barely took notice of the newcomer who entered.

Others did, however, and Halt, senses finely honed by years of living through dangerous situations, felt a change in the atmosphere in the room. A sense of apprehension and almost suspicion seemed to grip the people grouped around the musicians.

There was even a slight hesitation in the tune as the piper glanced up and saw the man who had entered. Just the slightest break in rhythm, almost imperceptible, but enough for Halt to notice.

He looked at the newcomer. A tall, well-built man, perhaps ten years younger than himself. Black beard and hair, and heavy, black brows that gave him an ominous appearance. He was obviously not one of the simple townsfolk. As he threw back his cloak, he revealed a chain mail shirt covered with a black surcoat that bore a white raven insignia.

The hilt of a sword was obvious at his waist, worked with gold wire and with a dully gleaming pommel in the same metal. High, soft leather riding boots marked him as a mounted warrior − a knight, judging by the insignia on his surcoat. Halt had no doubt that, tethered outside the tavern, he would find a battlehorse − most probably a jet black one, judging by the stranger's favoured colour scheme.

The newcomer was obviously looking for someone. His eyes swept the room quickly, passing over Halt without noticing the shadowy figure at the rear of the room, then finally lighting on Horace. The brows tightened fractionally and he nodded, almost imperceptibly, to himself. The boy, enthralled by the music, had barely taken note of the knight's arrival and now paid no attention to the intense study to which he was subjected.

There were others in the room who did. Halt saw the heightened awareness of the innkeeper and his wife, as they watched and waited for events to unfold. And several of the townspeople were showing signs of anxiety, signs that they might prefer to be somewhere else.

Halt's hand reached under the table for his quiver. As ever, his weapons were within easy reach, even when he was dining, and the longbow leaning against the wall behind him was already strung. Now, he eased an arrow from the quiver and laid it on the table before him as the tune came to an end.

This time, there was no chorus of applause from the

people in the room. Only Horace clapped enthusiastically, then, realising he was the only one to be doing so, he stopped, confused, a flush of embarrassment rising to his cheeks. Now he too became aware of the armed man in the room, standing half a dozen paces away from him, staring at him with an intensity that bordered on aggression.

The boy recovered his composure and nodded a greeting to the newcomer. Halt was pleased to notice that Horace had the presence of mind not to look in his direction. He had sensed that something unpleasant might be about to happen and understood the advantage that would come from Halt's not being noticed.

Finally, the newcomer spoke, his voice deep and gravelly. He was a tall man, as tall as Horace, and heavily built. This was no roadside warrior, Halt decided. This man was dangerous.

'You are the oakleaf chevalier?' he asked, with a hint of derision. He spoke the Araluan language well, but with a distinct Gallic accent.

'I believe I have been called that,' Horace replied, after a moment's pause. The knight seemed to consider the answer, nodding to himself, his lip curled in a half sneer.

'You believe so?' he said. 'But can you, yourself, be believed? Or are you a lying Araluan dog who barks in the gutters?'

Horace frowned, puzzled. It was a clumsy attempt to insult him. The other man was trying to provoke a fight for some reason. And that, to Horace, was sufficient reason not to be provoked.

'If you like,' he replied calmly, his face a mask of

indifference. But Halt had noticed how his left hand had touched lightly, and almost instinctively, to his left hip, where his sword normally hung ready. Now, of course, it hung behind the door of their room upstairs. Horace was armed with only a dagger.

The knight had noticed the involuntary movement as well. He smiled now, his lips curling in a cruel arc. And he moved a pace closer to the muscular young apprentice. He took stock of the young man now. Wide shoulders, slim at the waist and obviously well muscled. And he moved well, with a natural grace and balance that was the mark of an expert warrior.

But the face was young and absolutely without guile. This was not an opponent who had fought men to the death repeatedly. This was not a warrior who had learned the darker skills in the unforgiving school of mortal combat. The boy had barely begun to shave. He was undoubtedly a trained fighter, and one to be respected.

But not feared.

Having made his assessment, the older man moved a pace closer, yet again.

'I am Deparnieux,' he said. Obviously, he expected the name to mean something. Horace merely shrugged his shoulders good-naturedly.

'Good for you,' he replied. And those black brows contracted once more.

'I am no roadside yokel for you to defeat by trickery and knavish behaviour. You will not catch me unprepared with your cowardly tactics, as you have so many of my compatriots.'

He paused to see if the insulting words were having the

desired effect. Horace, however, was canny enough not to take exception. He shrugged once more.

'I'll definitely bear that in mind,' he replied mildly.

One more pace and the heavily built knight was within arm's reach. His face suffused with rage at Horace's answer, and the boy's refusal to be insulted.

'I am warlord of this province!' he shouted. 'A warrior who has despatched more foreign interlopers, more Araluan cowards, than any other knight in this land. Ask them if this is not so!' And he swept an arm around at the people sitting tensely at tables round the fire. For a moment, there was no reply, then he turned his fierce gaze on them, daring them to disagree with him.

As one, their eyes dropped and they mumbled a grudging acknowledgement of his claim. Then his gaze came back to challenge Horace once more. The boy returned it impassively, but a shade of red was beginning to colour his cheeks.

'As I said,' he replied carefully, 'I will bear it in mind.'

Deparnieux's eyes glittered at the boy. 'And I call you a coward and a thief who has killed Gallic warriors by subterfuge and deceit and stolen their armour and horses and belongings!' he concluded, his voice rising to a crescendo.

There was a long silence in the room. Finally, Horace replied.

'I think you are mistaken,' he said, in the same mild tone he had maintained throughout the confrontation. There was a collective intake of breath throughout the room. And now Deparnieux reared back in fury.

'You say I am a liar?' he demanded.

Horace shook his head. 'Not at all. I say you are mistaken. Somebody has apparently misinformed you.'

Deparnieux spread his hands and addressed the room at large.

'You have heard this! He calls me liar to my face! This is insupportable!'

And, just as he had planned, in the same movement with which he had spread his hands, he had plucked one of his leather gauntlets from where it had been secured under his belt and now, before anyone in the room could react, had drawn it back to slap it across Horace's face in a challenge that could not be ignored.

Feeling a sense of exultation, he began the forward sweep of his hand to bring the glove swiping across the boy's face.

Only to have it plucked from his grip by an invisible hand, and hurled across the room, where it came to a quivering halt, skewered to one of the upright oak beams that supported the ceiling.

Twenty-one

So they were to be separated after all, Will thought. Evanlyn was led away, stumbling as she turned to look back over her shoulder at him, a stricken expression on her face. He forced a grin of encouragement and waved to her, making the gesture casual and light-hearted, as if they would be seeing each other shortly.

His attempt at raising her spirits was cut short by a solid backhander to his head. He staggered a few feet, his ears ringing.

'Get moving, slave!' snarled Tirak, the Skandian supervisor of the yard. 'We'll see how much you have to smile about.'

The answer to that was precious little, Will soon discovered.

Of all the Skandians' captives, yard slaves had the hardest, most unpleasant assignment. House slaves — those who worked in the kitchens and dining rooms — at least had the comfort of working, and sleeping, in a warm area. They might fall into their blankets exhausted at the end of a day, but the blankets were warm.

Yard slaves, on the other hand, were required to look after all the arduous, unpleasant outdoor tasks that needed doing — cutting firewood, clearing snow from the paths, emptying the privies and disposing of the result, feeding and watering the animals, cleaning stables. They were all jobs that had to be done in the bitter cold. And when their exertions finally raised a sweat, the slaves were left in damp clothing that froze on them once their tasks were completed, leaching the heat from their bodies.

They slept in a draughty, dilapidated old barn that did little to keep out the cold. Each slave was given one thin blanket — a totally inadequate covering when the night temperatures fell below freezing point. They supplemented the covering with any old rags or sacks they could lay hands on. They stole them, begged them. And often, they fought over them. In his first three days, Will saw two slaves battered to the point of death in fights over ragged pieces of sacking.

Being a yard slave was more than uncomfortable, he realised. It was downright dangerous.

The system they worked under added to the danger. Tirak was nominally in charge of the yard, but he delegated that authority to a small, corrupt gang known as the Committee. These were half a dozen long-term slaves who hunted as a pack and held the power of life or death over their companions. In return for their authority and some extra comforts such as food and blankets, they maintained the brutal discipline of the yard and organised the work roster, assigning tasks to the other slaves. Those who pandered to them and obeyed them were given the easiest tasks. Those who resisted them found themselves carrying out the wettest, coldest, most dangerous jobs. Tirak ignored their excesses. He simply didn't care about the slaves in his charge. They were expendable as far as he was concerned and his life was much simpler if he used the Committee to maintain order. If they killed or crippled the occasional rebel, it was a small price to pay.

It was inevitable that Will, being the person he was, would clash with the Committee. It happened on his third day in the yard. He was returning from a firewood detail, dragging a heavily laden sled through the thin snow. His clothes were damp with sweat and from the melting snow and he knew that as soon as the exertion stopped, he would be shivering with cold. The marginal rations that they were fed would do little to restore his body heat and, with each day, he could feel his strength and resilience fading a little further.

Bent almost double, he dragged the sled into the yard, heaving it to a stop beside the kitchen, where house slaves would unload it, carrying the split logs in to the warmth of the massive cooking ranges. His head spun a little as he straightened up, then, from behind one of the kitchen outhouses, he heard a voice cursing, while another whimpered in pain.

Curious, he left the sled and went to see the cause of the commotion. A thin, ragged boy was huddled on the ground while an older, larger youth flayed at him with a length of knotted rope.

'I'm sorry, Egon!' the victim wept. 'I didn't know it was yours!'

They were both slaves, Will realised. But the big youth looked well fed and he was warmly dressed, in spite of the fact that his clothes were ragged and stained. Will estimated his age at about twenty. He'd noticed there were no older slaves in the yard. He had an uncomfortable suspicion that this was because yard slaves didn't live very long.

'You're a thief, Ulrich!' said the larger youth. 'I'll teach you to touch my belongings!'

He was aiming the knotted rope for his victim's head now, lashing furiously. The boy's face was heavily bruised, Will saw, and as he watched, a cut opened just under the smaller boy's eye and blood covered his face. Ulrich cried and tried to cover his face with his bare arms. His tormentor flailed all the more wildly. Will could stand by no longer. He stepped forward and caught the end of the knotted rope as Egon began another stroke, jerking it backwards.

Egon was thrown off balance. He staggered and let go the rope, turning to look in surprise to see who had dared interrupt him. He half expected to see Tirak or another Skandian standing there. Nobody else would dare interfere with a Committeeman. To his surprise, he found himself facing a short, slight youth who looked to be about sixteen years old.

'He's had enough,' Will said, tossing the rope into the slushy snow of the kitchen yard.

Furious, Egon started forward. He was bigger and heavier than Will and he was ready to punish this foolhardy stranger. Then something in the stranger's eyes, and in his ready stance, stopped him. He could see no fear there. And he looked fit and ready to fight. He was new to the yard, Egon realised, and still in relatively good condition. This was no easy target, like the unfortunate Ulrich.

'I'm sorry, Egon,' the ragged boy now snuffled. He crawled towards the Committeeman and placed his head against his worn boots. 'I won't do it again.' Egon by now had lost interest in his initial victim. He shoved him away with his foot. Ulrich looked up, saw that Egon's attention was diverted, and made his escape.

Egon barely noticed him go. He was glaring at Will, assessing him. This one would be no easy victim. But there were other ways to deal with troublemakers.

'What's your name?' he asked, his eyes slitted and his voice low with fury.

'I'm called Will,' the apprentice Ranger said and Egon nodded his head slowly, several times.

'I'll remember that,' he promised.

The following day, Will was assigned to the paddles.

The paddles were the most feared work assignment among the yard slaves.

Hallasholm's fresh water supply came from a large well in the centre of the square facing Ragnak's Lodge. As the colder weather set in, the water in the well, if left untended, would freeze over. So the Skandians had installed large wooden paddles to constantly agitate the water and break up the ice before it froze solid. It was a constant, grinding job, heaving on the crank handles that turned the clumsy wooden blades in the water. Like snow clearing, it was wet and cold work, thoroughly debilitating. Nobody lasted long on the paddles.

Will had been working for half the morning, but already he was exhausted. Every muscle in his arms, back and legs ached with the strain.

He heaved on the handle, worn smooth over the years by a succession of long-dead hands. It was barely minutes since he'd last agitated the surface of the well water but already a thin skin of ice had formed. It cracked now as the wooden blade stabbed into it and moved rapidly from side to side. On the far side of the well, his co-worker jerked and twisted at his own paddle, keeping the water moving, stopping it freezing. When he had first arrived, Will had nodded to the other slave. The greeting was ignored. Since then, they had worked in silence, apart from their constant groans of exertion.

A heavy leather strap, wielded by the overseer, snapped across his shoulders. He heard the noise, felt the impact. But there was no stinging sensation from the blow. That was numbed by the cold.

'Dig them in deeper!' the overseer snarled. 'The water will freeze underneath if you simply skim the surface like that.'

Groaning softly, Will obeyed, rising on tiptoe to drive the wooden paddle down into the frigid water, throwing up a wash of spray as he did so. He felt the icy touch of the water on his body. He was already wet through. It was almost impossible to remain dry. He knew that when he stopped for one of the brief rest periods they were allowed, the wet, freezing clothes would leach the body heat from him and the trembling would start again.

It was the unstoppable shivering that frightened him most. As he cooled down, his body would begin to shake. He tried to force it to stop, and found he couldn't. He had lost control over his own body, he realised dully. His teeth chattered and his hands shook and he was helpless to do anything about it. The only way to regain warmth was to start work again.

Eventually, it was over. Even the Skandians recognised that no one could work more than a four-hour shift on the paddles. Trembling and exhausted, utterly spent, Will staggered back to the barracks shed. He stumbled and fell as he approached his assigned sleeping space and lacked the energy to rise again. He crawled on hands and knees, longing for the meagre warmth of the thin blanket.

Then a hoarse cry of despair was torn from him. The blanket was gone!

He huddled on the cold floor, weeping. His knees were drawn up and he wrapped his arms around them in an attempt to contain his failing body heat. He thought of his warm Ranger cloak, lost when he was captured by Erak and his men. The shivering began and he felt his whole body give way to it. The cold burrowed deep into his flesh, reaching right into his bones, right into the very soul of him.

There was nothing but the cold. His world was circumscribed by cold. He was the cold. It was inescapable, unbearable. There was no slight flicker of warmth in his world.

Nothing but the cold.

He felt something rough against his cheek and opened his eyes to see someone leaning over him, spreading a piece of coarse sacking over his trembling body. Then a quiet voice was in his ear.

'Take it easy, friend. Be strong now.'

The speaker was a tall slave, bearded and unkempt. But it was the eyes that Will noticed. They were full of sympathy and understanding. Pathetically, Will drew the scratchy cloth closer around his chin.

'Heard what you tried to do for Ulrich,' said his saviour. 'We've got to stick together if we're going to make it in here. I'm Handel, by the way.'

Will tried to answer but his teeth were chattering uncontrollably and his voice shook as he tried to form words. It was useless.

'Here, try this,' said Handel, glancing around to make sure they were not observed. 'Open your mouth.'

Will forced his chattering teeth apart and Handel slipped something into his mouth. It felt like a bundle of dried herbs, Will thought dully.

'Put it under your tongue,' Handel whispered. 'Let it dissolve. You'll be fine.'

And then, after a few moments, as his saliva moistened the substance under his tongue, Will felt the most glorious, liberating sense of warmth radiating through his body. Beautiful warmth that forced the cold out, that spread to the very tips of his fingers and toes in a series of pulsing waves. He had never felt anything so wonderful in his life.

The trembling eased as successive waves of warmth swept gently over him. His tight muscles relaxed into a delightful sense of rest and wellbeing. He looked up to see Handel smiling and nodding at him. Those wonderful, warm eyes smiled reassuringly and he knew everything was going to be all right.

'What is it?' he said, speaking awkwardly around the sodden little wad in his mouth.

'It's warmweed,' Handel told him gently. 'It keeps us alive.'

And from the shadows of a far corner, Egon watched the two figures and smiled. Handel had done his work well.

Twenty-two

The black-clad knight cursed violently as the arrow ripped his gauntlet from his grasp and thudded, carrying the glove with it, into a heavy oak beam.

The solid impact of the arrow with the beam drew his eyes for a second, then he whirled suspiciously, to see where the missile had come from. For the first time, he registered the presence of a dark, indistinct shape in the shadows at the rear of the room. Then, as Halt moved from behind the table and out into the light, he also registered the longbow, with a second arrow nocked ready to the string. The archer hadn't bothered to draw the bow, but Deparnieux had just seen an example of his skill. He knew he was facing a master archer, capable of drawing and firing in a heartbeat. He stood very still now, controlling his rage with difficulty. He knew his life might well depend on his ability to do so.

'Unfortunately for the dictates of chivalry,' Halt said, 'Sir Horace, knight of the Order of the Oakleaf, is indisposed, with an injury to his left hand. He will therefore be unable to reply to the kind invitation you were about to issue.'

He had moved further into the light now and Deparnieux could make out his face more clearly. Bearded and grim, this was the face of an experienced campaigner. The eyes were cold and bore no hint of indecision. This, the knight knew instantly, was a man to be wary of.

There was a subdued chuckle from one of the townspeople in the room and, inwardly, the Gallic knight seethed with fury. His eyes flicked to the source of the sound and he saw a carpenter, lowering his face to hide his smile. Deparnieux noted the man mentally. His day of reckoning would come. Outwardly, however, he forced a smile.

'A pity,' he told the archer. 'I had hoped for a friendly trial of arms with the young chevalier — all in the spirit of good fellowship, of course.'

'Of course,' Halt replied levelly and Deparnieux knew that he wasn't for a moment deceived. 'But, as I say, we shall have to disappoint you, as we are travelling on a rather urgent quest.'

Deparnieux's eyebrows lifted in polite enquiry. 'Is that so? And where might you and your young master be bound?'

He added the 'young master' to see what effect it would have on the bearded man before him. It was obvious who was the master here, and it wasn't the young knight. He'd hoped that he might sting the other man's pride, and possibly goad him to a mistake.

The hope, however, was short-lived. He noticed a faint glint of amusement in the man's eyes as he recognised the gambit for what it was.

'Oh, here and there,' Halt replied vaguely. 'It's not a task of sufficient importance to interest a warlord such as yourself.' The tone of his voice left the knight in no doubt that he would not be answering casual questions about their end destination, or even their intended direction of travel.

'Sir Horace,' he added, aware that the boy was still within arm's reach of the black knight, 'why don't you sit yourself down over there and rest your injured arm?'

Horace glanced at him, then understanding dawned and he moved away from the knight, taking a seat by the edge of the fire. There was absolute silence in the room now. The townspeople gazed at the two men confronting each other, wondering where this impasse was going to end. Only two people in the room, Halt and Deparnieux, knew that the knight was trying to gauge his chances of drawing his sword and cutting down the archer before he could fire. As Deparnieux hesitated, he met the unwavering gaze of the Ranger.

'I really wouldn't,' said Halt, mildly. The black knight read the message in his eyes and knew that, fast as he might be, the other man's reply would be faster. He inclined his head slightly in recognition of the fact. This was not the time.

He forced a smile onto his face and made a mocking bow in Horace's direction.

'Perhaps another day, Sir Horace,' he said lightly. 'I would look forward to a friendly trial of arms with you when you are recovered.'

This time, he noticed, the boy glanced quickly at his older companion before replying. 'Perhaps another day,' he agreed.

Embracing the room with a thin smile, Deparnieux turned on his heel and walked to the door. He paused there a moment, his eyes seeking Halt's once more. The smile faded and the message he sent was clear. *Next time, my friend. Next time.*

The door closed behind him and a collective sigh of relief went round the room. Instantly, a babble of conversation broke out among those present. The musicians, sensing that their moment was over for the night, packed away their instruments and gratefully accepted drinks from the serving girl.

Horace moved to the beam where Halt's arrow had pinned the knight's gauntlet. He wrestled the shaft free, dropped the glove onto a table and returned the arrow to Halt.

'What was that all about?' he asked, a little breathlessly. Halt moved back to their table in the shadows, and leaned his longbow against the wall once more.

'That,' he told the boy, 'is what happens when you begin to acquire a reputation. Our friend Deparnieux is obviously the person who controls this area and he saw you as a potential challenge to that control. So, he came here to kill you.'

Horace shook his head in bewilderment. 'But . . . why? I don't have any quarrel with the man. Did I offend him somehow? I certainly didn't mean to,' he said. Halt nodded gravely.

'That's not the point,' he told the young apprentice. 'He doesn't give a toss about you. You were simply an opportunity for him.'

'An opportunity?' Horace asked. 'For what?'

'To re-affirm his hold over the people in the area,' Halt explained. 'People like him rule by fear, for the most part. So, when a young knight comes into the area with a reputation as a champion, somebody like Deparnieux sees it as an opportunity. He provokes a fight with you, kills you, and his own reputation is enlarged. People fear him more and are less likely to challenge his control over them. Understand?'

The boy nodded slowly. 'It's not the way it should be,' he said, a disappointed tone in his voice. 'It's not the way chivalry was intended to be.'

'In this part of the world,' Halt told him, 'it's the way it is.'

Twenty-three

Jarl Erak, wolfship captain and member of Ragnak's inner council of senior jarls, had been absent from Hallasholm for several weeks.

He was whistling as he strode back through the open gates to the Lodge, with a sense of satisfaction over a job well done. Borsa had sent him to sail down the coast to one of the southernmost settlements, to enquire over an apparent shortfall in taxes paid by the local jarl. Borsa had noticed a decline over the past four or five years. Nothing too sudden to be suspicious, but a little less every year.

It had taken a calculating mind like Borsa's to notice the creeping discrepancy. And to note that the gradual reduction in reported income had coincided with the election of a new jarl in the village. Smelling a rat, the hilfmann had assigned Erak to investigate — and to persuade the local jarl that honesty, in the case of taxes owed to Ragnak, was definitely the best policy.

It has to be admitted that Erak's version of investigating consisted of seizing the unfortunate jarl by his beard as he lay sleeping in the pre-dawn darkness. Erak then threatened to brain him with a battleaxe if he didn't make a rapid and upward adjustment to the amount of tax he was paying to Hallasholm. They were rough and ready tactics, but highly effective. The jarl was only too eager to hand over the delinquent tax.

It was sheer chance that Erak came striding back through the gates at the very moment that Will was stumbling, shovel in hand, to clear the walkways of the deep snow that had fallen overnight.

For a moment, Erak didn't recognise the emaciated, shambling figure. But there was something familiar about the shock of brown hair, matted and dirty as it was. Erak stopped for a closer look.

'Gods of darkness, boy!' he muttered. 'Is that you?'

The boy turned to look at him, the expression blank and incurious. He was reacting only to the sound of a voice. There was no sign that he recognised the speaker. His eyes were red-rimmed and dull as he regarded the burly Skandian. Erak felt a deep sadness come over him.

He knew the signs of warmweed addiction, of course, knew that it was used to control the yard slaves. And he'd seen many of them die from the combined effects of cold, malnutrition and the general lack of will to live that resulted from addiction to the drug. Warmweed addicts looked forward to nothing, planned for nothing. Consequently, they had no hope to bolster their spirits. It was that, as much as anything, that killed them in the long run.

It hurt him to see this boy brought so low. To see those eyes, once so full of courage and determination, reflecting nothing but the dull emptiness of an addict's lack of hope or expectation.

Will waited a few seconds, expecting to be given an order. Deep inside him, a faint memory stirred for a second or two. A memory of the face before him and the voice he had heard. Then, the effort of remembering became too great, the fog of addiction too thick and, with the slightest of shrugs, he turned away and shambled to the gateway to begin shovelling the snow. Within a few minutes, he would be soaked with sweat from the heavy work. Then the moisture would freeze on his body and the cold would eat deep into him again. He knew the cold now. It was his constant companion. And with the thought of the cold, there came the longing for his next supply of the weed. His next few moments of comfort.

Erak watched Will as he bent slowly and clumsily to his task. He swore softly to himself and turned away. Other yard slaves were already at work on the paddles at the fresh water well, smashing the thick ice that had formed during the freezing night.

He passed them by quickly, with barely a glance. He was no longer whistling.

Two days later, late in the evening, Evanlyn was summoned to Jarl Erak's quarters.

She had managed to claim a sleeping space for herself that was close enough to the great ovens to be warm through the night, but not so close that she roasted.

Now, at the end of a long day, she spread her blanket out on the hard rushes and sank gratefully onto it, rolling it round her. Her pillow was a small log from the firewood pile, padded with an old shirt. She lay back on it now, listening to the noises of those around her – the occasional thick, chesty coughs that were the inevitable result of living in the snow and ice of Skandia at this time of year, and the low muttering of conversation. This was one of the few times that the slaves were free to talk among themselves. Usually, Evanlyn was too tired to take advantage of it.

She became conscious of the fact that someone was calling her name and she sat up with a small groan. A chamber slave was moving through the rows of prone forms, occasionally stooping to shake a shoulder and ask if anyone knew where she would find the Araluan slave called Evanlyn. For the most part, she received blank stares and disinterested shrugs. Life among the slaves was not conducive to forming new friendships.

'Over here!' Evanlyn called, and the chamber slave looked to see where the voice came from, then picked her way carefully across the bodies to her.

'You're to come with me,' she said, a pompous tone in her voice. Chamber slaves, who looked after the living quarters in the Lodge, saw themselves as superior beings to mere kitchen slaves – a breed of people who lived in a world of grease and spilt wine and food.

'Where?' Evanlyn asked and the girl sniffed disdainfully at her.

'Where you're told,' she replied. Then, as Evanlyn made no move to rise, she was forced to add: 'Jarl Erak says.' After all, she had no personal authority over kitchen slaves, even though she might think herself above them. The Skandians recognised no such differentiation. A slave was a slave and, apart from the gang bosses in the yard, they were all the same as each other.

There was a small stir of interest from the others sitting and lying nearby. It was not unknown for the senior Skandian officers to recruit their personal slaves from the ranks of the more attractive young girls.

Wondering what this was all about, Evanlyn rose and carefully folded her blanket, leaving it to mark her space. Then, gesturing for the other girl to lead the way, she followed her out of the kitchen.

Ragnak's Lodge was, in effect, a veritable rabbit warren of passageways and rooms leading from the central, high-ceilinged Great Hall where meals were served and official business conducted. The girl led Evanlyn now through a series of low, dimly lit passageways, until they reached what appeared to be a dead end. There was a door set into the end of the wall and the chamber slave indicated it to her.

'In there,' she said briefly, then added, 'You'd better knock first.' And she turned away, hurrying back down the dim corridor. Evanlyn hesitated a moment, not sure what this was all about, then rapped with her knuckles on the hard oak of the door.

'Come in.' She recognised the voice that answered her knock. Erak's vocal chords were trained to carry to his men over the gales of the Stormwhite Sea. He never seemed to lessen the volume. There was a latch on the outside of the door. She raised it and went inside.

Erak's chambers were simple. Inevitably constructed from pine logs, there was a sitting room and, screened by a woven wool curtain, a bedchamber to one side. The sitting room had a small log fire burning at one end, giving the room a comfortable warmth, and several carved oak chairs. A very expensive and, she recognised, foreign tapestry covered the rush floor. She guessed it was the result of one of Erak's raids to Gallica. In her years at Castle Araluen, she had seen many similar pieces. Woven by the artists of the Tierre Valley over a period of years that often spanned one or two decades, the rugs usually changed hands for a small fortune. Somehow, she didn't think Erak had paid cash for his.

The Jarl was sitting by the fire, leaning back in one of the comfortable looking carved chairs. He motioned her in and indicated a bottle and glasses on a low table in the centre of the room.

'Come in, girl. Pour us some wine and sit down. We have some talking to do.'

Uncertainly, she crossed the room and poured the red wine into two glasses. Then, handing one to the Skandian, she sat on the other armchair. Unlike Erak, however, she didn't sprawl comfortably back. She perched nervously on the edge, as if poised for flight. The Jarl studied her with what appeared to be a hint of sadness in his look, then he waved a hand at her.

'Relax, girl. Nobody's going to harm you — least of all me. Drink your wine.'

Tentatively, she took a sip and found it surprisingly good. Erak was watching her and he saw the involuntary expression of surprise on her face.

'You know good wine then?' he asked her. 'I took a hogshead of this out of a Florentine ship in the last raiding season. Not bad, is it?'

She nodded her agreement. She was beginning to relax a little and the wine sent a soft glow through her. She hadn't touched alcohol in any form for months, she realised. The thought occurred to her that she had better watch her step. And her tongue.

She waited now for the Skandian captain to speak. He seemed to be hesitating, as if not sure how he should proceed. The silence grew between them until, eventually, she could bear it no longer. She took another quick sip of her wine, then asked:

'Why did you send for me?'

Jarl Erak had been staring into the flames of the small fire. He looked up in surprise now as she spoke. He must be unused to having slaves begin conversations with him, she thought. Then she shrugged. They could sit here in silence all night if someone didn't get the ball rolling. She was intrigued to see a slow smile break out on the bearded face. It occurred to her that in another place, under different conditions, she could grow to quite like the Skandian pirate.

'Probably not for the reason you're thinking,' he said, then, before she could reply, he continued, almost to himself, 'But somebody has to do something and I think you're the one for the job.'

'Do something?' Evanlyn repeated. 'Do something about what?'

Erak seemed to come to a decision then. He heaved a deep sigh, drained the last of the wine in his glass, and leaned forward, his elbows resting on his knees, his craggy, bearded face thrust towards her.

'Have you seen your friend lately?' he asked. 'Young Will?'

Her eyes dropped from his gaze. She had seen him all right — or rather, she had seen the shambling, mindless figure that he had become. Some days ago, he had been working outside the kitchen and she had taken him some food. He snatched the bread from her hands and devoured it like an animal. But when she spoke to him, he had merely stared at her.

In two short weeks, he had already forgotten Evanlyn, forgotten Halt and the little cottage by the edge of the woods outside Castle Redmont. He had forgotten even the major events that had happened at the Plains of Uthal, when King Duncan's army had faced and defeated Morgarath's implacable Wargal regiments.

Those events, and all the others of his young life, might as well have taken place on the far side of the moon for all he was concerned. Today, his life and his total being centred on one thought and one thought only.

His next supply of warmweed.

One of the other slaves, an older woman, had witnessed the encounter. As Evanlyn returned to the kitchen, she had spoken softly to her.

'Forget your friend. The drug's got him. He's already dead.'

'I've seen him,' she told Erak now in a low voice.

'I had nothing to do with that,' he said angrily, surprising Evanlyn with the intensity of his reply. 'Nothing. Believe me, girl, I hate that damn drug. I've seen what it does to people. No one deserves that sort of shadow life.'

She looked up to meet his gaze again. He was obviously sincere and, equally obviously, wanted her to acknowledge what he had said. She nodded.

'I believe you,' she said.

Erak rose from his chair. He strode restlessly about the small, warm room as if action, any form of physical action, would relieve the fury that had been building within him since he encountered Will.

'A boy like that, he's a real warrior. He may only be knee high to a gnat, but he's got the heart of a true Skandian.'

'He's a Ranger,' she told him quietly, and he nodded.

'That he is. And he deserves better than this. That damned drug! I don't know why Ragnak allows it!'

He paused for a long moment, gaining control of his temper. Then he turned to her and continued.

'I want you to know that I tried to keep you two together. I had no idea Borsa would send him to the yard. The man has no concept of how to treat an honourable enemy. But what can you expect? Borsa's no warrior. He counts sacks of grain for a living.'

'I see,' Evanlyn said carefully. She wasn't sure that she did, but she felt some response was expected of her. Erak looked at her keenly, assessing her, she thought. He seemed to be trying to make up his mind about something.

'Nobody survives the yard,' he added softly, almost to himself. As he said it, Evanlyn felt a cold hand wrap around her heart.

'So,' he said, 'it's up to us to do something about it.'

Evanlyn looked at him, hope rising inside her as he spoke those last words.

'Exactly what sort of thing do you have in mind?' she asked slowly, hoping against hope that she was judging this conversation correctly. Erak paused for a second or two, then decided, irrevocably, to commit himself.

'You're going to escape,' he said finally. 'You're taking him with you and I'm helping you do it.'

Twenty-four

The two travellers spent a restless night, taking it in turns to keep watch. Neither of them trusted the local warlord not to come sneaking back in the darkness. As it turned out, however, their fears were unfounded. There was no further sign of Deparnieux that night.

The next morning, as they were saddling their horses in the barn at the rear of the building, the innkeeper approached Halt nervously.

'I can't say, sir, that I am sorry to see you leave my inn,' he said apologetically. Halt patted him on the shoulder to show that he took no offence.

'I can understand your position, my friend. I'm afraid we haven't endeared ourselves to your local thug.'

The innkeeper glanced round nervously before agreeing with Halt, as if frightened that someone might be observing them and might report his disloyalty to Deparnieux. Halt guessed that such a thing had probably happened many times before in this town. He felt sorry for the man in the bar the previous night who had laughed – and been seen to do so by the black knight.

'He's a bad, bad man, right enough, sir,' the innkeeper admitted in a lowered voice. 'But what can the likes of us do about him? He has a small army at his back and we're just tradesmen, not warriors.'

'I wish we could help you,' Halt told him, 'but we do have to be on our way.' He hesitated just a second, then asked innocently, 'Does the ferry at Les Sourges operate every day?'

Les Sourges was a river town that lay to the west, some twenty kilometres away. Halt and Horace were travelling north. But the Ranger was sure that Deparnieux would return, asking for any clues as to the direction they had taken. He didn't expect the innkeeper would keep his question a secret. Nor would he blame him if he didn't. The man was nodding now in confirmation of the question.

'Yes, sir, the ferry will still be running at this time of year. Next month, when the water freezes, it will close down and travellers will have to use the bridge at Colpennieres.'

Halt swung up into the saddle. Horace was already mounted, and held the lead rein for their string of captured horses. After the previous night's events, they had decided it would be wiser to leave the town as quickly as possible.

'We'll make for the ferry then,' he said in a carrying voice. 'The road forks a few miles to the north, I take it?'

Again, the innkeeper nodded. 'That's right, sir. It's the first major crossroads you come to. Take the road to the right and you're headed for the ferry.'

Halt raised a hand in thanks and farewell and, nudging

Abelard with his knee, he led the way out of the stableyard.

They travelled hard that day. Reaching the crossroads, they ignored the right turn and continued straight ahead, heading north. There was no sign on the road behind them that there was any pursuit. But the hills and the woods that surrounded them could have concealed an army if need be. Halt wasn't entirely convinced that Deparnieux, who knew the countryside, wasn't travelling parallel to them somewhere, perhaps outflanking them to set up an ambush at some point further along the road.

It came as something of an anticlimax when, in mid-afternoon, they arrived at yet another small bridge, with yet another knight in attendance, barring their passage across and offering them the choice of paying tribute or contesting with him.

The knight, astride a bony chestnut horse that should have been retired two or three years ago, was a far cry from the warlord they had confronted the night before. His surcoat was muddy and tattered. It may have been yellow once but now it had faded to a dirty off-white. His armour had been patched in several places and his lance was obviously a roughly trimmed sapling, with a decided kink about a third of the way along its length. His shield was inscribed with a boar's head. It seemed appropriate for a man as rusty, tattered, and generally grubby as he was.

They came to a halt, surveying the scene. Halt sighed wearily.

'I am getting so very tired of this,' he muttered to Horace, and began unslinging his longbow from where he wore it across his shoulders.

'Just a moment, Halt,' said Horace, shrugging his round buckler from its position on his back and onto his left arm. 'Why don't we let him see the oakleaf insignia and see if that changes his mind about things?'

Halt scowled at the tatterdemalion figure in the road ahead of them, hesitating as his hand reached for an arrow.

'Well, all right,' he said reluctantly. 'But we'll give him one chance only. Then I'm putting an arrow through him. I'm heartily sick of these people.'

He slouched back in his saddle as Horace rode to meet the scruffy knight. So far, there had been no sound from the figure in the middle of the road and that, thought Halt, was unusual. As a general rule, the road warriors couldn't wait to issue challenges, usually peppering their speech with generous helpings of 'Ho, varlet!' and 'Have at thee then, sir knight' and other antiquated claptrap of the sort.

And even as the thought occurred to him, warning bells went off in his mind and he called to the young apprentice who was now some twenty metres away, trotting Kicker to meet his challenger.

'Horace! Come back! It's a . . .'

But before he could say the last word, an amorphous shape dropped from the branches of an oak tree that overhung the road, draping itself around the head and shoulders of the boy. For a moment, Horace struggled uselessly in the folds of the net that enveloped him. Then an unseen hand tugged on a rope and the net tightened around him and he was jerked out of the saddle, to crash heavily onto the road.

Startled, Kicker reared away from his fallen rider,

trotted a few paces, then, sensing he was in no danger himself, stopped and watched, eyes pricked warily.

'. . . trap,' finished Halt quietly, cursing his lack of awareness. Distracted by the ridiculous appearance of the shabby knight, he had allowed his senses to relax, leading them into this current predicament.

He had an arrow on the bowstring now, but there was no visible target, save the knight on the ancient battlehorse, who still sat silently in the middle of the road. He was part of the entire elaborate setup, without a doubt. He had shown no sign of surprise when the net had fallen onto Horace.

'Well, my friend, you can pay for your part in this deception,' Halt muttered, and brought the bow up smoothly, bringing it back in a full draw until the feathered end touched his cheek, just above the corner of his mouth.

'I don't think I'd do that,' said a familiar gravelly voice. The ragged, rusty knight pushed back his visor, revealing the dark features of Deparnieux.

Halt swore to himself. He hesitated, the arrow still at full draw, and heard a series of small noises from the underbrush on either side of the road. Slowly, he released the tension on the string as he became aware that at least a dozen shapes had risen from the bushes, all of them holding deadly little crossbows.

All of them pointing towards him.

He replaced the arrow in the quiver at his back and lowered the bow until it rested across his thighs. He glanced hopelessly to where Horace still struggled against the fine woven mesh that had wrapped itself around him. Now more men were emerging from the bushes and trees that flanked the road. They approached the helpless apprentice and, as four of them covered him with crossbows, the others worked to loosen the folds of the net and bring him, red-faced, to his feet.

Deparnieux, grinning widely with satisfaction, urged his bony horse down the road towards them. Stopping within easy speaking distance, he performed a cursory bow from the waist.

'Now, gentlemen,' he said mockingly, 'I will be privileged to have you as my guests at Chateau Montsombre.'

Halt raised one eyebrow. 'How could we possibly refuse?' he asked, of no one in particular.

Twenty-five

It had been five days since Evanlyn had been summoned to Erak's quarters.

While she waited for further contact from him, she went ahead with the other part of the plan he had outlined to her, complaining loudly at the prospect of being assigned to be one of his personal slaves. According to the story they had concocted, she would finish the week in the kitchen, then take up her new assignment. She professed her disgust with him in general, with his standard of cleanliness in particular, and spoke as often as she could of the cruelty he had shown her on the voyage to Hallasholm.

To hear Erak described by Evanlyn in those few days, he was the worst of the devils of hell, and with bad breath to boot.

After several days of this, Jana, one of the senior kitchen slaves, said to her wearily, 'There could be worse things for you, my girl. Get used to it.'

She turned away, tired of Evanlyn's constant complaints. For in truth, the life of a personal slave had some advantages: better food and clothing and more comfortable quarters among them.

'I'll kill myself first,' Evanlyn called after her, glad of the chance to make her abhorrence of the Jarl more public. A passing kitchenhand, a freeman, not a slave, cuffed her heavily around the back of the head, setting her ears ringing.

'I'll do it for you, you lazy slacker, if you don't get back to work,' he told her. She shook her head, glaring her hatred after his retreating back, and hurried off to serve ale to Ragnak and his fellow diners.

As ever, she felt a distinct surge of anxiety as she entered the dining hall under Ragnak's gaze. Although reason told her that he was unlikely to single her out from the dozens of other hurrying slaves busily serving food and drink, she still lived in the constant fear that, somehow, she would be recognised as Duncan's daughter. It was that anxiety, as much as the nonstop work, that left her drained and exhausted at the end of each night.

After the evening's work was completed, the slaves moved gratefully to their sleeping spaces. Evanlyn noted wryly that Jana, obviously bored with Evanlyn's constant complaints about Erak, had moved her blanket to the far side of the room. She spread her own blanket and went to re-roll the cloth around her log pillow. As she did so, a small piece of paper fell from the folds of the old shirt she used to pad the wood.

Her heart racing, Evanlyn quickly covered the scrap with her foot, glancing round to see if any of her neighbours had noticed. Nobody seemed to. They all continued with their own preparations for sleep. As casually as she could, Evanlyn lay down, retrieving the small scrap of paper as she did so, and pulled her blanket up to her chin, taking the opportunity to glance at the one word message written on the paper:

'Tonight.'

A kitchenhand came in a few minutes later and doused the lanterns, leaving only the flickering flames of the banked fire to light the room. Exhausted as she was, Evanlyn lay on her back, eyes wide open, pulses racing, waiting for the time to pass.

Gradually, the voices around the room fell silent, replaced by the deep, regular breathing of sleeping slaves. Here and there were soft snores or the occasional cough, and, once or twice, a voice spoke out, slurred and indistinct, as an elderly Teuton slave muttered in her sleep.

The fire died away to a dull red glow and Evanlyn heard the watch sounding the horn for midnight from the harbour. That would be the last signal horn until dawn, at around seven o'clock. She settled back to wait. Erak had told her to wait till an hour after the midnight signal. 'That gives them time to settle down and sleep deeply,' he'd said to her, when he outlined his plan. 'Leave it any longer and the light sleepers and the older slaves will start waking up and needing to use the privies.'

In spite of the tension she felt, her eyelids were beginning to droop and, with a panicky start, she realised she had nearly dropped off to sleep. That would be perfect, she thought bitterly, to have the Jarl waiting for her outside the Great Hall while she was snoring soundly in her blanket.

She shifted on the hard floor, moving to a less comfortable position, digging her nails into her palms so that the pain would keep her alert. She began to count to measure the time passing, then realised, almost too late, that the soporific effect of counting had nearly put her to sleep again.

Finally, with a shrug of annoyance, she decided that an hour must have passed. There was no sign of anyone being awake in the kitchen, as she cautiously pushed back her blanket and stood up. If anyone stirred, she reasoned, she could always claim that she was heading for the privy herself. She had gone to bed fully dressed, apart from her boots. She carried them with her now, wrapping the blanket around her. As the fire had died down, the room had grown progressively colder and she shivered as the chill air struck at her.

The door to the yard seemed to be loud enough to wake the dead as she tried to ease it open. It swung on the heavy hinges with what seemed to be a deafening shriek. Wincing, she shut it as carefully as she could, marvelling that nobody had seemed to be disturbed by the noise.

There was no moon. The night was overcast with thick clouds but still the snow that covered the ground reflected what little light there was, making it easy to see details. The black mass that was the yard slaves' sleeping quarters, a cold and draughty barn, was easily visible, thirty or forty metres away.

Hopping from one foot to the other, she tugged on her boots. Then, hugging the wall of the main building, she moved to her left, making for the corner as Erak had instructed. As she reached the end of the wall, she let out an involuntary gasp. There was a burly figure waiting there, huddled close in to the shadow of the building.

For a moment, she felt a shaft of fear stab at her. Then she realised it was Jarl Erak.

'You're late,' he whispered in an angry tone. She realised that he was possibly as keyed up as she was. Jarl or no Jarl, he was risking his life to help a slave escape and he'd be well aware of the fact.

'Some of them hadn't settled down,' she lied. It seemed pointless to tell him that she'd had no way of measuring time. He grunted in reply and she guessed her excuse was accepted. He thrust a small sack into her hands.

'Here,' he said. 'There are a few silver coins in there. You'll probably have to bribe one of the Committeemen to get the boy out of there. This should be enough. If I give you more, they'll only get suspicious and wonder where it came from.'

She nodded. They had discussed all this in his quarters five nights before. The escape would have to be accomplished without any suspicion falling on Erak. This was the reason why he had instructed her to spend the last few days complaining about the prospect of becoming his slave. It would create an apparent reason for her attempt to escape.

'Take this as well,' he said, handing her a small dagger in a leather sheath. 'You might need it to make sure he sticks to the bargain after you've bribed him.'

She took the weapon, shoving it through the wide belt she wore. She was dressed in breeches and a shirt, with the blanket draped round her shoulders like a cloak.

'Once I get him out, what then?' she asked softly. Erak pointed to the path that led down to the harbour, and to the township of Hallasholm itself.

'Follow that path. Not far from the gate, you'll see another path branching off to the left, uphill. Take that. I've tethered a pony along the path, with food and warm clothing. You'll need the horse to keep Will moving.' He hesitated, then added, 'You'll also find a small supply of warmweed in the saddle pack.'

She looked up at him, surprised. The other night, he had made no secret of his distaste for the narcotic.

'You'll need it for Will,' he explained briefly. 'Once a person's addicted to the stuff, you can kill him by stopping the supply all at once. You'll have to wean him off it gradually, reducing the amount each week, until his mind recovers and he can do without it.'

'I'll do my best,' she said and he gripped her wrist encouragingly. He glanced at the low clouds above them, sniffing the air.

'It'll snow before dawn,' he said. 'That will cover your tracks. Plus I'll lay a false trail as well. Just keep heading up into the mountains. Follow the path until you come to a fork in the trail by three boulders, with the largest in the middle. Then branch left and you'll reach the hut in another two days' travel.'

There was a small hut up in the mountains, used as a base for hunters during the summer season. It would be unoccupied now and would provide a relatively safe refuge for them through the winter.

'Remember,' he told her, 'once the spring thaw starts, get moving. The boy should have recovered by then. But you can't afford to be caught up there by hunters. Get out once the snow's gone and keep heading south.' He hesitated, then shrugged apologetically. 'I'm sorry I can't do more,' he said. 'This is the best I could come up with at short notice and if we don't do something now, Will won't survive much longer.'

She reached up on tiptoe and kissed his bearded cheek.

'You're doing plenty,' she said. 'I'll never forget you for this, Jarl Erak. I can't begin to thank you for what you're doing.'

Awkwardly, he shrugged away her thanks. He glanced at the sky once more, then jerked his thumb at the yard slaves' barracks.

'You'd better get going,' he told her. Then he added, 'Good luck.'

She grinned quickly at him, then hurried across the bare patch of ground to the barracks. She felt glaringly exposed as she crossed the snow-covered yard, and half expected to hear a challenge from somewhere behind her. But she made it to the building without incident and shrank gratefully into the shadows at the base of the wall.

She paused a few seconds to regain her breath and let her heart settle to a more normal pace. Then she edged her way along the wall to the door. It was locked, of course, but only from the outside and only with a simple bolt. She slid it back now, holding her breath as the metal rasped on metal, then swung the rickety door open and slipped inside.

It was dark in the barracks, with no fire to light the gloom. She waited, letting her eyes grow accustomed to the darkness. Gradually, she could make out the sleeping forms of the slaves, sprawled on the dirt floor, wrapped in rags and scraps of blankets. Light fell across them in bars, coming through the gaps in the rough pine walls of the building.

The Committeemen, Erak had told her, had a separate room at the end of the barracks, where they even kept a small fire burning for warmth. But there was always a chance that one of them might stay on watch in the main barracks. That was why he had given her the silver.

And the dagger.

She touched her hand to the cold hilt of the weapon now, feeling it for reassurance. She had reconnoitred the barracks several days ago and she knew roughly where Will had his sleeping space. She began to head towards it, picking her way carefully among the prone bodies. Her eyes moved this way and that, seeking him out, and she felt a growing sense of desperation as she searched. Then she made out that unmistakable shock of hair above a ragged blanket and, with a sigh of relief, she made her way to him.

At least there would be no problem getting Will to move. Yard slaves, their senses dulled and their minds slowed by the drug, would obey any command they were given.

She crouched beside Will, shaking his shoulder to wake him — gently at first, then, realising that in his drugged state he would sleep like the dead, increasingly roughly.

'Will!' she hissed, leaning close to his ear. 'Get up. Wake up!'

He muttered once. But his eyes remained tight shut and his breathing heavy. She shook him again with a growing sense of panic.

'Please, Will,' she begged. 'Wake up!' And she hit him across the cheek with the palm of her hand.

That did the trick. His eyes opened and he stared

foggily at her. There was no sign of recognition but at least he was awake. She dragged at his shoulder.

'Get up,' she commanded. 'And follow me.'

Her heart leapt in triumph as he obeyed. He moved slowly, but he moved, rising groggily to his feet and standing, swaying unsteadily, beside her, waiting for further instructions.

She pointed to the door, swinging open and letting a band of white light into the barracks.

'Go. To the door,' she ordered and he began to trudge towards it, uncaring where he put his feet, kicking and treading on the other sleeping slaves. Remarkably, they showed little reaction, at most muttering or tossing in their sleep. She turned to follow him but a cold voice from the far end of the room stopped her in her tracks.

'Just a moment, missy. Where do you think you're going?'

It was a Committeeman. Even worse, it was Egon. Jarl Erak had been right. They did take turns to stand watch over the other slaves. She turned to face him as he made his way through the crowded room. Like Will, he paid no heed to the sleeping figures on the floor, treading on them as he came.

Evanlyn drew herself up, took a deep breath and said, in as steady a voice as she could manage: 'Jarl Erak sent me to fetch this slave. He needs firewood brought into his quarters.'

The gang boss hesitated. It was not impossible that she was telling the truth. If one of the senior jarls ran out of firewood in the middle of the night, he'd have no compunction about sending a slave to bring a new stack in.

However, he was suspicious and he thought he recognised this girl.

'He sent for this slave in particular?' he challenged.

'That's right,' Evanlyn replied, trying to sound unconcerned. It was the one part of their story that was thin. There was no reason why Erak, or any other Skandian, would have specified a particular yard slave for a menial carrying task.

'Why this slave?' he pressed and she knew the bluff wouldn't work. She tried another tack.

'Well, he didn't actually say *this* one. He just said a slave. But Will's a friend of mine and he'll get to work inside where it's warm for a few hours and maybe a decent meal, so I thought . . .' She let the sentence hang, shrugging her shoulders, hoping he'd be satisfied. Egon, however, simply continued to stare at her. Then, finally, his eyes narrowed in recognition.

'That's right,' he said. 'You were in here the other day. I saw you looking around, didn't I?'

Inwardly, Evanlyn cursed him. She decided she had to break this impasse quickly. She tugged out the small sack of coins and jingled it.

'Look, I'm just trying to do a friend a good turn,' she said. 'I'll make it worth your while.'

He glanced quickly over his shoulder to make sure none of the other Committeemen were witness to the scene. Then his hand shot out and he grabbed the sack from her.

'That's more like it,' he said. 'I do something for you, and you do something for me.' He shoved the coins inside his shirt and moved closer to her, standing only a few centimetres away. Glancing over her shoulder, she saw that

Will was waiting, an uninterested spectator, by the doorway. Suddenly Egon grabbed her by the shoulders and pulled her closer to him.

'Maybe you can find a few more coins hidden somewhere,' he suggested. Then a frown came over his face as he felt a sharp pain in his belly — and a warm trickle running down his skin from the spot where the pain was centred. Evanlyn smiled without any warmth.

'Maybe I can gut you like a herring if you don't let go,' she said, jabbing the razor-sharp dagger into his skin once more.

She wasn't totally sure that herrings were gutted. But neither did he seem to be. He backed off quickly, waving at the door and cursing her.

'All right,' he said. 'Get out of here. But I'll make your friend pay for this when he comes back.'

With a vast sigh of relief, Evanlyn hurried to the door, grabbing Will's arm and dragging him outside. Once there, she turned and slid the bolt home again.

'Come on, Will. Let's get out of here,' she said, and led the way towards the path to the harbour.

From the shadows, Jarl Erak watched the figures leave and heaved his own sigh of relief.

Then, after a few minutes, he followed them. There was still work for him to do this night.

Twenty-six

The small cavalcade followed the road north. Halt and
Horace rode in the centre with Deparnieux, who had
changed into his customary black armour and surcoat. The
raddled old hack that he had been riding was now
consigned to the rear of the column, and he was astride
a large, aggressive and, as Halt had expected, black
battlehorse.

They were surrounded by at least two dozen men at
arms, marching silently ahead and behind. In addition,
there were ten mounted warriors, split into two groups of
five and stationed at either end of the column.

Halt noticed that the men nearest them kept their
crossbows loaded and ready for use. He had no doubt that
at the first indication that they wanted to escape, he and
Horace would be bristling with crossbow bolts before they
had gone ten steps.

His own longbow was slung across his shoulder, while
Horace had retained his sword and lance. Deparnieux had

shrugged at them as he took them captive, indicating the mass of armed men around them.

'You can see it's no use resisting,' he said, 'so I'll allow you to hold onto your weapons.' He had then glanced meaningfully at the longbow resting lightly across Halt's saddle pommel. 'However,' he added, 'I think I'd feel more at ease with that bow unstrung, and slung over your shoulder.'

Halt had shrugged and complied. His look told Horace that there was a time to fight, and a time to accept the inevitable. Horace had nodded and they had fallen in beside the Gallic warlord, finding themselves immediately bunched in by his retainers. Halt noted wryly that Deparnieux's generosity did not extend to their string of captured horses and armour. He gruffly ordered for their lead rein to be handed to one of his mounted retainers, who now rode at the rear of the column with them. Their captor noted with interest that the shaggy little pack horse did not have a lead rope, and stayed calmly alongside Halt's mount. He raised an eyebrow, but made no comment.

To Halt's surprise, the black-clad knight turned his horse's head to the north and they began their march.

'May I ask where you are taking us?' he said.

Deparnieux bowed from the saddle with mock courtesy.

'We are heading for my castle at Montsombre,' he told them, 'where you will remain as my guests for a short while.'

Halt nodded, digesting that piece of information. Then he asked further: 'And why might we be doing that?'

The black knight smiled at him. 'Because you interest me,' he said. 'You travel with a knight and you carry a yeoman's weapons. But you're no simple retainer, are you?'

Halt said nothing this time, merely shrugging. Deparnieux, eyeing him shrewdly, nodded as if confirming his own thought.

'No. You are not. You're the leader here, not the follower. And your clothing interests me. This cloak of yours . . .' He leaned across from his saddle and fingered the folds of Halt's dappled Ranger cloak. 'I've never seen one quite like it.'

He paused, waiting to see if Halt would comment this time. When he didn't, Deparnieux didn't seem too surprised by the fact. He continued, 'And you're an expert archer. No, you're more than that. I don't know any archer who could have pulled off that shot you made last night.'

This time, Halt made a small gesture of self-deprecation. 'It wasn't such a great shot,' he replied. 'I was aiming for your throat.'

Deparnieux's laugh rang out loud and long.

'Oh, I think not, my friend. I think your arrow went straight where you aimed it.'

And he laughed again. Halt noticed that the merriment, loud as it was, didn't reach his eyes. 'So,' Deparnieux said, 'I decided that such an unusual fish might deserve more study. You may be useful to me, my friend. After all, who knows what other skills and abilities may lie hidden under that unusual cloak of yours?'

Horace watched the two men. The Gallic knight seemed to have lost all interest in him and he wasn't unhappy about that fact. In spite of the light, bantering words between the two men, he could sense the deadly serious undertones of the conversation. The whole thing was getting beyond him and he was content to follow Halt's lead and see where this turn of events took them.

'I doubt I'll be of any use to you,' Halt replied evenly to the warlord's last statement. Horace wondered if Deparnieux read the underlying message there: that Halt had no intention of using his skills in his captor's service.

It seemed that he had, for the black knight regarded the short figure riding beside him for a moment, then replied, 'Well, we'll see about that. For the meantime, let me offer you my hospitality until your young friend's arm has healed.' He looked around to smile at Horace, including him in the conversation for the first time. 'After all, these are not safe roads to ride if you're not fully fit.'

They made camp that night in a small clearing close to the road. Deparnieux posted sentries, but Halt noticed that the number assigned to watch inwards exceeded those who were tasked with guarding the camp from attack. Deparnieux must feel relatively safe within these lands, Halt thought. Significantly, as they settled for the night, their captor demanded that their weapons be surrendered for safekeeping. With no real alternative, the two Araluans were forced to comply.

At least the warlord made no further pretence of cordiality, choosing instead to eat and sleep alone in the pavilion — made from black canvas, of course — that his men pitched for him.

Halt found himself facing something of a quandary. If he were travelling alone, it would be a matter of the utmost simplicity for him to just melt away into the night, retrieving his weapons as he went.

But Horace was totally unskilled in the Ranger arts of unseen movement and evasion and there was no possibility that Halt could spirit him away as well. He had no doubt that, if he were to disappear alone, Horace would not survive very long. So Halt contented himself with waiting and seeing what might transpire. At least they were heading north, which was the direction they wanted to follow.

In addition, he had learned in the tavern the night before that the high passes between Teutlandt, the neighbouring land to the north, and Skandia above it, would be blocked by snows at this time of the year. So they might as well find quarters in which to spend the next month or two. He guessed that Chateau Montsombre would fit that bill as well as any other. Halt had no doubt that Deparnieux had some inkling of his real occupation. Obviously, he hoped to enlist him in his battle against neighbouring warlords. For the moment, he mused, they were safe enough, and heading in the right direction.

When the time came, he might have to ring a few changes. But that time wasn't yet.

The following day, they came to the warlord's castle. After his initial display of goodwill, Deparnieux had decided not to return their weapons in the morning and Halt felt strangely naked without the comforting, familiar weight of the knives at his belt and the two dozen arrows slung over his shoulder.

Chateau Montsombre reared above the surrounding forest on a plateau reached by a narrow, winding path. As they climbed higher and higher up the path, the ground fell away on either side in a sheer slope. The path itself was barely wide enough for four men travelling abreast. It was a width that allowed reasonable access to friendly forces, but prevented any invader from approaching in large numbers. It was a grim reminder of the state of affairs in Gallica, where neighbouring warlords battled constantly for supremacy and the possibility of attack was ever-present.

The castle itself was squat and powerful, with thick walls and heavy towers at each of the four corners. It had none of the soaring grace of Redmont or Castle Araluen. Rather, it was a dark, brooding and forbidding structure, built for war and for no other reason. Halt had told Horace that the word Montsombre translated to mean 'dark mountain'. It seemed an appropriate name for the thick-walled building at the end of the winding, tortuous pathway.

The name became even more meaningful as they climbed higher. There were poles lining the side of the road, with strange, square structures hanging from them. As they drew closer, Horace could make out, to his horror, that the structures were iron cages, only an armspan wide, containing the remains of what used to be men. They hung high above the roadway, swaying gently in the wind that keened around the upper reaches of the path.

Some had obviously been there for many months. The figures inside were dried-out husks, blackened and shrivelled by their long exposure, and festooned in fluttering rags of rotting cloth. But others were newer and the men inside were recognisable. The cages were constructed from iron bars arranged in squares, leaving room for ravens and crows to enter and tear at the men's flesh. The eyes of most of the bodies had been plucked out by the birds.

He glanced, sickened, at Halt's grim face. Deparnieux saw the movement and smiled at him, delighted with the impression his roadside horrors were having on the boy.

'Just the occasional criminal,' he said easily. 'They've all been tried and convicted, of course. I insist on a strict rule of law in Montsombre.'

'What were their crimes?' the boy asked. His throat was thick and constricted and it was difficult to form the words. Again, Deparnieux gave him that unconcerned smile. He made a pretence of trying to think.

'Let's say, "various",' he replied. 'In short, they displeased me.'

Horace held the other man's amused gaze for a few seconds, then, shaking his head, he turned away. He tried to keep his own gaze from the tattered, sorry figures hanging above him. There must have been more than twenty of them all told. Then, his horror increased as he realised that not all of them were dead. In one of the cages, he saw the imprisoned figure moving. At first, he thought it was an illusion, caused by the movement of the man's clothing in the wind. Then one hand reached through the bars as they drew closer and a pitiful croaking sound came from the cage.

Unmistakably, it was a cry for mercy.

'Oh my God,' said Horace softly, and he heard Halt's sharp intake of breath beside him.

Deparnieux reined in his black horse and sat, easing his weight to one side in the saddle.

'Recognise him?' he asked, an amused tone in his voice. 'You saw him the other night, in the tavern.'

Horace frowned, puzzled. The man wasn't familiar to him. But there had been at least a dozen people in the tavern on the night when they had first encountered the warlord. He wondered why he should be expected to remember this man more than any of the others. Then Halt said, in a cold voice:

'He was the one who laughed.'

Deparnieux gave a low chuckle. 'That's right. He was a man of rare humour. Strange how his sense of fun seems to have deserted him now. You'd think he might while away the hours with the odd merry jest.'

And he shook his reins, slapping them on his battlehorse's neck and moving off once again. The entourage moved with him, stopping when he stopped, moving when he moved, and forcing Halt and Horace to keep pace.

Horace looked at Halt once more, seeking some message of comfort there. The Ranger met his gaze for a few seconds, then slowly nodded. He understood how the boy was feeling, sickened by the depravity and abject cruelty he was witnessing. Somehow, Horace found a little comfort from Halt's nod. He touched his knee to Kicker's side and urged him forward.

And together, they rode towards the dark and forbidding castle that waited for them.

Twenty-seven

$\mathcal{T}$he pony was where Erak had told her it would be.

It stood tethered to a sapling, its hindquarters turned patiently to the icy wind that was bringing the snow clouds lower over Hallasholm. Evanlyn untied the rope bridle and the little horse came docilely along. Above their heads, the wind sighed through the pine needles, sounding like some strange inland surf as it stirred the snowclad branches.

Will followed her dumbly, staggering in the calf-deep snow that covered the path. It was hard going for Evanlyn, but even harder for the boy, exhausted and worn out as he was from weeks of hard labour with insufficient food or warmth. Soon, she knew, she should stop and find the warm clothing that Erak had said was inside the pack on the pony's back. And she'd probably need to let Will ride the pony if they were to make any distance before dawn. But, for the moment, she wanted no delay, no matter how short. All her instincts told her to continue, to put as much distance as possible between them and the Skandian township, and to do it as fast as she could.

The path wound up into the mountains and she leaned forward, into the wind, leading the pony with one hand and holding Will's icy cold hand in the other. Together, they stumbled on, slipping on the thick snow, staggering over tree roots and rocks that were hidden beneath its smooth surface.

After half an hour's travelling, she felt the first tentative flakes of snow brushing her face as they fell. Then they were tumbling down in earnest, heavy and thick. She paused, looking at the path behind them, where their footprints were already half obscured. Erak had known it would snow heavily tonight, she thought. He had waited until his sailor's instincts had told him that all signs of their passage would be covered. For the first time since she had crept out of the Lodge's open gateway, she felt her heart lift with hope. Perhaps, after all, things would work out for them.

Behind her, Will stumbled and, muttering incoherently, fell to his knees in the snow. She turned to him and realised that he was shivering and blue with the cold, virtually done in. Moving to the pack slung over the pony's back, she unlaced the fastenings and rummaged inside.

There was a thick sheepskin vest, among other items, and she draped it around the shivering boy's shoulders, helping him push his arms through the arm holes. He stared at her dully as she did so. He was a dumb animal, mutely accepting whatever befell him. She could hit him, she knew, and he would make no attempt to avoid the blow, or to strike back at her. Sadly, she contemplated him, remembering him as he had been. Erak had said he could possibly recover, although very few warmweed addicts ever got the chance. Isolated in the mountains as they would be, Will was going to have every opportunity to break the vicious cycle of the drug. She prayed now that the Skandian Jarl was right, and that it was possible for an addict, deprived of warmweed, to make a full recovery.

She shoved the unresisting boy towards the pony, motioning for him to climb astride. For a moment he hesitated, then, clumsily, he hauled himself up into the saddle and sat there, swaying uncertainly, as she headed out again, following the forest pathway as it led them up into the mountains.

Around them, the fat flakes of snow continued to tumble down.

Erak watched the two figures move furtively off into the forest, taking the fork that he had described to Evanlyn. Satisfied that they were on their way, he followed them out of the stockade but continued past the point where they had turned off and headed for the harbour instead.

There were no sentries posted at the Great Hall at this time of year. There was no fear of attackers, as the thick snows covering the mountains around them were more effective than any human sentries. But Erak was more cautious as he approached the harbourfront. A watch was kept here, to ensure that the wolfships rode safely at their moorings. A sudden squall could see the ships dragging their anchors and being cast up on shore, and so a few men were posted to give warning and rouse the duty crews in case of danger.

But they could just as easily see him and wonder what he was doing at this time of night, so he stayed in the shadows wherever he could.

His own ship, *Wolfwind*, was moored to the harbour quay and he boarded her silently, knowing that there was no duty crew present. He'd dismissed them that afternoon, relying on his reputation as a weather forecaster to reassure them that there would be no strong winds that night. He leaned over the outboard bulwark and there, floating in the lee of the ship, was the small skiff he had moored there earlier in the day. He glanced at the way the boats in the harbour rode to their moorings and saw that the tide was still running out. He had timed his arrival to coincide with the falling tide and now he climbed quickly down into the smaller craft, felt around in the stern for the drainage plug and pulled it loose. The icy water cascaded in over his hands. When the boat was half full, he replaced the plug and heaved himself back over the rail onto the wolfship. Drawing his dagger, he cut through the painter holding the skiff alongside.

For a moment, nothing happened. Then the little craft, already sitting lower in the water, began to slide astern, slowly at first, then with increasing speed as the tide drew it along. There was one oar in the boat, set in the rowlock. He'd arranged it that way in case the boat was found in the next few days. The combination of an empty boat, apparently swamped and half full of water, with one oar missing, would all point to an accident.

The skiff drifted downharbour, becoming lost to sight among the larger craft that crowded the anchorage.

Satisfied that he had done all he could, Erak slipped back ashore and retraced his steps to the Great Hall. As he went, he noticed with satisfaction that the heavy snow had already obliterated the tracks he had made earlier. By morning, there would be no sign that anyone had passed this way. The missing boat and the cut painter would be the only clues as to where the escaped slaves had gone.

The going was harder as the pathway through the forest grew steeper. Evanlyn's breath came in ragged gasps, and hung on the frigid air in great clouds of steam. The slight wind that had stirred the pines earlier had died away as the snow began to fall. Her throat and mouth were dry and there was an unpleasant, brassy taste in her mouth. She'd tried to ease her thirst several times with handfuls of snow, but the relief was short-lived. The intense cold of the snow undid any benefit that she might have got from the small amount of water that trickled down her throat as the snow melted.

She glanced behind her. The pony was trudging doggedly in her tracks, head down and seemingly unaffected by the cold. Will was a huddled shape on the pony's back, wrapped deep in the folds of the sheepskin vest. He moaned softly and continuously.

She paused for a moment, breathing raggedly, taking in huge gulps of the freezing air. It bit almost painfully at the back of her throat. The muscles in the backs of her thighs and calves were aching and trembling from the effort of driving on through the thick snow but she knew she had to keep going as long as she could. She had no idea how far she had travelled from the Lodge at Hallasholm but she suspected it was not far enough. If Erak's attempt to lay a false trail was unsuccessful, she had no doubt that a party of able-bodied Skandians could cover the ground she and Will had travelled in less than an hour.

Erak's instructions were to get as far up the mountain as possible before dawn came. Then they must get off the pathway and into the cover of the thick trees, where she and Will could hide for the day.

She looked up at the narrow gap through the trees above her. The thick overcast hid any sign of the moon or stars. She had no idea how late it was or how soon the dawn might come.

Miserably, with every muscle in her legs protesting, she started upward again, the pony trailing stolidly behind her. For a moment, she considered climbing up onto the saddle behind Will and riding double. Then she dismissed the notion. It was only a small pony and, while he might carry one person and their packs uncomplainingly, a double load in these conditions would quickly tire him. Knowing how much depended on the shaggy little beast, she reluctantly decided that it was best for her to continue on foot. If she exhausted the pony, it could well be a death sentence for Will. She'd never keep him moving, exhausted and weakened as he was.

She trudged on, lifting each foot clear of the snow, planting it down, slipping slightly as it crunched through the ever-thickening ground cover, compacting it until she had a firm footing once more. Left foot. Right foot. Left foot. Right foot. Mouth drier than ever. Breath still clouding on the air and hanging in the still night behind her, briefly marking where she had passed. Unthinkingly, she began to count the paces as she took them. There was no reason to it. She wasn't consciously trying to measure distance. It was an instinctive reaction to the constant, repetitive rhythm she had established. She reached two hundred and started again. Reached it again and started from one once more. Then, after several more times, she realised that she had no idea how many times she had reached that two hundred mark and she stopped counting. Within twenty steps, she became aware that she was counting again. She shrugged. This time, she decided, she'd count to four hundred before starting back at one again. Anything for a little variety, she thought with grim humour.

The thick flakes of snow continued falling, brushing her face and matting her hair pure white. Her face was growing numb and she rubbed it vigorously with the back of her hand, realised the hand was numb as well and stopped to look through the pack once more.

She'd seen gloves in there when she'd found the vest for Will. She located them again, thick wool gauntlets, with a thumb piece and a single space for the rest of her fingers. She pulled them onto her freezing hands, swinging her arms, slapping her hands against her ribs and up under her armpits to stimulate the circulation. After a few minutes of this, she felt a brief tingle of returning sensation and began walking again.

The pony had stopped when she did. Now, patiently, it moved off again in her footprints.

She reached four hundred and started back at one.

Twenty-eight

Halt looked around the large chambers they had been shown to.

'Well,' he said, 'it's not much, but it's home.'

In fact, he wasn't being quite fair with his statement. They were high in the central tower of Chateau Montsombre, the tower Deparnieux told them he kept exclusively for his own use — and that of his guests, he added sardonically. The room they were in was a large one and quite comfortably furnished. There was a table and chairs that would do quite well for eating meals, as well as two comfortable-looking wooden armchairs arranged either side of the large fireplace. Doors led off either side to two smaller sleeping chambers and there was even a small bathing room with a tin tub and a washstand. There were a couple of halfway decent hangings on the stone walls and a serviceable rug covering a large part of the floor. There was a small terrace and a window, which afforded a view of the winding path they had followed to reach the castle and the forest lands below. The window was unglazed, with wooden shutters on the inside to provide relief from the wind and weather.

The door was the only jarring note in the scheme of things. There was no door handle on the inside. Their quarters might be comfortable enough. But they were prisoners for all that, Halt knew.

Horace dumped his pack on the floor and dropped gratefully into one of the wooden armchairs by the fire. There was a draught coming through the window, even though it was still only midafternoon. It would be cold and draughty at night, he thought. But then, most castle chambers were. This one was no better or worse than the average.

'Halt,' he said, 'I've been wondering why Abelard and Tug didn't warn us about the ambush. Aren't they trained to sense things like that?'

Halt nodded slowly. 'The same thought occurred to me,' he said. 'And I assume it had something to do with your string of conquests.'

The boy looked at him, not understanding, and he elaborated. 'We had half a dozen battlehorses tramping along behind us, laden down with bits of armour that clanked and rattled like a tinker's cart. My guess is that all the noise they were making masked any sound Deparnieux's men might have made.'

Horace frowned. He hadn't thought of that. 'But couldn't they scent them?' he asked.

'If the wind were in the right direction, yes. But it was blowing from us to them, if you remember.' He regarded Horace, who was looking vaguely disappointed at the horses' inability to overcome such minor difficulties. 'Sometimes,' Halt continued, 'we tend to expect a little too much of Ranger horses. After all, they are only human.' The faintest trace of a smile touched his mouth as he said that but Horace didn't notice. He merely nodded and moved on to his next question.

'So,' he said, 'what do we do now?'

The Ranger shrugged. He had his own pack open and was taking out a few items — a clean shirt and his razor and washing things.

'We wait,' he said. 'We're not losing any time — yet. The mountain passes into Skandia will be snowed over for at least another month. So we may as well make ourselves comfortable here for a few days until we see what our gallant Gall has in mind for us.'

Horace used one foot to remove the boot from the other and wiggled his toes in delight, enjoying the sudden feeling of freedom.

'There's a thing,' he said. 'What do you suppose this Deparnieux is up to, Halt?'

Halt hesitated a moment, then shook his head. 'I'm not sure. But he'll probably show his hand sometime over the next few days. I think he has a vague idea that I'm a Ranger,' he added thoughtfully.

'Do they have Rangers here?' Horace asked, surprised. He'd always assumed that the Ranger Corps was unique to Araluen. Now, as Halt shook his head, he realised his assumption was correct.

'No, they don't,' Halt replied. 'And we've always been at some pains not to spread word of the Corps too far and wide. Never know when you're going to end up at war with someone,' he added. 'But of course, it's impossible to keep something like that a total secret, so he may have got some word of it.'

'And if he has?' Horace asked. 'I thought he was originally only interested in us because he wanted to fight me — you know, like you said.'

'That was probably the case at first,' Halt agreed, 'but now he's got wind of something and I think he's trying to work out how he can use me.'

'Use you?' Horace repeated, frowning at the idea. Halt made a dismissive gesture.

'That's usually the way people like him think,' he told the boy. 'They're always looking to see how they can turn a situation to their own advantage. And they think that everyone can be bought, if the price is right. Do you think you could put that boot back on?' he added mildly. 'The window can only let in a limited amount of fresh air and your socks are a touch ripe, to put it mildly.'

'Oh, sorry!' said Horace, tugging the riding boot back on over his sock. Now that Halt mentioned it, he was aware of a rather strong odour in the room.

'Don't knights in this country take vows of chivalry?' he asked, returning to the subject of their captor. 'Knights vow to help others, don't they? They're not supposed to "use people".'

'They take the vows,' Halt told him. 'Keeping them is another matter altogether. And the idea of knights helping the common people is one that works in a place like Araluen, where we have a strong King. Here, if you've got the power, you can pretty much do as you please.'

'Well, it's not right,' Horace muttered. Halt agreed with him but there didn't seem to be anything to gain by saying so.

'Just be patient,' he told Horace now. 'There's nothing we can do to hurry things along. We'll find out what Deparnieux wants soon enough. In the meantime, we may as well relax and take it easy.'

'Another thing . . .' Horace added, ignoring his companion's suggestion. 'I didn't like those cages by the roadside. No true knight could ever punish anyone that way, no matter how bad their crime might be. Those things were just terrible. Inhuman!'

Halt met the boy's honest gaze. There was nothing he could offer by way of comfort.

Inhuman was an apt description of the punishment.

'Yes,' he said, finally, 'I didn't like those either. I think that before we leave here, my lord Deparnieux might have a little explaining to do on that matter.'

They dined that night with the Gallic warlord. The table was an immense one, with room for thirty or more diners, and the three of them were dwarfed by the empty space around them. Serving boys and maids scurried about their tasks, bringing extra helpings of food and wine as required.

The meal was neither good nor bad, which surprised Halt a little. Gallic cuisine had a reputation for being exotic and even outlandish. The plain fare that was served up to them seemed to indicate that the reputation was an unfounded one.

The one thing he did notice was that the serving staff went about their tasks with their eyes cast down, avoiding eye contact with any of the three diners. There was a palpable air of fear in the room, accentuated when any of the servants had to move close to their master to serve him with food or to fill his goblet.

Halt sensed also that Deparnieux was not only aware of the tension in the atmosphere, he actually enjoyed it. A satisfied half smile would touch his cruel lips whenever one of the servants came close to him, eyes averted and holding his or her breath until the task was completed.

They spoke little during the meal. Deparnieux seemed content to observe them, rather as a boy might observe an interesting and previously unknown bug that he had captured. In the circumstances, neither Halt nor Horace were inclined to offer any small talk.

When they had eaten, and the table had been cleared, the warlord finally spoke what was on his mind. He glanced dismissively at Horace and waved a languid hand towards the stairway that led to their chambers.

'I won't keep you any longer, boy,' he said. 'You have my leave to go.'

Flushing slightly at the ill-mannered tone, Horace glanced quickly at Halt and saw the Ranger's small nod. He rose, trying to retain his dignity, trying not to show the Gallic knight his confusion.

'Good night, Halt,' he said quietly, and Halt nodded again.

''Night, Horace,' he said. The apprentice warrior drew himself up, looked Deparnieux in the eye, and abruptly turned and left the room. Two of the armed guards who had been standing by in the shadows instantly fell in behind him, escorting him up the stairs.

It was a small gesture, Horace thought as he climbed to his chambers, and it was probably a childish one. But ignoring the master of Chateau Montsombre as he left made him feel a little better.

Deparnieux waited until the sound of Horace's footsteps on the stone flagged stairs had receded. Then, pushing his chair back from the table, he turned a calculating gaze on the Ranger.

'Well, Master Halt,' he said quietly, 'it's time we had a little chat.'

Halt pursed his lips. 'About what?' he asked. 'I'm afraid I'm just no good at all with gossip.'

The warlord smiled thinly. 'I can tell you're going to be an amusing guest,' he said. 'Now tell me, exactly who are you?'

Halt shrugged carelessly. He toyed with a goblet that was sitting, almost empty, on the table in front of him, twirling it this way and that, watching the way the faceted glass caught the light from the fire in the corner.

'I'm an ordinary sort of person,' he said. 'My name's Halt. I'm from Araluen, travelling with Sir Horace. Nothing much more to tell, really.'

The smile stayed fixed on Deparnieux's face as he continued to regard the bearded man sitting opposite him. He appeared nondescript enough, that was for sure. His clothes were simple — verging on drab, in fact. His beard and hair were badly cut. They looked as if he had cut them with a hunting knife, thought Deparnieux, unaware that he was only one of many people to have that very same thought about Halt.

He was a small man, too. His head barely came up the warlord's shoulder. But he was muscular for all that and, in spite of the grey hairs in his beard and hair, he was in excellent physical condition. But there was something about the eyes — dark and steady and calculating — that belied the claim of ordinariness that the man made now. Deparnieux prided himself that he knew the look of a man who was used to command, and this man had it, definitely.

Plus there was something about his equipment. It was unusual to see a man with this unmistakable air of command who was not armed as a knight. The bow was a commoner's weapon, in Deparnieux's eyes, and the double knife scabbard was something he had not encountered before. He had taken the opportunity to study the two knives. The larger one reminded him of the heavy saxe knives carried by the Skandians. The smaller knife, razor-sharp like its companion, was a perfectly balanced throwing knife. Unusual weapons indeed for a commander, Deparnieux thought.

The strange cloak fascinated him as well. It was patterned in irregular daubs of green and grey and he could see no reason for the colours or the pattern. The deep cowl served to hide the man's face when he pulled it up in place. Several times during their ride to Montsombre, the Gallic knight had noticed that the cloak seemed to shimmer and merge with the forest background, so that the small man almost disappeared from sight. Then, the illusion would pass.

Deparnieux, like many of his countrymen, was more than a little superstitious. He suspected that the cloak's strange properties could be some form of sorcery.

It was this last thought that had led to his somewhat equivocal treatment of Halt. It didn't pay to antagonise sorcerers, the warlord knew. So he determined to play his cards carefully until he knew exactly what to expect of this mysterious little man. And, should it prove that Halt had no dark powers, there was always the possibility that he might be persuaded to turn his other talents to Deparnieux's own ends.

If not, then the warlord could always kill the two travellers as he pleased.

He realised now that he had been silent for some time following Halt's last statement. He took a sip of wine and shook his head at the sentiments Halt had expressed.

'Not ordinary in any way, I think,' he said. 'You interest me, Halt.'

Again, the Ranger shrugged. 'I can't see why,' he replied mildly.

Deparnieux twirled his wine goblet between his fingers. There was a tentative knock at the door and his head steward entered apologetically and a little fearfully. He had learned by bitter experience that his master was a dangerous and unpredictable man.

'What is it?' Deparnieux said, angry at the intrusion.

'Your pardon, my lord, but I wondered would there be anything more?'

Deparnieux was about to dismiss him when a thought struck him. It would be an interesting experiment to provoke this strange Araluan, he thought. To see which way he jumped.

'Yes,' he said. 'Send for the cook.'

The steward hesitated, puzzled.

'The cook, my lord?' he repeated. 'Do you require more food?'

'I require the cook, you fool!' Deparnieux snarled at him. The man hastily backed away.

'At once, my lord,' he said, backing nervously towards the door. When he had gone, the Gallic warlord smiled at Halt.

'It's almost impossible to find good staff these days,' he said. Halt eyed him contemptuously.

'It must be a constant problem for you,' he said evenly. Deparnieux glanced keenly at him, trying to sense any sarcasm behind the words.

They sat in silence until there was a knock at the door and the steward returned. The cook followed a few paces behind him, nervously wringing her hands in the hem of her apron. She was a middle-aged woman, and her face showed the strain that came from working in Deparnieux's household.

'The cook, my lord,' the steward announced.

Deparnieux said nothing. He stared at the woman the way a snake stares at a bird. Her wringing of the apron became more and more pronounced as the silence between them grew. Finally, she could bear it no longer.

'Is something wrong, my lord?' she began. 'Was the meal not —'

'*You* do not speak!' Deparnieux shouted, rising from his chair and pointing angrily at her. 'I am the master here! You do not speak before me! So remain silent, woman!'

Halt's eyes narrowed as he watched the unpleasant scene. He knew that this was all being done for his benefit. He sensed that Deparnieux wanted to see how he might react. Frustrating as it might be, there was nothing he could do to help the woman right now. Deparnieux shot a quick glance at him, confirming his suspicions, seeing that the smaller man was as calm as ever. Then he resumed his seat, turning back to the unfortunate cook.

'The vegetables were cold,' he said, finally.

The woman's expression was equal parts fear and puzzlement.

'Surely not, my lord? The vegetables were —'

'Cold, I tell you!' Deparnieux interrupted. He turned to Halt. 'They were cold, were they not?' he challenged. Halt shrugged.

'The vegetables were fine,' he said evenly. No matter what happened, he must keep any sense of anger or outrage out of his voice. Deparnieux smiled thinly. He looked back at the cook.

'Now see what you have done?' he said. 'Not only have you shamed me in front of a guest, you have made that guest lie on your behalf.'

'My lord, really, I didn't . . .'

Deparnieux cut her off with an imperious wave of the hand.

'You have disappointed me and you must be punished,' he said. The woman's face grew grey with fear. In this castle, punishment was no light matter.

'Please, my lord. Please, I will try harder. I promise,' she babbled, hoping to forestall his pronouncement of her punishment. She looked appealingly to Halt.

'Please, master, tell him that I didn't mean it,' she begged.

'Leave her be,' the Ranger said finally.

Deparnieux's head cocked expectantly to one side.

'Or?' he challenged. Here was an opportunity to assess his prisoner's powers — or lack thereof. If he truly were a sorcerer, then perhaps he might show his hand now.

Halt could see what the other man was thinking. There was an air of expectancy about him as he watched Halt carefully. The Ranger realised, reluctantly, that he was in no position to enforce threats. He decided to try another tack.

'Or?' he repeated, shrugging. 'Or what? The matter is unimportant. She is nothing but a clumsy servant who deserves neither your attention or mine.'

The Gallican fingered his lip thoughtfully. Halt's apparent lack of care might be real. Or it might be simply a way of masking the fact that he had no powers. The principal reason for doubt in Deparnieux's mind was the fact that he couldn't really believe that any person of power or authority would really have more than a passing concern for a servant. Halt might be backing down. Or he might actually not care enough to make an issue of the matter.

'Nevertheless,' he replied, watching Halt, 'she must be punished.'

He looked at the head steward now. The man had shrunk back against one wall, trying to make himself as inconspicuous as possible while all this went on.

'You will punish this woman,' he said. 'She is lazy and incompetent and she has embarrassed her master.'

The steward bowed obsequiously. 'Yes, my lord. Of course, my lord. The woman will be punished,' he said. Deparnieux raised his eyebrows in mock wonder.

'Really?' he said. 'And what will the punishment be?'

The servant hesitated. He had no idea what the knight had in mind. He decided that, on the whole, it would be better to err on the side of harshness.

'Flogging, my lord?' he replied, and, as Deparnieux seemed to nod in agreement, he continued, more definitely, 'She will be flogged.'

But now the warlord was shaking his head and beads of perspiration broke out on the balding steward's forehead.

'No,' Deparnieux said in a silky tone. '*You* will be flogged. She will be caged.'

Powerless to intervene, Halt watched the cruel tableau unfold before his eyes. The head servant's face crumpled with fear as he heard he was to be flogged. But the woman, on hearing her own punishment, sank to the floor, her face a mask of despair. Halt recalled the winding road they had travelled to Montsombre, lined with the pitiful wretches suspended in iron cages. He felt sickened by the black-clad tyrant in front of him. He stood abruptly, shoving his chair back so that it toppled over and crashed to the flagstones.

'I'm going to bed,' he said. 'I've had enough.'

Twenty-nine

Evanlyn had no idea how long they had been stumbling up the snow-covered path. The pony trudged, head down and uncomplaining, with Will swaying uncertainly on its back, moaning quietly. Evanlyn herself continued to stagger mindlessly, her feet squeaking and crunching the new-fallen dry snow underfoot.

Finally, she knew she could go no further. She stumbled to a halt and looked for a place to shelter for what remained of the night.

The prevailing north wind over the previous days had piled the snow thickly against the windward side of the pines, leaving a corresponding deep trough in their lee. The lower branches of the bigger trees spread out above these hollows, creating a sheltered space below the surface of the snow. Not only would they find shelter from the weather as the snow continued to fall, the deep hole would conceal them from the casual glance of passers-by on the path.

It was by no means an ideal hiding place, but it was the

best available. Evanlyn led the pony off the track, looking for one of the larger trees, set three or four rows back from the path.

Almost at once, she sank waist deep in the snow. But she struggled forward, leading the pony behind her in the path she made. It took almost the last reserves of her strength but she finally stumbled into a deep hollow behind a tree. The pony hesitated, then followed her. Will at least had the presence of mind to lean down over the pony's neck to avoid being swept out of the saddle by the huge, snow-laden overhanging branches of the pine.

The space under the tree was surprisingly large and there was plenty of room for the three of them. With their combined body heat in the more or less enclosed space, it was also nowhere near as cold as she had thought it might be. It was still bitterly cold, mind you, but not life threatening. She helped Will down from the pony's back and motioned for him to sit. He sprawled, shivering, his back against the rough bark of the tree, while she searched the pack and found two thick wool blankets. She draped them around his shoulders, then sat beside him and pulled the rough wool around herself as well. She took one of his hands in hers and rubbed his fingers. They felt like ice. She smiled at him in encouragement.

'We'll be fine now,' she told him, 'Just fine.'

He looked at her and, for a moment, she thought he had understood her. But she realised he was simply reacting to the sound of her voice.

As soon as he seemed to have warmed up a little, and his shivering had died down to an occasional spasm, she unwrapped herself and stood to loosen the pony's pack saddle. The animal grunted and snorted in relief as the straps loosened around its belly, then slowly settled to its knees to lie down in the shelter.

Perhaps, in this snow-covered land, horses were trained to do this. She had no idea. But the reclining pony offered a warm resting spot for her and Will. She dragged the unresisting boy away from the bole of the tree and re-settled him, leaning back against the warm belly of the horse. Then, wrapping herself in the blankets again, she nestled close to him. The horse's body heat was bliss. She could feel it in the small of her back and, for the first time in hours, she felt warm. Her head drooped against Will's shoulder and she slept.

Outside, the heavy flakes of snow continued to tumble down from the low clouds.

Within thirty minutes, all sign of their passage through the deep snow was obliterated.

The news that two of the slaves had gone took some time to be relayed to Erak the following morning.

That was hardly surprising, as such an event wasn't considered important enough to bother one of the senior jarls. In fact, it was only after one of the kitchen slaves recalled that Evanlyn had spent the previous few days bemoaning her assignment to his household that Borsa, who had been informed of the girl's disappearance, thought to mention it to him.

As it was, he only mentioned the fact in passing, as he saw the bearded ship's captain leaving the dining hall after a late breakfast.

'That damn girl of yours has gone,' he muttered, brushing past Erak. As hilfmann, of course, Borsa had been informed of the slave's disappearance as soon as the kitchen steward had discovered it. It was the hilfmann's job to deal with such administrative hiccups, after all.

Erak looked at him blankly. 'Girl of mine?'

Borsa waved a hand impatiently. 'The Araluan you brought in. The one you were going to have for a servant. Apparently, she's run off.'

Erak frowned. He felt it was logical for him to look a little annoyed about such a turn of events.

'Where to?' he asked and Borsa replied with an irritated shrug.

'Who knows? There's nowhere to run to and the snow was falling like a blanket last night. There are no signs of tracks anywhere.'

And, at that piece of news, Erak breathed an inner sigh of relief. That part of his plan had succeeded, at any rate. His next words, however, belied the sense of satisfaction that he hid deep inside.

'Well, find her!' he snapped irritably. 'I didn't haul her all the way across the Stormwhite so you could lose her!'

And he turned on his heel and strode away. He was, after all, a senior jarl and a warleader. Borsa might well be the hilfmann and Ragnak's senior administrator, but in a battle-orientated society such as this, Erak outranked him by a significant margin.

Borsa glared after his retreating back and cursed. But he did it quietly. Not only was he aware of their comparative ranks, he also knew that it was an unwise man who would insult the Jarl to his face — or to his back as the case might be. Erak had been known to lay about him with his battleaxe on the slightest of provocations.

The thought of Erak's voyage from Araluen with the girl brought the other slave to his mind — the boy who had been a Ranger apprentice. He had heard that the girl had been asking about him in the past few days. Now, swinging his heavy fur cloak around him, he headed for the door and the quarters of the yard slaves.

Wrinkling his nose against the stink of unwashed bodies, Borsa stood in the doorway of the yard slaves' barracks and surveyed the cringing Committeeman in front of him.

'You didn't see him go?' he asked incredulously. The slave shook his head, keeping his eyes cast down. His manner showed his guilt. Borsa was sure he had heard or seen the other slave escaping and had done nothing about it. He shook his head angrily and turned to the guard beside him.

'Have him flogged,' he said briefly, and turned back to the main Lodge building.

It was barely an hour later that the report came in of the missing skiff. The end of the painter, cut with a knife, told its own story. Two missing slaves, one missing boat. The conclusion was obvious. Bleakly, Borsa thought about the chances of surviving in the Stormwhite at this time of year in an open boat — particularly close to the coast.

For, contrary to the way it might seem, the fugitives would have a better chance of survival in the open sea. Close to the coast, and driven by the prevailing winds and heavy waves, it would be a miracle if they weren't smashed along the rocky coast before they had gone ten kilometres.

'Good riddance,' he muttered, and sent word that the patrols sent to search the mountain paths to the north should be recalled.

Later that day, Erak overheard two slaves talking in muted tones about the two Araluans who had stolen a boat and tried to escape. Around noon, the search parties returned from the mountains. The men were obviously grateful to be in from the deep snow and the biting wind that had sprung up shortly after dawn.

His heart lifted. At least now the fugitives would be safe until spring.

As long as they managed to find the mountain cabin, he thought soberly, and didn't freeze to death in the attempt.

Thirty

L ife in Chateau Montsombre had taken on a pattern.

Their host, the warlord Deparnieux, saw his two unwilling guests only when he chose to, which was usually over the evening meal, once or twice a week. It also generally coincided with those occasions when he had thought of some new way of baiting Halt, to try to draw him out.

At other times, the two Araluans were confined mainly to their tower room, although each day they were allowed a short time for exercise in the castle courtyard, under the suspicious gaze of the dozen or so men at arms who stood sentry over them in the tower. They had asked several times if they might venture outside the castle walls, and perhaps explore the plateau a little.

They expected no more than the answer they received, which was a stony silence from the sergeant of the men set to guard them, but it was still extremely frustrating.

Now Horace paced up and down the terrace, high in the central tower of Chateau Montsombre.

Inside, Halt was sitting cross-legged on his bed as he put the finishing touches to a new bow he was making for Will. He had been working on the project since they had landed in Gallica. He had carefully selected strips of wood and glued and bound them tightly together, so that their different grains and natural shapes were opposed to each other and bent the composite piece into a smooth curve. Then he had attached two similar, but shorter, composites to either end, so that their curve opposed the main shape of the bow. This formed the recurve shape that he wanted.

When they had first arrived at Montsombre, Deparnieux had seen the pieces in Halt's pack, but he had seen no reason to confiscate them. Without arrows, a half-made bow constituted no threat to him.

The wind curled around the turrets of the castle, keening its way among the figures of gargoyles carved in the stone. Below the terrace, a family of rooks soared and planed on the wind, coming and going from their nest, set in a cranny in the hard granite wall.

Horace always felt slightly queasy to find himself looking down on birds flying. He moved back from the balustrade, pulling his cloak more tightly around him to keep out the wind. The air carried the threat of rain with it and, in the north, there were banks of heavy cloud driving towards them on the wind. It was midafternoon on another wintry day in Montsombre. The forest that spread out below them was dull and featureless — from this height it looked like a rough carpet.

'What are we going to do, Halt?' Horace asked and his companion hesitated before answering. Not because he was uncertain of the answer itself; rather, because he was unsure how his young friend's temperament would greet it.

'We wait,' he said simply, and immediately saw the frustration in Horace's eyes. He knew the boy was expecting something to precipitate matters with Deparnieux.

'But Deparnieux is torturing and killing people! And we're just sitting back watching him do it!' the boy said angrily. He expected more from the resourceful ex-Ranger than the simple injunction to wait.

The forced inactivity was galling to Horace. He wasn't coping well with the boredom and frustration of day-to-day life in Montsombre. He was trained for action and he wanted to act. He felt the compulsion to *do* something – anything. He wanted to punish Deparnieux for his cruelty. He wanted a chance to ram the black knight's sarcastic comments back down his throat.

Most of all, he wanted to be free of Montsombre and back on the road in search of Will.

Halt waited until he judged Horace had calmed down a little. 'He's also lord of this castle,' he replied mildly, 'and he has some fifty men at his beck and call. I think that's a few more than we could comfortably deal with.'

Horace picked a crumbled piece of granite from a corner of the balustrade and tossed it far out into the void below, watching it fall, seeming to curve in towards the castle walls until it was lost from view.

'I know,' he said moodily, 'but I wish we could do something.'

Halt glanced up from his task. Although he hid the fact, his sense of frustration was even sharper than Horace's. If he were on his own, Halt could escape from this castle with the greatest ease. But to do so, he would have to abandon Horace — and he couldn't bring himself to do that. Instead, he found himself torn by conflicting loyalties — to Will, and to the young man who had unselfishly chosen to accompany him in search of a friend. He knew that Deparnieux would show no mercy to Horace if Halt were to escape. At the same time, every fibre of his being ached to be on the road and in pursuit of his lost apprentice. He dropped his eyes to the almost completed bow again, careful to keep any sense of his own frustration out of his voice.

'The next move is up to our host, I'm afraid,' he told Horace. 'He's not sure what to make of me. He's not sure whether I might be useful to him. And while he's uncertain, he's on his guard. That makes him dangerous.'

'Then surely we might as well fight him?' Horace asked but Halt shook his head emphatically.

'I'd rather he relaxed a little,' he said. 'I'd rather he felt we were not as dangerous, or as useful, as he first assumed. I can sense he's trying to make his mind up about me. That business with the cook was a test.'

The first drops of rain spattered onto the flagstones. Horace looked up, realising with some surprise that the clouds, seemingly so far away only a few minutes ago, were already scudding overhead.

'A test?' he repeated.

Halt twisted his face into a grimace. 'He wanted to see what I would do about it. Maybe he wanted to see what I *could* do about it.'

'So you did nothing?' Horace challenged, and instantly regretted the hasty words. Halt, however, took no offence. He met the boy's gaze steadily, saying nothing. Eventually, Horace dropped his eyes and mumbled, 'Sorry, Halt.'

Halt nodded, registering the apology. 'There wasn't much I could do, Horace,' he explained gently. 'Not while Deparnieux was keyed up and on his guard. That's not the time to take action against an enemy. I'm afraid,' he added in a warning tone, 'the next few weeks are going to bring us more of these tests.'

That gained Horace's attention immediately. 'What do you think he has in mind?'

'I don't know the details,' Halt said. 'But you can bet that our friend Deparnieux will perform more unpleasant acts, just to see what I do about them.' Again, the ex-Ranger grimaced. 'The point is, the more I do nothing, the more he will relax, and the less careful he will be around me.'

'And that's what you want?' Horace queried, beginning to understand. Halt nodded grimly in reply.

'That's what I want,' he said. He glanced at the dark clouds that were whipping overhead. 'Now come inside before you get soaked,' he suggested.

The rain came and went over the next hour, pelting in on the wind, driven almost horizontally through those open window spaces of the Chateau where the occupants had neglected to close the wooden shutters.

An hour before dark, the rain cleared as the ever-present wind drove the clouds further south, and the low sun broke through in the west, in a spectacular display against the dispersing storm clouds.

The two prisoners were watching the sunset from their windswept terrace when they heard a commotion below them.

A lone horseman was at the main gate, hammering on the giant brass bell that hung on a post there. He was dressed as a knight, carrying sword and lance and shield. He was young, they could see — probably only a year or two older than Horace.

The newcomer stopped hammering and filled his lungs to shout. He spoke, or rather shouted, in Gallic, and Horace had no idea what he was saying, although he certainly recognised the name 'Deparnieux'.

'What's he saying?' he asked Halt, and the Ranger held up a hand to hush him as he listened to the last few words from the knight.

'He's challenging Deparnieux,' he said, his head cocked to one side to make out the strange knight's words more clearly. Horace made an impatient gesture.

'I gathered that!' he said with some asperity. 'But why?'

Halt waved him to silence as the newcomer continued to shout. The tone was angry enough but the words were a little difficult to make out, as they ebbed and flowed on the swirling wind.

'From what I can make out,' Halt said slowly, 'our friend Deparnieux murdered this fellow's family — while he was away on a quest. They're very big on quests here in Gallica.'

'So what happened?' Horace wanted to know. But the Ranger could only shrug in reply.

'Apparently Deparnieux wanted the family's lands, so he got rid of the lad's parents.' He listened further and said, 'They were on the elderly side and relatively helpless.'

Horace grunted. 'That sounds like what we know about Deparnieux.'

Abruptly, the stranger ceased shouting, turned his horse and trotted away from the gate to wait for a reaction. For a few minutes, there was no sign that anyone other than Halt and Horace had paid the slightest attention. Then a sally port in the massive wall crashed open and a black armoured figure on a jet black battlehorse emerged.

Deparnieux cantered slowly to a position a hundred metres from the other knight. They faced each other while the young knight repeated his challenge. On the castle ramparts, Horace and Halt could see Deparnieux's men eagerly taking up vantage positions to watch the coming battle.

'Vultures,' Halt muttered at the sight of them.

The black-clad knight made no reply to the stranger. He simply reached up with the edge of his shield and flicked the visor on his helmet closed. That was enough for his challenger. He slammed down his own visor and set spurs to his battlehorse. Deparnieux did the same and they charged towards each other, lances levelled.

Even at a distance, Halt and Horace could see that the young man was not very skilled. His seat was awkward and his positioning of shield and lance was clumsy. Deparnieux, by contrast, looked totally co-ordinated and frighteningly capable as they thundered together.

'This doesn't look good,' Horace said in a worried tone.

They struck with a resounding crash that echoed off the walls of the castle. The young knight's lance, badly positioned and at the wrong angle, shattered into pieces. By contrast, Deparnieux's lance struck squarely into the other knight's shield, sending him reeling in the saddle as they passed. Yet strangely, Deparnieux appeared to lose his grasp on his own lance. It fell away into the grass behind him as he wheeled his horse for the return pass. For a moment, Horace felt a surge of hope.

'He's injured!' he said eagerly. 'That's a stroke of luck!'

But Halt was frowning, shaking his head.

'I don't think so,' he said. 'There's something fishy going on here.'

The two armoured warriors now drew their broadswords and charged again. They crashed together. Deparnieux took the other knight's stroke on his shield. His own sword struck ringingly against his opponent's helmet, and again the young man reeled in the saddle.

The battlehorses screamed in fury as they circled and reared now, with each rider trying to gain a winning position. The warriors struck at each other again and again as they came within reach, Deparnieux's men cheering every time their lord landed a blow.

'What's he doing?' Horace asked, his earlier excitement gone. 'He could have finished him off after that first stroke!' His voice took on a tone of disgust as he realised the truth. 'He's playing with him!'

Below them, the ringing, slithering screech of sword on sword continued, interspersed by the duller clang as they struck each other's shields. To experienced spectators like Halt and Horace, who had seen many tournaments at

Castle Redmont, Deparnieux was obviously holding back. His men, however, didn't seem to notice. They were peasants who had no real knowledge of the skills involved in a duel such as this. They continued to roar their approval with each stroke Deparnieux landed.

'He's playing to the audience,' Halt said, indicating the men at arms on the ramparts below them. 'He's making the other man look better than he really is.'

Horace shook his head. Deparnieux was showing yet another side of his cruel nature by prolonging the battle like this. Far better to give the young knight a merciful end than to toy with him.

'He's a swine,' he said in a low voice. Deparnieux's behaviour went against all the tenets of chivalry that meant so much to him. Halt nodded agreement.

'We knew that already. He's using this lad to boost his own reputation.'

Horace threw him a puzzled look and he explained further.

'He rules by fear. His hold over his men depends on how much they respect and fear him. And he has to keep renewing that fear. He can't let it slip. By making his opponent look better than he really is, he enhances his own reputation as a great warrior. These men,' he gestured contemptuously at the ramparts below, 'don't know any better.'

Deparnieux seemed to decide that he had prolonged matters long enough. The two Araluans detected a subtle change in the tempo and power of his blows. The young knight swayed under the onslaught and tried to give ground. But the black armoured figure urged his battlehorse after him, following him relentlessly, raining blows on sword, shield or helmet at will. Finally, there was a duller sound as Deparnieux's sword struck a vulnerable point — the chain mail protecting his opponent's neck.

The black knight knew it was a killing stroke. Contemptuously, he wheeled his horse towards the castle gate, without a backward glance at his opponent, who was crumpling sideways from the saddle. The ramparts resounded with cheers as the limp figure crashed onto the turf and lay, unmoving. The gate slammed shut behind the victor.

Halt stroked his beard thoughtfully.

'I think,' he said, 'we might have found the key to our problem with Lord Deparnieux.'

Thirty-one

$\mathfrak{I}$t was midmorning when Evanlyn woke, although she had no way of knowing it.

There was no sign of the sun. It was hidden behind the low-lying snow clouds. The light was so flat and diffused that it seemed to come from every direction and no direction. It was daylight and that was all she knew.

She eased her cramped muscles and looked around. Beside her, Will sat upright and wide awake. He may have been that way for hours or he may have woken only minutes before her. There was no way of knowing. He simply sat, eyes wide, rocking slowly back and forwards and staring straight ahead.

It tore at her heart to see him that way.

As she stirred, the horse sensed her movement and began to heave itself back upright. She moved away from the animal to give it room, taking Will's hand and pulling him away too. The horse came to its feet and stamped once or twice, then shook itself and snorted violently, blowing a huge cloud of steam into the frigid air.

The snow had stopped during the night but not before it had obliterated all sign of their passage to the hollow under the tree. It would be a hard slog back to the path, Evanlyn realised, but at least she was rested now. She thought briefly about eating — there was a small supply of food in the pack — then she discarded the idea, in favour of moving on and putting more distance between them and Hallasholm. She had no way of knowing that the search parties had already been recalled by Borsa.

She decided that she could live for a few more hours with the empty feeling in her belly, but not with the raging thirst that had dried her mouth. Moving to a point where the snow lay thick and new, she took a handful and put it in her mouth, letting it melt there. It produced a surprisingly small amount of water, so she repeated the action several more times. She considered showing Will how to do the same but suddenly felt impatient to be on their way. If he was thirsty, she reasoned, he could work it out for himself.

She strapped the pack saddle onto the pony's back again, tightening the girths as much as she could. The pony, canny in the way of its kind, tried to suck air and expand his belly, so he could exhale and allow the straps to loosen. But Evanlyn had been awake to that trick since she had been eleven years old. She kneed the horse firmly in the belly, forcing him to gasp the air out, then, as his body contracted, she jerked the straps tight. The pony turned a reproachful eye on her but otherwise accepted his fate philosophically.

As she led the way out from under the tree, forcing a path once more through the waist-deep snow, Will made a move to mount the pony. She stopped him, holding up a hand and saying, 'No', gently to him. They needed the pony and Will should be rested after an undisturbed night in the relative warmth of the snow hollow. Later, she might need to let him ride the horse again. She knew his reserves of strength couldn't be very deep. But for now, he could walk and they could preserve the little horse's strength as much as possible.

It took five minutes' hard work to reach the relatively easy going of the path once more and, already breathing hard and wet with perspiration, she doggedly resumed her uphill path.

The horse plodded patiently behind her and Will walked half a pace to her right. His low-level, nonstop keening was beginning to set her teeth on edge, but she did her best to ignore it, knowing that he couldn't help it. For the hundredth time since they had left Hallasholm, she found herself wishing for the day when he might have finally expelled all traces of the drug from his system.

That day was to be further postponed, unfortunately. After a couple of hours of solid, dogged plodding through the fresh fallen snow, Will was suddenly seized by an uncontrollable fit of shivering.

His teeth clattered and his body shook and trembled and heaved as he fell to the ground, rolling helplessly in the snow, his knees drawn up to his chest. One hand flailed uselessly at the snow, while the other was jammed firmly in his mouth. She watched in horror as the moaning turned to a shuddering cry, dragged deep from his soul and torn with agony.

She dropped to her knees beside him, putting her arms around him and trying to soothe him with her voice. But he jerked away from her, rolling and thrashing again, and she realised that there was nothing for it but to give him a little of the warmweed Erak had put in the pack. She'd seen it already when she had searched for warm clothes and blankets. There was a small amount of the dried leaf packed in an oiled linen pouch. Jarl Erak had warned her that Will would not be able to quit the drug straight away. Warmweed built up a physical dependence in its addicts, so that total deprivation meant actual pain.

She would have to gradually wean the boy off the drug, he had told her, by giving him ever-decreasing amounts at ever-increasing intervals until he could cope with the deprivation.

Evanlyn had hoped that Erak might be wrong. She knew that each dose of the drug extended the time of the dependence further and she had hoped that she might just be able to cut off Will's supply straight away and help him cope with the pain and torment.

But there was no help for him as he was now and, reluctantly, she let him have a small amount of the dried leaf, shielding the pouch with her body as she took it from the pack, then again when she returned it.

Will seized the small handful of the grey, herb-like substance with horrifying eagerness. For the first time, she saw a glint of expression in his normally dull gaze. But his attention was totally focused on the drug and she came to realise how completely it ruled his life and his mind these days. Silently, tears forming in her eyes, she watched the hollow shell who had once been such a vital, enthusiastic companion. She condemned Borsa and the other Skandians who had caused this to the hottest corner of whatever hell they believed in.

The apprentice Ranger crammed the small amount of leaf into his mouth, forcing it into one cheek and allowing the saliva to soak it and release the juice that would carry the narcotic through his system. Gradually, the shuddering spasms calmed down, until he knelt in the snow beside the path, hunched over, rocking gently backwards and forwards, eyes slitted, once again moaning softly to himself in whatever lonely, pain-filled world he inhabited.

The pony watched these events incuriously, from time to time pawing a hole in the snow and nibbling at the sparse strands of grass exposed there. Eventually, Evanlyn took Will's hand and pulled him, unresisting, to his feet.

'Come on, Will,' she said in a dispirited voice. 'We've still got a long way to go.'

As she said it, she realised she was talking about a lot more than just the distance to the hunting cabin in the mountains.

Crooning softly and tunelessly to himself, Will followed her as she led the way upwards yet again.

The daylight was nearly gone by the time she found the cabin.

She had gone past it twice, following the instructions that Erak had made her commit to memory: a left fork in the trail a hundred paces after a lightning blasted pine; a narrow gully that led downwards for a hundred metres, then curved back up again, and a shallow ford across a small stream.

Mentally, she ticked off the landmarks, peering this way and that through the gloom of evening as it settled over the trees. But she could see no sign of the hut — only the featureless white of the snow.

Finally she realised that, of course, the hut would not be visible as a hut. It would be virtually buried in snow itself. Once she saw that simple fact, she became aware of a large mound not ten metres away from her. Dropping the pony's lead rein, she blundered forward, the snow catching at her legs, and made out the edge of a wall, then the slope of a roof, then the hard angle of a corner, more regular and even than any shape that nature might have concealed under the snow.

Moving round the large mound, she found the leeward side was more exposed and she could see the door and a small window, covered with a wooden shutter. She reflected that it was lucky the door had been built on the lee side of the cabin, then realised that this would have been intentional. Only a fool would place a door on the side where the prevailing north winds would pile the snow deeply.

Heaving a sigh of relief, she retraced her steps and took the pony's bridle. Will's meagre strength had given out hours before and he was once more slumped on the pack saddle, swaying and moaning in that continuous undertone. She led the pony to stand by the tiny porch that adjoined the doorway, tying the lead rein to a tether post that was set in the ground there. There was probably no need for that, she reflected. The pony had shown no inclination to leave her so far. However, it did no harm to take precautions. The last thing she wanted was to have to hunt for the pony and its rider through the gathering dusk.

Satisfied that the bridle was tied firmly, she shoved the ill-fitting door open and entered the hut to take stock of their new refuge and its contents.

It was small, just one main room with a rough table and two benches either side. Against the far wall, there was a wooden cot, with what appeared to be a straw-filled mattress on it. The room smelt of damp and mustiness and she wrinkled her nose momentarily, then realised that once she had a fire burning in the stone fireplace that comprised most of the western wall, she could do something to dispel the smells.

There was a handy supply of firewood stacked by the fireplace, with a flint and iron as well.

She spent a few minutes kindling a fire and the cheerful crack of the flames, and the flickering yellow light they cast over the interior of the hut, raised her spirits.

In a corner that was obviously a pantry, she found flour and dried meat and beans. There was some evidence that small scavengers had been at the supplies but she felt that they would probably be sufficient for the next month or two. She and Will wouldn't be feasting, she knew, but they would survive.

Particularly if he recovered any of his old skill as he shook off the effects of the drug. Because now, she saw, there was a small hunting bow and a leather quiver of arrows hanging behind the door of the hut. Even in the deep winter there would be some small game available — snowshoe rabbits and snow hares, mainly. They might well be able to supplement the food that had been stored here.

If not — she shrugged at the thought. At least they were free and at least she had a chance to break Will's warmweed addiction. She would face other problems as they arose.

The interior of the hut was becoming warmer now and she went back outside, motioning for Will to dismount. As he did so, she frowned at the sight of the pony. He could hardly stay outside, she realised. Yet the thought of sharing the single-roomed hut with him for the winter held little appeal. The previous night, even though she had been grateful for his warmth, she had been totally conscious of the powerful animal odour that came from him.

Telling Will to wait by the door, she moved around the hut to the side she had so far not inspected, and found her answer there.

There was a low lean-to built onto the hut at this point. It was open at one side but would provide sufficient shelter for the pony through the winter. There were a few items of abandoned tack and leather harness hanging on iron nails there, along with some simple tools. Obviously, it was intended as a stable.

It had another use as well, she was grateful to see. Along the outer wall of the hut, against which the lean-to abutted, there was a large stack of cut firewood. She was relieved to see it there. Already she had wondered what she might do when she had exhausted the small supply in the hut itself.

She brought the pony to the lean-to, and removed the pack saddle and bridle from him. There was a feed tub there and a small supply of grain, so she let him have some.

He stood gratefully, munching on the grain, grinding his teeth together in that peaceful way that horses have.

At this stage, she could find no water for him. But she'd seen him licking at the snow during the day and reasoned that he could satisfy himself that way until she could arrange some alternative. The small supply of grain in the stable would obviously not last him until spring and she worried about that fact for a moment. Then, in line with her new philosophy of not worrying about matters she couldn't rectify, she shrugged the thought away.

'Worry about it later,' she told herself, and returned to the cabin proper.

She found that Will had had the good sense to move inside and was seated on one of the benches, close to the fire. She took that as a good sign and prepared a simple meal from the remains of the provisions Erak had placed in the pack for them.

There was a battered kettle on a hanging arm by the fireplace and she rammed it full of snow, swinging the arm in until the kettle was suspended over the flames and the snow began to melt, then the water to boil. She had seen a small box of what looked like tea in the pantry area of the hut. At least they could have a warm drink to drive the last traces of cold and dampness away, she thought.

She smiled at Will as he chewed stolidly at the food she had placed before him. She felt strangely optimistic. Once more, she cast her glance over the interior of the hut. The light had gone outside now and they were lit solely by the uncertain but cheerful yellow glow of the fire. In the light it threw, the hut looked somehow welcoming and reassuring and, as she'd hoped, the heat of the fire and the smell of the pine smoke had overpowered the dampness and mustiness that had filled the room when she'd first entered.

'Well,' she said, 'it isn't much, but it's home.'

She had no idea she was echoing the words spoken by Halt, hundreds of kilometres to the south.

Thirty-two

Halt and Horace weren't surprised when, the evening following the one-sided combat, the sergeant of the guards told them that the lord Deparnieux expected their company in the dining hall that night. It was a command, not an invitation, and Halt felt no need to pretend that it was anything else. He made no acknowledgement of the sergeant's message, but merely turned away to gaze out the tower window. The sergeant seemed unconcerned by this. He turned and resumed his post at the top of the spiralling staircase that led to the dining hall. He had passed on the message. The foreigners had heard it.

That evening, they bathed, dressed and walked together down the spiral staircase to the lower floors of the castle, their boot heels ringing on the flagstones as they went. They had spent the latter part of the afternoon discussing their plan of action for the night and Horace was eager to put it into effect. As they reached the three-metre-high double doors to the dining hall, Halt put a hand on his arm and stopped him. He could see the impatience on the young man's face. They had been cooped up here for weeks now, listening to Deparnieux's sneering, veiled insults and watching his savagely cruel treatment of his staff. The incidents with the cook and the young knight were only two of many. Halt knew that Horace, with the impatience of all young men, was keen to see Deparnieux given his come-uppance. He also knew that the plan they had agreed on would depend on patience and proper timing.

Halt had realised that Deparnieux's need to appear invincible to his men was a weakness they could exploit. Deparnieux himself had created a situation where he was forced to accept any challenge that might be issued, so long as it were made before witnesses. There could be no carping or quibbling on the warlord's part. If he appeared to show fear, or reluctance to accept a challenge, it would be the beginning of a long, downward spiral.

Now, as they stopped, Halt met Horace's eager, antici-patory gaze with his own — steady, patient and calculating.

'Remember,' he said, 'nothing until I give you the signal.'

Horace nodded. His cheeks were slightly flushed with excitement. 'I understand,' he said, holding in his eagerness with some difficulty. He felt the Ranger's hand on his arm, realised those steady eyes were still on his. He took three deep breaths to steady his pulse, then nodded again, this time more deliberately.

'I do understand, Halt,' he said again. He met the Ranger's gaze this time, holding it with his own. 'I won't spoil things,' he assured his friend. 'We've waited too long for this moment and I'm aware of it. Don't worry.'

Halt studied him for another long moment. Then, satisfied with the unspoken message he saw in the boy's eyes, he nodded and released his arm. He shoved the double doors back so that they crashed against the wall on either side. Together, Horace and Halt marched into the dining hall to where Deparnieux waited for them.

The meal they were served was another disappointing example of the much vaunted Gallic cuisine. To Halt's taste, the dishes placed before them depended far too much on a rich and slightly sickly combination of too much cream and an excess of garlic. He ate sparingly, noticing, however, that Horace, with a young man's appetite, wolfed down every morsel that was placed before him.

Throughout the meal, the warlord kept up a constant stream of sarcasm and disdain, referring to the clumsiness and stupidity of his own serving staff and to the inept display made by the unknown knight the day before. As was their custom, Halt drank wine with the meal, while Horace contented himself with water. As they had finished eating the over-rich, heavy food, servants brought jugs of coffee to the table.

This, Halt had to admit, was one thing the Galls did with great skill. Their coffee was ambrosia, far better than any he had ever tasted in Araluen. He sipped appreciatively at the fragrant, hot drink, looking over the rim of his cup to where Deparnieux regarded him and Horace with his usual, disdainful smile.

By now, the Gallic knight had come to a decision about Halt. There was, he believed, nothing to fear from the grey-bearded foreigner. Obviously, the man had some skill with a bow. And he probably had skills in wood craft and stalking as well. But as for his original fears that Halt might have some arcane skills as a sorcerer, he felt comfortable that he had been mistaken.

Now that he felt it was safe to do so, Deparnieux could not resist the temptation to berate Halt with sneers and insults even more than before. The fact that he had been wary of the bearded man for some time merely served to redouble his efforts to discomfort him. The warlord enjoyed toying with people. He loved to hold people helpless, loved to see them suffer or rage impotently under the scourge of his sarcastic tongue.

And, as his disdain for Halt grew, so too did his total dismissal of Horace. Each time the three of them dined together like this, he waited expectantly for the moment when he could brusquely dismiss the muscular young man and send him, cheeks flaming with rage and embarrassment, back to the tower. Now, he judged, it was time to do so once more.

He tilted his heavy chair back on its hind legs, draining the silver goblet that he held in his left hand. He waved the other hand disdainfully in the boy's direction.

'Leave us, boy,' he commanded, refusing to even look at Horace. He felt a distinct thrill of pleasure when the boy, after a slight pause, and a quick glance at his companion, stood slowly and replied with one word.

'No.'

The word hung in the air between them. Deparnieux exulted in the boy's rebellion, but he allowed no sign to show on his face. Instead, he affected a heavy frown of apparent displeasure. He turned slowly to face the youth. He could see Horace's breath coming faster as the adrenalin surged through his veins, now that this vital moment had finally arrived.

'No?' Deparnieux repeated, as if he could not believe what he was hearing. 'I am the lord of this castle, and my word here is law. My pleasure is the command of all others. You do me the discourtesy of telling me "no" in my own castle?'

'The time is past when your word is to be obeyed without question,' Horace replied carefully, frowning as he strove to make sure he stayed to the exact wording Halt had laid out. 'You have forfeited your right to obedience by your unchivalrous actions.'

Deparnieux still maintained a pretence of displeasure. 'You challenge my right to command in my own fief?'

Horace hesitated once more, making sure he phrased his reply exactly. As Halt had told him, accuracy now was of paramount importance. In fact, as Horace realised only too well, it was a matter of life and death.

'It's time that right was challenged,' he replied, after a pause. Deparnieux, allowing a wolfish smile to show on his dark features, now rose from his seat, leaning forward over the table, resting both hands on the bare wood surface.

'So you challenge me?' he asked, the pleasure in his voice all too obvious. Horace, however, made an uncertain gesture.

'Before any challenge is issued, I would demand that you respect it,' he said, and the warlord frowned slightly.

'Respect it?' he repeated. 'What do you mean, you whining pup?'

Horace shook his head doggedly, dismissing the insult.

'I want an undertaking that you will abide by the terms of the challenge. And I want it made before your own men.'

'Oh, you do, do you?' Now the hint of anger in Deparnieux's voice wasn't assumed. It was real. He could see where the boy was going.

'I think,' Halt interrupted quietly, 'that the boy feels you rule by fear, Lord Deparnieux,' he said. The Gall turned to face him.

'And what is that to either of you, bowman?' he asked, although he thought he already knew.

Halt shrugged, then replied casually, 'Your men are with you because of your reputation as a warrior. I believe Horace would prefer to see the challenge issued and accepted before your men.'

Deparnieux frowned. With the challenge more or less issued in front of some of his men already, he knew he had no choice but to comply. A warlord who even seemed to show fear of a sixteen-year-old youth would find little respect from the men he commanded, even if he were to win the resultant battle.

'You feel I am afraid of this boy's challenge?' he asked sarcastically. Halt held up a cautioning hand.

'No challenge has been issued . . . yet,' he said. 'We're merely concerned to see that you have the courage to honour any challenge that might eventuate.'

Deparnieux snorted in disgust at the Ranger's careful words. 'I can see your true calling now, bowman,' he replied. 'I thought you might be a sorcerer. I see now you are no more than a grubby lawyer, bickering over words.'

Halt smiled thinly and inclined his head slightly. He

made no other reply and the silence stretched between them. Deparnieux glanced quickly at the two sentries who stood inside the large double doors of the dining hall. Their faces betrayed their interest in the scene being played out. The details would spread throughout the castle within the hour if he were to refuse the challenge now, or try to gain any unfair advantage over the boy. He knew his men had little love for him and he knew that, should he not treat the challenge fairly, he would begin to lose them. Not immediately, perhaps, but gradually, by ones and twos as they deserted his banner and flocked to his enemies. And Deparnieux had all too many enemies.

He glared at the boy now. He had no doubt whatever that he could best Horace in a fair fight. But he resented the fact that he had been manipulated into this position. In Chateau Montsombre, it was Deparnieux who preferred to do the manipulating. He forced a smile and tried to look as if he were bored with the entire affair.

'Very well,' he said, in a careless tone, 'if this is what you wish, I will abide by the terms of the challenge.'

'And you give that undertaking in front of your own men here?' Horace said quickly, and the warlord scowled at him, abandoning any pretence that he didn't dislike the quibbling boy and his bearded companion.

'Yes,' he spat at them. 'If I must spell it out to please you, I guarantee my acceptance, in front of my men.'

Horace heaved a large sigh of relief. 'Then,' he said, beginning to tug one of his gloves free from where it was tucked securely into his belt, 'the challenge may be issued. The combat will take place in two weeks' time.'

'Agreed,' Deparnieux replied.

'. . . on the grassed field before Chateau Mont-sombre . . .'

'Agreed.' The word was almost spat out.

'. . . in view of your own men and the other people of the castle . . .'

'Agreed.'

'. . . and it shall be mortal combat.' Horace's voice hesitated slightly over the phrase, but he glanced quickly at Halt and the Ranger nodded slightly to give him courage. And now, the smile returned to the warlord's lips, thin and bitter and savage.

'Agreed,' he said again. Yet this time, the word was almost purred. 'Now get on with it, boy, before you lose your courage and wet your pants.'

Horace cocked his head at the warlord and, for the first time, felt in control of the situation.

'What a thoroughly unpleasant piece of work you are, Deparnieux,' he said softly and the black knight leaned forward across the table, thrusting his chin out for the ritual blow with a glove that would issue the challenge and make the entire event irrevocable.

'Frightened, boy?' he sneered, and then flinched as a glove slapped stingingly across his cheek.

Not that the pain made him flinch. Rather, it was the unexpectedness of it all. For the boy across the table hadn't moved. Instead, the bearded, grizzled bowman had come to his feet with a speed and agility that left the warlord no time to react, and struck him across the face with the glove that he had held under the table for the past few minutes.

'Then I challenge you, Deparnieux,' the Ranger said. And for a few seconds the warlord felt a surge of uncertainty as he saw the light of satisfaction deep behind those steady, unwavering eyes.

Thirty-three

A small patch of sunlight crept across the single room of the hut. Evanlyn, dozing in a chair, felt the warmth of the sun on her face and smiled, unconsciously. Outside, the snow was still deep on the ground, but the sky was a brilliant, cloudless blue in the midafternoon.

Half asleep, she enjoyed the warmth as it slowly moved across her. Behind closed eyelids, she saw the bright red of the sun's glare.

Then, abruptly, the light was blocked and she opened her eyes.

Will stood before her, in the attitude that had become familiar to her over the past week. His hands were clasped together and his dark brown eyes, once so alight with amusement and fun, held nothing but a wistful plea. He stood patiently, waiting for her to react, and she smiled at him, a little sadly.

'All right,' she told him gently.

The faintest trace of a smile touched his lips, seeming

for a moment to reflect in those dark eyes, and she felt a renewal of the surge of hope that had been growing within her over the past days. Gradually, but noticeably, Will was changing. At first, as she withheld the drug from him, he had convulsed in those awful shuddering fits, only recovering when she doled out a small portion of the warmweed.

But, as the intervals between doses had grown longer and the doses themselves smaller, she had begun to hope that he would eventually recover. The seizures were a thing of the past. Now, instead of being ruled by his body as it craved the drug, Will was becoming more mentally attuned to a smaller supply. There was still a need there, but it was reflected in the pleading, almost childlike, behaviour that she was seeing now.

After three days without a taste of the weed, he would come to her and simply stand in front of her, the message clear in his eyes. And, in response, she would measure out a helping of the ever-decreasing stock of drug that remained in the oiled cotton pouch. It was a race, she knew, to see whether his dependence would outlast the supply. If that were the case, she could see some hard times ahead for the two of them. She had no idea what his reaction would be if she refused him. But she sensed that further deprivation would result in another bout of uncontrollable shivering and crying.

Perhaps, she reasoned, that was the next necessary stage in his rehabilitation. But, rightly or wrongly, she simply could not bring herself to witness that helpless, naked need again. Time enough for that when the warmweed finally ran out, she thought.

'Stay here,' she told him, rising from the wood frame chair and heading for the door. Again, she thought she saw a dim glint of pleasure in his eyes. It was gone almost as soon as she thought she had seen it, but she told herself that it had really been there, that she wasn't simply seeing what she hoped to see.

She kept the supply of warmweed in the stable, behind a loose board on one of the side walls. Initially, she was planning to conceal the oiled cloth pouch in the pile of firewood logs. But then she realised that she would use Will to fetch firewood and the possibility of his finding the supply of the drug was too awful to contemplate.

She had no clear idea what would happen to him if he took an excessively large dose.

At the least, she reasoned, his dependence would soar once again to a new level. And there might possibly be more permanent side effects as well — even fatal ones. What she did know was that if Will found the warmweed and used it all in one massive binge, she would face weeks of the convulsions and shuddering fits that had seized him when he had been deprived of the drug before.

She wondered if his dulled mind could process the fact that she always left the cabin and returned with the weed; whether he was capable of putting together a cause and effect sequence and reasoning that the weed must be kept somewhere outside the cabin. She wasn't sure, but in any event, she took no risk, taking great care to check that he hadn't followed her when she took the pouch from the small concealed space in the timber wall.

She looked carefully over her shoulder as she entered the stable and the pony looked up and snorted a greeting to her. But there was no sign that Will was showing any interest in her movements. Apparently, he was content to wait where he was, knowing that she would shortly return with the drug that he craved. How this happened, or where she found it, didn't seem to be questions that concerned him. They were abstractions and he dealt only in absolute facts these days.

She measured a minute amount of the dried weed into the palm of her hand, rewrapped the remaining supply and replaced it behind the loose board. Again, halfway through the sequence, she turned suddenly to see if she might be being observed. But there was no sign of her companion — only the pony, watching her with liquid, intelligent eyes.

'Don't say a word,' she said to the horse in a lowered tone. Remarkably, it chose that very moment to shake its head, as ponies do from time to time. Evanlyn shrugged after a second of startled reaction. It was as if the horse had heard and understood her. She replaced the pouch in the hollow and jammed the section of board back to conceal it. Stooping to the earth floor of the stable, she gathered a handful of dirt and smeared it over the jagged line that marked the join in the wood. Then, satisfied that the hiding place was concealed as well as it could be, she returned to the cabin.

Will smiled as she entered and, for one moment, she thought he had recognised her from the old days. The old days, she thought ruefully. They were barely a few months ago, but now she thought of them as ancient history. Then she realised that his gaze was riveted on her clenched right hand. The smile was for the drug, not for her.

Still, it was a beginning, she thought.

She held out the clenched hand and he eagerly stepped forward, cupping both his hands underneath hers, anxious that not a grain should be spilt. She allowed the grey-green herb to trickle into his hands, watching his face as his eyes followed the thin stream of the drug. Unconsciously, his tongue darted across his lips in anticipation. When she had given him all of it — and allowed him to carefully brush the few minute crumbs that remained fastened on her palm into his own — he looked up at her and smiled again.

This time, he smiled at *her*, she was sure.

'Good,' he said briefly, and then his gaze fell to the tiny mound of dried warmweed in his hand. He turned away from her, hunching over the hand as he brought it to his mouth.

Evanlyn felt that sudden glow of hope burn brightly within her once more. It was the first time Will had actually spoken to her in the time since they had escaped from Hallasholm.

It wasn't much. Just the one word. But it was a beginning. She smiled after him as he hunkered down in a corner of the cabin. Animal-like, he instinctively cowered away as he took the drug, seemingly nervous that she might take it from him.

'Welcome back, Will,' she said softly.

But he said nothing in reply. The warmweed had him once again.

Thirty-four

Horace rose in his stirrups as Kicker reached a full gallop. He held the long ash pole out to his right-hand side, at right angles to his body and the line of travel. Ahead of him, standing unmoving in the middle of the field situated in front of the castle, Halt drew back the string of his longbow until the feathered end of the arrow touched the corner of his mouth.

Horace urged the battlehorse to an even faster pace, until they had reached maximum speed. He glanced out to his right, to make sure the helmet that he had attached to the end of the pole was still in the correct position, facing Halt. Then he looked back at the small figure on the grass before him.

He saw the first arrow released, spitting from the bow with incredible force and speeding towards the moving target. Then, in an almost incomprehensible blur of motion, Halt's hands moved and another arrow was on the way.

Almost at the same time, Horace felt a double concussion transmitted down the length of the ash pole he held out, as the two shafts slammed into the helmet within the space of half a second.

He allowed Kicker to ease down to a canter as they passed Halt, taking the horse in a wide circle to come to a stop before the Ranger. Halt now stood with his bow grounded, waiting patiently to see the result of his practice. Horace let the pole and the attached helmet dip to the ground in front of him. Both shafts, incredibly, had found their way through the helmet's vision slits and into the soft padding that Halt had put inside to protect the razor-sharp arrowheads.

As Halt took the old helmet in his hands, Horace swung his leg over the pommel and slid to the ground beside him. The grizzled Ranger nodded once as he inspected the result of his target practice.

'Not bad,' he said. 'Not bad at all.'

Horace dropped the end of his reins, allowing Kicker to wander off and crop the short, thick grass that grew on the tournament field. He was puzzled and more than a little worried by Halt's actions.

After the challenge had been issued and accepted, Deparnieux had agreed to return their weapons. Halt claimed that he had not fired an arrow in weeks and would need to hone his skills for the combat. Deparnieux, who practised his own combat skills daily, saw nothing unusual in the request. So the weapons had been returned, although the two Araluans were watched closely by at least half a dozen crossbowmen whenever they practised.

For the past three days, Halt had instructed Horace to gallop down the field, the helmet held out on the end of a pole, as he fired shafts at the eyeholes. Every time, at least one of the two shafts had found its mark. Generally, Halt managed to put both arrows through the tiny spaces he was aiming at.

Yet this was no more than Horace expected of the Ranger. Halt's skill with a longbow was legendary. There was no need for him to practise now, particularly when, by doing so, he was revealing his tactics to the Gallic warlord.

'Is he watching?' Halt asked quietly, seeming to read Horace's thoughts. The Ranger had his back to the castle walls and couldn't see. But Horace, moving his eyes only and not his head, could make out the black silhouette at one of the castle's many terraces, hunched over the balustrade watching them – as he had done every time they had taken the field.

'Yes, Halt,' he said now. 'He's watching. But is it wise for us to do this where he can see?'

The very faintest trace of a smile seemed to touch the Ranger's lips.

'Possibly not,' he replied. 'But he'd make sure he saw us no matter where we practised, wouldn't he?'

'Yes,' Horace admitted reluctantly, 'but surely you don't need to practise, do you?'

Halt shook his head sadly. 'Spoken like a true apprentice,' he said. 'Practice never hurt anyone, young Horace. Bear that in mind when we get back to Castle Redmont.'

Horace eyed Halt unhappily as he eased the two arrows free from the straw and leather padding that filled the inside of the helmet.

'There's something else,' he began, and Halt held up a hand to stop him.

'I know, I know,' he said. 'Your precious rules of chivalry are bothering you again, aren't they?' Horace was forced to nod reluctant agreement. It was a bone of contention between the two of them, and had been ever since Halt had arranged to challenge Deparnieux to a duel.

At first, the warlord had been enraged, then sarcastically amused, that a commoner might assume to challenge him.

'I am a consecrated knight,' he spat at Halt. 'A nobleman! I cannot be challenged to combat by any ruffian from the forest!'

The Ranger's brows had darkened at that. His voice, when he spoke, was low and dangerous. Inadvertently, both Deparnieux and Horace had leaned forward to listen more carefully to his words.

'Guard your tongue, you lowborn cur!' Halt had replied. 'You're speaking to a member of the royal house of Hibernia, sixth in line to the throne and with a lineage that was noble when you and yours were scouring the kennels for scraps to eat!'

And, as he had spoken, an unmistakable Hibernian burr had accented his words. Horace had looked at him in considerable surprise. He had never had the slightest idea that Halt was descended from a royal line. Deparnieux was equally taken aback by the news. He was right, of course. No knight was obliged to honour a challenge from one beneath him. But the grizzled archer's claim to royal blood put a different aspect on matters. His challenge must be treated seriously and with respect. Deparnieux could not ignore it — particularly as it had been issued in the presence of several of his men. To refuse the challenge would undermine his position seriously.

As a result, he had accepted and the combat was set down for a week from that day.

Later, in their tower chambers, Horace had expressed his surprise about Halt's background.

'I had no idea you were descended from Hibernian royalty,' he said. Halt snorted dismissively as he replied.

'I'm not,' he said. 'But our friend doesn't know that and there's no way he can prove I'm not. Therefore he has to take my challenge as binding.'

And it was this disregard for the strict conventions of chivalry that had Horace so concerned, as much as the fact that Halt seemed to be letting his enemy know exactly what tactics he had for the combat, which was now only a day away. Training in the Battleschool placed great store upon the conventions and obligations of knighthood. They were, so Horace had been taught for the past eighteen months, binding and inflexible. They placed obligations on those who would be knights and, while they gave them great privileges, those privileges had to be earned. A knight had to observe the rules. To live by them and, if necessary, to die for them.

Among the most binding and inflexible of those conventions was that of a knight's recourse to trial by combat. It was a course that could be followed only by those who were followers of one of the various chivalrous orders. Even Horace, as an unknighted warrior, wasn't strictly speaking entitled to challenge Deparnieux. But Halt certainly wasn't and the Ranger's cavalier attitude to a system that Horace held in the highest esteem had shocked the boy — and continued to do so now.

'Look,' said Halt, not unkindly, as he put an arm around Horace's brawny shoulders, 'the rules of chivalry are a fine thing, I admit that. But only for those who abide by all the rules.'

'But . . .' Horace began, but Halt stopped him by squeezing his shoulder.

'Deparnieux has used those rules to kill, to plunder and to murder for god knows how many years. He accepts those parts of the rules that suit him and discards the ones that don't. You've seen that already.'

Horace nodded unhappily. 'I know, Halt. It's just I've been taught that —'

Halt interrupted him again, but gently. 'You've been taught by men who are noble,' he said. 'By men who uphold the rules of chivalry — all the rules — and live according to them. Let me tell you, I know no finer man than Sir Rodney, or Baron Arald, for that matter. Men like that are the embodiment of everything that is right about chivalry and knighthood.'

He paused, looking intently at the boy's troubled face. Horace nodded agreement. Halt had chosen two of his role models in Rodney and the Baron. Seeing that he had made his point, Halt continued: 'But a murdering, cowardly swine like Deparnieux cannot be allowed to claim the same standards as men like that. I have no compunction at all about lying to him as long as it helps me bring him to the point where I can fight him — and defeat him, with any luck.'

And at that point, Horace turned to him, his face still troubled, but perhaps a little less so.

'But how can you hope to defeat him when he knows exactly what you plan to do?' he asked miserably. Halt shrugged and replied, without any trace of a smile:

'Perhaps I'll get lucky.'

Thirty-five

The hunting bow was awkward in Evanlyn's grip. She fumbled as she tried to set one of the arrows on the string, almost dropping it into the snow at her feet as she tried to keep her eyes on the small animal moving slowly across the clearing before her.

Unthinkingly, she hissed her annoyance and instantly the rabbit sat up on its hind legs, its ears twitching this way and that to see if they could catch another hint of the foreign sound it had just picked up, and the nose twitching this way and that as it sampled the air for any trace of a foreign scent.

Evanlyn froze, waiting till the animal had reassured itself that there was no immediate danger, then went back to scrabble with its forepaws in the snow, scraping it away to expose the wet, stunted grass underneath. Scarcely daring to breathe, she watched as the rabbit began to graze again, then, looking down this time, slipped the arrow onto the string, just under the nock mark that the bow's original maker had placed there.

At this point, the string had been built up in thickness, with a fine cord wound round and round it, so that the nock fitted snugly, holding the arrow in place without any need for her fingers to do so. It was a snug hold, but a light one nevertheless, and the force of the string's release would instantly break the grip and send the arrow on its way.

She brought the bow up now and began to draw back on the string with her right hand. She knew she wasn't doing this correctly. She'd seen enough archers in her time to know that this simply wasn't the way it was done. However, as she was beginning to appreciate, watching a trained archer and emulating his movements were two completely different matters. Will, she remembered, could nock and draw an arrow in one smooth, practised and seemingly effortless movement. She could picture the movement now in her mind, but it was totally beyond her abilities to re-create it. Instead she held the bow upright and quivering, gripping the arrow's nock between her finger and thumb, and attempting to draw the string back with the strength of her fingers and arm alone.

Doing it that way, she could barely manage to bring the arrow to half draw. She pursed her lips in anger. That would have to do. She closed one eye and squinted down the arrow, trying to aim it at the small creature, which was feeding contentedly and oblivious to the mortal danger lurking in the trees fringing the clearing. With more hope than conviction, she finally released her grip on the arrow.

Three things happened.

The bow jerked in her grip, throwing the arrow off its

aim by at least three metres. The arrow itself flipped out of the bow, with barely enough power behind it to cause it to pierce flesh, and the string slapped painfully against the soft inside skin of her right forearm. She yelped in pain and dropped the bow. The arrow skated off the bole of a tree and disappeared into the forest on the far side of the clearing.

The rabbit came upright again and peered at her, a look of total puzzlement seeming to come over it as it cocked its head to see her more clearly. Then, dropping to all fours, it ambled slowly out of the clearing and into the trees.

So much, she thought bitterly, for the mortal peril hanging over its head.

She picked up the bow, rubbing the painful spot on her forearm where the string had slapped her, and went to look for the arrow. After ten minutes' searching, she decided it would have to remain lost. Glumly, she headed back to the small cabin.

'I guess I'm going to have to practise more,' she muttered.

This had been her second attempt at hunting. Her first had been equally fruitless and every bit as discouraging. For what must have been the fiftieth time, she sighed over the thought that if Will were healthy, he would have no difficulty at all in using the bow to provide food for their table.

She had shown him the bow, of course, hoping that the sight of the weapon might awaken some spark of memory within him. But he had done nothing other than stare at it with that disinterested, disingenuous expression that had become all too familiar to her.

There had been a fresh snowfall overnight and the snow was knee deep as she trudged back to the cabin. It had been the first snow in over a week and that had also set her to thinking. Winter must be more than halfway over and, eventually, when the spring came, the Skandians from Hallasholm would again begin to move through these mountains. Perhaps some might even arrive to use the cabin she and Will were wintering in. He would have to be recovered by then so they could begin the long trek south, and she had no idea how long his recovery might take. He seemed to be improving with each day, but she couldn't be sure. Nor could she really be sure how long they had until the spring thaw began to melt the snow.

They were in a race, she knew. But it was a race where she had no sight of the finish line. It could be on her any day.

The cabin came into view. She was relieved to see that a thin whisper of woodsmoke still issued from the chimney. She'd banked the fire before she'd left earlier in the day, hoping that she'd put enough fuel on to keep it burning through her absence. Nothing was more disheartening, she had already discovered, than arriving home cold and wet to a dead fire.

Naturally, there was no way she could expect Will to tend the fire while she was away. Even a simple task like that seemed beyond him. It was not, she realised, that he was unwilling. He was simply totally uninterested in doing or saying anything beyond the most basic functions. He ate, slept and occasionally came to her with that pleading expression in his eyes, asking for more warmweed. At least, she consoled herself, it had been some time since he had done that.

For the rest of the time, he simply sat wherever he might be, staring at the floor, or his hand, or a piece of wood, or whatever might have formed a focus point for his eyes at the time.

The old leather hinges on the cabin door creaked as she swung it inward. The noise was enough to draw Will's attention to her. He was sitting cross-legged on the floor in the middle of the cabin, much as he had been when she left, some hours earlier.

'Hullo, Will. I'm back,' she said, forcing a smile onto her face. She always tried, living in the hope that one day he would answer her.

This was not to be that day. The boy showed no sign of reply or interest. Sighing to herself, she leaned the small bow against the wall, just inside the door. Vaguely, she realised that she should unstring the bow, but she was too dispirited to do so right at the moment.

She crossed to the pantry and took out a small piece of their dwindling supply of dried beef. There was rice there too and she began preparing the beef-flavoured rice that had become their staple meal over the last few weeks, setting water to boil so that she could steep the meat in it and prepare a thin stock with at least a little flavour to it.

She had measured out a cup of the rice and was setting it into another pan when she heard a slight noise behind her. Turning, she realised that Will had moved from the position he'd occupied for most of the afternoon. He was now sitting near the doorway. She wondered what had caused him to move, then decided that it was probably a random inclination on his part.

Then she saw what it was, and she gave a jerk of surprise, spilling some of the precious rice onto the table.

The little bow was still leaning against the wall by the door. But now, it had been unstrung.

Thirty-six

Deparnieux's men had been out since early that morning, sweeping scythes through the long grass that covered the field in front of Chateau Montsombre. The Gallic knight was taking no chances on the planned combat. He had seen battlehorses brought down by tangles of long grass and he wanted to make sure that the fighting ground was clear of any such danger.

Now, an hour after noon, he emerged from the sally port that he had used on the occasion of his last combat. He had no doubt that he would defeat Halt. But he also had no misconceptions about the small stranger. He had watched the constant practice sessions that Halt and Horace had been conducting and he knew the Araluan was an archer of rare skill. He had no doubt of the tactics that his opponent would be employing. The practice sessions had made them plain. Deparnieux smiled to himself. Halt's psychological tactics were interesting, he thought. The constant sight of an arrow slamming though the vision slit of a rapidly moving helmet might well be enough to unnerve most opponents. But, while Deparnieux had little doubt about Halt's abilities, he had even less about his own. His reflexes were as sharp as a cat's and he was confident that he could deflect Halt's arrows with his shield.

The grey-haired Araluan seemed to have misjudged his opponent, he thought, and felt vaguely disappointed by the fact. He had expected so much of the stranger. Now, it seemed, those early impressions had come to very little. Halt was an expert bowman, that was all. He had no supernatural powers or arcane skills. In fact, thought the warlord, he was a rather limited, rather boring man with a high opinion of himself. He doubted the archer's claim to royal lineage but that no longer mattered to him. The man deserved to die, and Deparnieux would be happy to oblige him.

There were none of the usual flourishes of trumpets or ruffles of side drums as Deparnieux cantered his black charger slowly onto the combat field. This was not a day for ceremony. This was a simple working day for the black knight. An interloper had challenged his authority and his pre-eminence in the area. It was necessary to dispatch such people with maximum efficiency.

For all that, virtually every member of the staff of Chateau Montsombre, and a good many of Deparnieux's fighting men, were present to witness the combat. He smiled wolfishly as he wondered how many of them were watching in the hope that they would see him defeated. More than a few, he thought. But they were doomed to disappointment. In fact, the despatch of the archer would serve a useful purpose for him. Nothing would serve discipline so well as the sight of the chateau's lord and master dealing a quick death to an upstart interloper.

Speak of the devil, there he was now. The archer was cantering onto the far end of the field now, on his absurd little barrel of a horse. He wore no armour, only a studded leather vest that would give him no protection at all against Deparnieux's lance and sword. And, of course, his ever-present grey and green dappled cloak.

His young companion rode a few paces behind him. He was fitted out in chain mail and had his helmet slung at the saddle bow of his battlehorse. He wore his sword and carried the round buckler emblazoned with the oakleaf symbol.

Interesting, thought Deparnieux. Obviously, in the event of Halt's inevitable defeat, his young fellow traveller would attempt to avenge his friend. All the better, thought the black knight. If one death would serve as a salutary lesson to his more unruly retainers, two would be doubly effective. After all, that was how this entire disappointing business had started in the first place.

He brought his horse to a stop now, testing his grip on the lance in his right hand, ensuring that he had it at just the right point of balance. At the far end of the field, his opponent continued to ride forward, slowly and steadily. He seemed ridiculously small, dwarfed by the muscular youth and the huge battlehorse that paced beside him.

'I hope you know what you're doing,' Horace said, trying to speak without moving his lips, in case Deparnieux was watching — which he undoubtedly was. Halt turned in the saddle and almost smiled at him.

'So do I,' he said quietly. He noticed that Horace's right hand was easing his sword in its scabbard once more. He had done that same thing at least half a dozen times as they rode forward. 'Relax,' he added calmly. Horace glanced at him openly now, no longer caring if Deparnieux saw him or not.

'Relax?' he repeated incredulously. 'You're going to fight an armoured knight with nothing more than a bow and you tell me to relax?'

'I'll have one or two arrows as well, you know,' Halt told him mildly and Horace shook his head in disbelief.

'Well . . . I just hope you know what you're doing,' he said again. Halt smiled at him now. Just the briefest flash of a smile.

'So you keep saying,' he replied. Then he nudged Abelard with his knee and the little horse came to a stop, ears pricked and ready for more signals. Halt's eyes locked on the distant figure in the black armour and he raised his right leg over the saddle bow and slid off the horse.

'Take him out of harm's way,' he told the apprentice, and Horace leant down and took the Ranger horse's rein. Abelard twitched his ears and looked inquisitively at his master.

'Go along,' Halt told him quietly and the horse allowed himself to be led away. Halt glanced once at the youth sitting astride the battlehorse. He could see the worry in every line of the boy's body.

'Horace?' he called and the apprentice warrior stopped and looked back at him.

'I do know what I'm doing, you know.'

Horace managed a wan smile at that.

'If you say so, Halt,' he said.

As they were talking, Halt carefully selected three arrows from the two dozen in his quiver and slid them, point down, into the top of his right boot. Horace saw the movement and wondered at it. There was no need for Halt to place his arrows ready to hand in that way. He could draw and fire from the quiver on his back in a fraction of a second.

He didn't have time to wonder about it any further. Deparnieux was calling from the far end of the field.

'My lord Halt,' his accented voice came to Horace clearly as he reined in, off to one side. 'Are you ready?'

Not bothering to speak, Halt raised a hand in reply. He looked so small and vulnerable, Horace thought, standing all alone in the centre of the mown field, waiting for the black-clad knight on his massive battlehorse to bear down on him.

'Then may the best man win!' shouted Deparnieux mockingly, and this time Halt did reply.

'I plan to,' he called back, as Deparnieux clapped his spurs to the horse and it began to lumber forward, building up to a full gallop as it came.

It struck Horace then that Halt had not said anything to him about what he should do if Deparnieux were victorious. He had half expected the Ranger to instruct him to try to escape. He certainly expected that Halt would forbid him to challenge Deparnieux immediately after the combat — which was precisely what Horace planned to do if Halt lost. He wondered now if the Ranger hadn't said anything because he knew that Horace would ignore any such instruction, or if it were simply because he was totally confident of emerging as the victor.

Not that there seemed any way that he could. The earth shook under the hooves of the black battlehorse and Horace's expert eye could see that the Gallic warlord was a warrior of enormous experience and natural ability. Perfectly balanced in his seat on the horse, he handled the long, heavy lance as if it were a lightweight staff, leaning forward and rising slightly in his stirrups as the point of his lance drew ever closer to the small figure in the grey-green cloak.

It was the cloak that first sent a slight feeling of misgiving through Deparnieux's mind. Halt was swaying slightly as he stood his ground, and the uneven patterns on the cloak, set against the grey-green of the mown winter grass, seemed to send his figure in and out of focus. The effect was almost mesmerising. Angrily, Deparnieux thrust the distracting thought aside and tried to centre his attention on the archer. He was close now, barely thirty metres away, and still the archer hadn't . . .

He saw it coming. A blur of movement as the bow came up and the first arrow spat towards him at incredible speed, coming straight towards the vision slits in his helmet and bringing instant oblivion with it.

Yet, fast as the arrow was travelling, Deparnieux was even faster, raising the shield in a slant to deflect the arrow. He felt it slam against the shield, steel screeching on steel as it gouged a long furrow in the gleaming black enamel then went hissing off as the shield deflected it.

But the shield was now blocking his sight of the little man and he lowered it quickly.

All the devils in hell take him! It was what Halt had planned on, firing a second arrow even as the shield was still up! Deparnieux's incredible reflexes saved him again, bringing the shield back up to deflect the treacherous second shot. How could anyone manage to fire so quickly, he thought, then cursed as he realised that, unsighted as he was, he had already been carried past the spot where the archer stood, calmly stepping out of the line of the lance point.

Deparnieux let the battlehorse slow to a canter, wheeling him in a wide arc. It wouldn't do to risk injury to the horse by trying to wheel it too quickly. He'd take his time and . . .

At that moment there was a bright flash of pain in his left shoulder. Twisting awkwardly, his vision constricted by the helmet, he realised that, as he had galloped past, Halt had sent another arrow spitting at him, this time aiming for the gap in his armour at the shoulder.

The chain mail that filled the gap had taken most of the force of the arrow, but the razor-sharp broadhead had still managed to shear through a little way and penetrate the flesh. It was painful, but only minor, he realised, moving the arm quickly to ensure that no major muscles or tendons had been damaged. If the fight were to be a prolonged one, it could stiffen and affect his shield defence.

As it was, the wound was a nuisance. A painful nuisance, he amended, as he felt the hot blood trickling down his armpit. Halt would pay for that, he promised himself. And he would pay dearly.

Because now, Deparnieux believed he understood Halt's plan. He would continue to blind him as he came charging in, forcing him to raise the shield to protect his eyes at the last minute, then sidestepping as Deparnieux went charging past.

Except the knight had no intention of playing Halt's game. He would abandon the wild high-speed charge with a lance for a slow, deliberate approach. After all, he didn't need the force and momentum of a charge. He wasn't facing another armoured knight, trying to knock him from the saddle. He was facing a man standing alone in the middle of the field.

As the plan came to him, he tossed the long, unwieldy lance to the ground, reached round and broke the arrow shaft off close to his shoulder, and tossed it after the lance.

Then, drawing his broadsword, he began to trot slowly to where Halt stood, waiting for him.

He kept Halt to his left, so that the shield would be in position to deflect his arrows. The long sword in his right hand swung easily in circles as he felt its familiar weight and perfect balance.

Watching, Horace felt his heart thud faster in his chest. There could only be one end to the contest now. Once Deparnieux had abandoned the headlong charge for a more deliberate approach, Halt was in serious trouble. Horace knew that nine out of ten knights would have continued to charge, outraged by Halt's tactics and determined to crush him with their superior force. Deparnieux, he could see now, was the one in ten who would quickly see the folly in that course, and find a tactic to nullify Halt's biggest advantage.

The mounted knight was only forty metres away from the small figure now, moving slowly towards him. As before, the bow came up and the arrow was on its way. Deftly, almost contemptuously, Deparnieux flicked his shield up to deflect the arrow. This time, he heard the ringing screech of its impact and lowered the shield again. He could see the next arrow, already aimed at his head. He saw the archer's hand begin the release and again brought the shield up as the arrow leapt towards him.

But there was one important item he didn't see.

This arrow was one of the three that Halt had placed in the cuff of his boot. And this arrow was different, with a much heavier head, made from heat-hardened steel. Unlike the normal war arrows in Halt's quiver, it was not a leaf-shaped broadhead. Rather, it was shaped like the point of a cold chisel, surrounded by four small spurs that would stop it deflecting from Deparnieux's plate armour and allow it to punch through into the flesh behind.

It was an arrowhead designed to pierce armour and Halt had learnt its secrets years before, from the fierce mounted archers of the eastern steppes.

The arrow flew from the bow. As Deparnieux raised his shield, he never saw the extra weight of the head already causing it to drop below its point of aim. The arrow arced in underneath the slanted shield and punched into the breastplate exposed there, with barely a check to its speed and force.

Deparnieux heard it. A dull impact of metal on metal — more a metallic thud than a ringing tone. He wondered what it was. Then he felt a small core of intense pain, a bright flare of agony, that began in his left side and expanded rapidly until it engulfed his entire body.

He never felt the impact as his body hit the grassy field.

Halt lowered the bow. He eased the string and replaced the second armour-piercing arrow, already nocked and ready, back in his quiver.

The lord of Chateau Montsombre lay unmoving. A stunned silence hung over the small crowd of onlookers who had come out of the castle to watch the combat. None of them knew how to react. None of them had expected this result. The servants, cooks and stable hands felt a cautious sense of pleasure. Deparnieux had never been a popular master. His use of the lash and the iron cages on any servant who displeased him had seen to that. But their expectations of the man who had just killed him were not necessarily any higher. Logically, they assumed that the bearded stranger had killed their master so that he could take control of Montsombre. That was the way of things here in Gallica and former experience had shown them that a change in master brought no improvement to their lot. Deparnieux himself had defeated a former tyrant some years back. So, while they felt satisfaction to see the sadistic and pitiless black knight dead, they viewed his successor with no great sense of optimism.

For the men at arms who had served under Deparnieux, it was a slightly different matter. They, at least, felt a closer bond to the dead man, although to class that feeling as loyalty would be overstating matters. But he had led them to many victories and a considerable amount of booty over the years, so now three of them started towards Halt, their hands dropping to their sword hilts.

Seeing the movement, Horace spurred Kicker forward to come between them and the grey-cloaked archer. There was a ringing hiss of steel on leather as his sword came free of the scabbard, catching the early afternoon sun on its blade as it did so. The soldiers hesitated. They knew of Horace's reputation and none of them fancied himself swordsman enough to contest matters with the younger man. Their normal battleground was the confusion of a pitched battle, not the cold, calculating atmosphere of a duelling ground such as this.

'Get the horse,' Halt called to Horace. The apprentice glanced round in surprise. Halt hadn't moved. He stood, feet slightly apart, side on to the approaching soldiers. Once again, an arrow was nocked to his bowstring, although the bow remained lowered.

'What?' Horace asked, puzzled, and the Ranger jerked his head at the warlord's battlehorse, shifting its weight from foot to foot, tossing its head uncertainly.

'The horse. It's mine now. Get it for me,' Halt repeated, and Horace trotted Kicker slowly to a point where he could lean down and gather the black horse's reins. He had to re-sheath his sword to do so and he glanced warily at the three soldiers — and the dozen others who stood behind them, as yet uncommitted one way or the other.

'Captain of the guard!' Halt called. 'Where are you?'

A stockily built man in half armour took a pace forward from the larger group of warriors. Halt looked at him a moment, then called again:

'Your name?'

The captain hesitated. In the normal course of events, he knew, the victor of such a combat would simply demand a continuation of the status quo, and life at Montsombre would go on, relatively unchanged. But the captain also knew that, often as not, a new commander could choose to demote or even eliminate the ranking officers from the previous regime. He was wary of the bow in the stranger's hands. But he saw no point in not making himself known. The others would be quick to isolate him if it meant possible advancement for them. He came to a decision.

'Philemon, my lord,' he said. Halt's eyes bored into him and there was a long, uncomfortable, silence.

'Step over here, Philemon,' Halt said finally and, replacing the arrow in his quiver, he slung the longbow over his left shoulder. That gesture was encouraging for the captain, although he had no doubt that, if Halt wished, he could unsling the bow and have several arrows on the way in less time than he, Philemon, could blink. Cautiously, every nerve end tingling with anticipation, he moved closer to the small man. When he was within easy talking distance, Halt spoke.

'I have no wish to stay here any longer than I need,' he said quietly. 'In a month, the passes into Teutlandt and Skandia will be open and my companion and I will be on our way.'

He paused and Philemon frowned, trying to understand what he was being told.

'You want us to come with you?' he asked, at last. 'You expect us to follow you?'

Halt shook his head. 'I have no wish to ever see any of you again,' he said flatly. 'I want nothing of this castle, nothing of its people. I will take Deparnieux's battlehorse, because I am entitled to it as the victor in this combat. As for the rest, you're welcome to it: castle, furnishings, booty, food, the lot. If you can keep it from your friends, it's yours.'

Philemon shook his head in disbelief. This was phenomenal luck! The stranger was moving on, and handing over the castle, lock, stock and barrel, to him — a mere captain of the guard. He whistled softly to himself. He would replace Deparnieux as the controller of this region. He would be a lord, with a castle, and men at arms and servants to do his bidding!

'Two things,' Halt interrupted his thoughts. 'You'll release those people in the cages immediately. As for the rest of the castle servants and slaves, I'll give them their choice of whether they stay or go. I'll not bind them to you in any way.'

The captain's heavy brows darkened at the statement. He opened his mouth to protest, then hesitated as he saw the look in Halt's eyes. It was cold, determined and utterly without pity.

'To you or your successor,' he amended. 'The choice is yours. Argue about it and I'll put the choice to whoever replaces you after I kill you.'

And as he heard the words, Philemon realised that Halt would have no hesitation in carrying out the threat. Either he or the muscular young swordsman on the battlehorse would have no trouble taking care of him.

He weighed the alternatives: jewels, gold, a well-stocked castle, a force of armed men who would follow him because he would have the wherewithal to pay them, and a possible lack of servants.

Or death, here and now.

'I accept,' he said.

After all, Philemon realised, most of the servants and slaves would have nowhere to go. The chances were good that the majority would choose to stay on at Chateau Montsombre, trusting to a weary fatalism that things couldn't really be much worse and they might just possibly be a little better.

Halt nodded slowly. 'I rather thought you would.'

Thirty-seven

Evanlyn was concentrating hard. The tip of her tongue protruded through her teeth and there was a small frown on her face as she began to trim the piece of soft leather to the correct shape.

She couldn't afford to make mistakes, she knew. She had found the piece of leather in the stable lean-to and there was only just enough for the purpose she had in mind. It was soft, supple and thin. There were other odds and ends of harness and tack in the shed but they were dried out and stiff. This was the piece she needed.

Evanlyn was making a sling.

She had finally given up trying to learn any skill with the bow. By the time she could hit the side of a barn, she thought, she and Will would have been long dead from hunger. She sighed. Being brought up as a princess had definite disadvantages. She could do fine needlework and embroidery, judge good wine and host a dinner party for a dozen nobles and their wives. She could organise servants and sit for hours, straight-backed and apparently attentive, through the most boring official ceremonies.

All valuable skills in their right place, but none of them were much use to her in her present situation. She wished she had spent a few hours learning even the rudiments of archery. The bow, she admitted ruefully, was beyond her.

But a sling! That was a different matter. As a little girl she and her two male cousins had made slings and wandered through the woods outside Castle Araluen, hurling stones at random targets. She recalled that she had been pretty good, too.

On her tenth birthday, to her intense fury, her father had decided that it was time for his daughter to stop being a tomboy and to begin to learn the ways of a lady. The wandering and slinging ceased. The embroidering and hostessing began.

Still, she thought, she could probably remember enough of the technique to serve her now, with a little practice.

She smiled a little, remembering those privileged days at Castle Araluen. They were a far cry from all this. These days, she had new skills, she thought wryly. She could drag a pony through thigh-deep snow, sleep rough, bathe a lot less frequently than polite society might think appropriate and, with any luck, even kill, clean and cook her own food.

That is, of course, if she could get the damn sling right. She shaped the soft leather patch around a large round stone, wrapping the stone in it and pulling the soft leather tight to create a pouch. She wrapped and released over and over again, forcing the shape of the rock into the leather. Her hands were starting to ache with the effort and she seemed to recall that, as a child, servants had done this part for her.

'I'm not really much use, am I?' she said to herself.

In fact, she was selling herself short. Her reserves of courage, determination and loyalty were vast, as was her ingenuity.

Unlike someone raised to these conditions, she might not always find the best way to solve their problems. But somehow, she would find *a* way. She would never give in. And it was that strength of purpose and ability to adapt that would make her a great ruler, if she were ever to make her way back to Araluen.

She heard a noise behind her and turned. Her heart sank as she saw Will standing close to her. His eyes were empty, his expression blank. For one awful moment, she thought he was looking for another dose of warmweed and she felt a real surge of fear. It had been two weeks since his last dose of the drug. When she had given him that, the packet was left virtually empty. She had no idea what would happen the next time the need clawed at him.

Each day, she lived with the constant dread that he would ask for more, mixed with a desperate growing hope that perhaps he was cured of the addiction. Since the day he had unstrung the bow, she had looked for some further sign of awareness or memory from him. But in vain.

He pointed to the water jug on the bench and she heaved a sigh of relief. She poured him a mug of water and he shambled away, his mind still locked in that faraway place only addicts know. Not cured, she thought, but at least the moment she was dreading had been postponed a little longer.

Her eyes blurred with tears. She dashed them away and turned back to her work. Earlier, she had cut two long thongs from the saddle pack, and now she attached one to either side of the pouch. She placed the stone in the pouch and swung the sling experimentally. It had been a long time, but it felt vaguely familiar. The weight of the rock felt comfortable and it nestled securely in the pouch. She glanced across at Will. He was huddled against the wall of the cabin, his eyes closed, lost to the world. He'd stay like that for hours, she knew.

'No point wasting any more time,' she said to herself, then called to Will, 'I'm going hunting, Will. I'll be a while.'

She collected a supply of pebbles and set out. Her previous attempts with the bow had taught her that the local wildlife tended to give the cabin a wide berth now that it was inhabited. Bitter experience in the past, she thought. It was certainly nothing to do with her attempts at hunting.

As she went, she took the opportunity to practise her technique, loading a rock into the sling, whirling it round her head till it made a dull droning sound, then releasing to cast at nearby tree trunks.

At first, the results were less than encouraging. The velocity was fine but the accuracy was sadly lacking. But as she continued to practise, her old skill began to return. More and more often, the stones she flung slammed into their targets.

She did even better when she loaded two stones into the sling, doubling her chances of a hit. Eventually, satisfied that she was ready, she set out, heading for a clearing by a stream, where she had seen rabbits feeding and sunning themselves on the warm rocks.

She was in luck. A large buck rabbit was sitting on the rocks, eyes closed, ears and nose twitching as he basked in the sunlight and the heat of the sun-warmed rock beneath it.

She felt a thrill of satisfaction as she loaded two of the larger stones into the sling and began to whirl it above her head. The dull, droning sound built as the sling gathered speed and the rabbit's eyes came open as he heard it. But he sensed no danger in the sound and remained where he was. Evanlyn saw his eyes open and resisted the temptation to cast instantly. She let the sling whip around two or three more times, then released, following through with a full arm cast, straight at her target.

Perhaps it was beginner's luck, but both stones hit the rabbit with the full force of the whirling sling behind them. The larger of the two broke its right hind leg, so that when it tried to flee, it flopped awkwardly over in the snow. Evanlyn, with a surge of fierce triumph, was across the clearing, grabbing the struggling animal and wringing its neck to put it out of its misery.

The fresh meat would be a welcome addition to their meagre diet. Flushed with success, she decided she might as well try another hunting spot and see if her luck held. Two rabbits would definitely be better than one.

She moved cautiously, and the soft snow underfoot aided her stealthy progress. As she drew closer to the next clearing, she began to walk with greater care, setting her feet carefully and making sure that, as she held tree branches aside to pass by, she allowed them to return to their initial position noiselessly.

In all likelihood, it was this extreme caution that saved her life.

She was about to step clear of the trees when some sixth sense made her hesitate. Something wasn't right. She had heard something, or felt something, that was out of place here. She hung back, staying in the shadows inside the tree-line and waiting to see if she could identify the cause of her unease. Then she heard it again, and this time she recognised it. The soft fall of a horse's hooves on the thick snow that still blanketed the ground.

Mouth dry, heart suddenly pounding, Evanlyn froze in place. She remembered Will's instructions on Skorghijl.

She was still well concealed from anyone or anything in the clearing. The pines grew thickly and the midmorning sunshine cast deep shadows between the trees. Her hair had risen on the back of her neck as she stood, motionless. Her eyes darted this way and that, straining to see through the alternating patches of bright, sunlit snow and deep shadow. Now she heard the soft, snuffling snort of a horse breathing and she knew she hadn't been mistaken. Across the clearing, a cloud of steam hung on the air and, as she watched, she saw the horse and its rider emerge from the deep shadows behind it.

For one brief moment, she felt a surge of joy as she thought the horse was Will's Ranger horse, Tug. Small, sturdy and shaggy in the coat, it was barely more than a pony in size. As she saw him, she nearly stepped forward into the sunlight but then, just in time, she stopped, as she saw the rider.

He was dressed in furs, with a flat-topped fur hat on his head and a bow slung over his shoulder. She could make out his face quite clearly: brown, weatherbeaten skin and high, prominent cheekbones, which made the eyes appear as little more than slits above them. He was small and stocky, she realised, like his horse, and something about him spelt danger. His head turned as he looked at the trees on his right and Evanlyn took the opportunity to shrink further back into the cover of the forest. Satisfied that there was nobody watching, the rider urged his horse forward a few paces, into the centre of the clearing.

He paused there, and his eyes seemed to pierce through the shadows to where the girl stood, concealed behind the rough-barked bole of a large pine. For a few breathless seconds, she thought he had seen her. But then he touched the horse's flank with the heel of one of his fur-trimmed boots and wheeled him to the right, trotting quickly out of the clearing and into the trees. In a moment, he was lost to her sight, the only sign of his presence the clouds of steam left hanging on the freezing air by the horse's warm breath.

For several minutes, Evanlyn stayed huddled against the pine tree, fearing that the rider might suddenly turn and backtrack. Then, long after the soft thud of his horse's hoofbeats on the snow had died away, she turned and began to run back through the forest towards the cabin.

Will had been sleeping.

He woke slowly, consciousness gradually filtering through to him as he became aware that he was sitting on a hard wood floor. His eyes opened and he frowned at the unfamiliar surroundings. He was in a small cabin, where the bright sunlight of late winter struck through an unglazed window and formed an elongated square on the floor, wider at its base than at the top.

Groggily, still half asleep, he stood, realising that for some reason he had been sleeping while sitting on the floor, his back against one of the walls. He wondered why he had chosen such a spot, when he could see that the cabin contained one rough bunk and two chairs. As he came slowly to his feet, something fell clattering from his lap to the floor. He looked down and saw a small hunting bow lying there. Curious, he picked it up, studying it. It was a low-powered affair, without any recurve, and without the long, heavy limbs of a proper longbow. Useful for small game, he thought vaguely, and precious little else. He wondered where his own recurve bow had got to. He couldn't remember having ever owned this toy.

Then he remembered. His bow had been lost, taken from him by the Skandians at the bridge. And as that memory came back, so did others: the flight through the swamps and marshes of the fenlands as a prisoner of the Skandians; the voyage across the Stormwhite Sea on Erak's wolfship; the harbour at Skorghijl, where they had sheltered through the worst of the storm season; and then the trip onwards to Hallasholm.

And then ... And then, nothing.

He racked his brain, trying to find some memory of events after they had reached the Skandian capital. But there was no memory there. Nothing but a blank wall that defied all his efforts to pierce it.

A jolt of fear hit him. Evanlyn! What had become of

her? He remembered, as if through a fog, that there was some great danger hanging over her. Her identity must never be revealed to their captors. Had they actually reached Hallasholm? He was sure that, if they had, he would remember. But where was the green-eyed blonde girl who had come to mean so much to him? Had he inadvertently betrayed her? Had the Skandians killed her?

A Vallasvow! He remembered it now. Ragnak, Oberjarl of the Skandians, had sworn a vow of vengeance on every member of the Araluan royal family. And Evanlyn was, in reality, Cassandra, princess of the realm. In an agony of uncertainty and lost memory, Will pounded the heels of his fists into his forehead, trying to remember, trying to reassure himself that Evanlyn had not suffered because he had somehow failed her.

And then, even as he thought about her, the door of the cabin slammed back on its crude leather hinges and she was there, framed against the bright sunlight reflecting from the snow outside and as breathtakingly beautiful as he knew he would always remember her to be, no matter how long he lived nor how old they might both become.

He moved towards her now, a smile of utter relief breaking out across his features, holding out his hands to her as she stood, wordless, staring at him as if he were some kind of a ghost.

'Evanlyn!' he said. 'Thank god you're safe!'

And, saying it, he wondered why her eyes had filled, and why her shoulders were shaking as tear after tear spilled uncontrollably down her cheeks.

After all, he couldn't really see that there was anything to cry about.

Epilogue

alt and Horace rode carefully down the winding path
that led from Chateau Montsombre. Neither of
them spoke, but both felt the same intense satisfaction.
They were on their way again. The worst of winter was
over and, by the time they reached the border, the passes
into Skandia would be open.

Horace glanced back once at the grim building where
they had been trapped for so many weeks. Then he shaded
his eyes to look more carefully.

'Halt,' he said, 'look at that.'

Halt eased Abelard to a stop and swivelled around.
There was a thin banner of grey smoke rising from the
castle keep, and as they watched, it thickened and turned
black. Dimly, they could hear the shouts of Philemon's
men as they ran to fight the fire.

'Looks to me,' said Halt judiciously, 'as if some careless
person left a torch burning in a pile of oily rags in the
basement store room.'

Horace grinned at him. 'You can tell all that just by looking, can you?'

Halt nodded, keeping a deadpan expression.

'We Rangers are gifted with uncanny powers of perception,' he replied. 'And I think Gallica will be better off without that particular castle, don't you?'

Only the warlord had actually lived in the keep. The soldiers and domestic staff lived in other parts of the building and they would have plenty of time to stop the fire spreading that far. But the keep, the central tower that had been Deparnieux's headquarters, was doomed. And that was as it should be. Montsombre had been the site of too much cruelty and horror over the years, and Halt had no intention of leaving it unscathed, so that Philemon could continue the ways of his old master.

'Of course, the stone walls won't burn,' said Horace, with a tinge of disappointment.

'No,' Halt agreed. 'But the timber floors and their support beams will. And all the ceilings and stairways will burn and collapse. And the heat will damage the walls as well. Shouldn't be surprised if some of them just collapse.'

'Good,' said Horace, and there was a world of satisfaction in the single word.

Together, they turned their backs on the memory of Deparnieux. They urged their horses forward and the little cavalcade moved off, Tug following close behind the two riders.

'Let's go and find Will,' said Halt.

READ ON FOR A PREVIEW OF BOOK 4

One

It was a constant tapping sound that roused Will from his deep, untroubled sleep.

He had no clear idea at what point he first became aware of it. It seemed to slide unobtrusively into his sleeping mind, magnified and amplified inside his subconscious, until it crossed over into the conscious world and he realised he was awake, and wondering what it might be.

Tap-tap-tap-tap . . .

It was still there, but not so loud now that he was awake and aware of other sounds in the small cabin.

From the corner, behind a small curtain of sacking that gave her a modicum of privacy, he could hear Evanlyn's even breathing. Obviously, the tapping hadn't woken her. There was a muted crackle from the heaped coals in the fireplace at the end of the room and, as he became more fully awake, he heard them settle with a slight rustling sound.

Tap-tap-tap . . .

It seemed to come from close to him. He stretched and yawned, sitting up on the rough couch he'd fashioned from wood and canvas. He shook his head to clear it and, for a moment, the sound was obscured. Then it was back once more and he realised it was coming from outside the window. The oiled cloth panes were translucent — they would admit the grey light of the pre-dawn, but he couldn't see anything more than a blur though them. He knelt on the couch and unlatched the frame, pushing it up and craning his head through the opening to study the small porch of the cabin.

A gust of chill air entered the room and he heard Evanlyn stir as it eddied around, causing the sacking curtain to billow inwards and the embers in the fireplace to glow more fiercely, until a small tongue of yellow flame was released from them.

Somewhere in the trees, a bird was greeting the first light of a new day, and the tapping sound was obscured once more.

Then he had it. It was water, dripping from the end of a long icicle that depended from the porch roof, and falling onto an upturned bucket that had been left on the edge of the porch.

Tap-tap-tap . . . tap-tap-tap.

Will frowned to himself. There was something significant in this, he knew, but his mind, still fuddled with sleep, couldn't quite grasp what it was. He stood, still stretching, and shivered slightly as he left the last warmth of his blanket and made his way to the door.

Hoping not to wake Evanlyn, he eased the latch upwards and slowly opened the door, holding it up so that the sagging leather hinges wouldn't allow the bottom edge to scrape the floor of the cabin.

Closing the door behind him, he stepped out onto the rough boards of the porch, feeling them strike icy cold against his bare feet. He moved to the spot where the water dripped endlessly onto the bucket, realising as he went that other icicles hanging from the roof were dripping water also. He hadn't seen this before. He was sure they usually didn't do this.

He glanced out at the trees, where the first rays of the sun were beginning to filter through.

In the forest, there was a slithering thump as a load of snow finally slid clear of the pine branches that had supported it for months and fell in a heap to the ground below.

And it was then that he realised the significance of the endless tap-tap-tap that had woken him.

Behind him, he heard the door creak and he turned to see Evanlyn, her hair wildly tousled, her blanket wrapped tight around her against the cold.

'What is it?' she asked him. 'Is something wrong?'

He hesitated a second, glancing at the growing puddle of water beside the bucket.

'It's the thaw,' he said finally.

After their meagre breakfast, they sat in the early morning sun as it streamed across the porch. Neither of them had wanted to discuss the significance of Will's earlier discovery, although they had since found more signs of the thaw.

There were small patches of soaked brown grass showing through the snow cover on the ground surrounding the cabin and the sound of wet snow sliding from the trees to hit the ground was becoming increasingly common.

The snow was still thick on the ground and in the trees, of course. But the signs were there that the thaw had begun and that, inexorably, it would continue.

'I suppose we'll have to think about moving on,' Will said finally, voicing the thought that had been in both their minds.

'You're not strong enough yet,' Evanlyn told him. It had been barely three weeks since he had thrown off the mind-numbing effects of the warmweed given to him as a yard slave in Ragnak's Lodge. Will had been weakened by inadequate food and clothing and a regimen of punishing physical work before they had made their escape. Since then, their meagre diet in the cabin had been enough to sustain life, but not to restore his strength or endurance. They had lived on the cornmeal and flour that had been stored in the cabin, along with a small stock of vegetables and the stringy meat from whatever game Evanlyn and he had been able to snare.

There was little enough of that in winter, and what game they had managed to catch had been in poor condition itself, providing little in the way of nourishment.

Will shrugged. 'I'll manage,' he said simply. 'I'll have to.'

And that, of course, was the heart of the problem. They both knew that once the snow in the high passes had melted, hunters would again begin to visit the high country where they found themselves. Already, Evanlyn had seen one such — the mysterious rider in the forest on the day when Will's senses had returned to him. Fortunately, since that day, there had been no further sign of him. But it was a warning. Others would come and, before they did, Will and Evanlyn would have to be long gone, heading down the far side of the mountain passes and across the border into Teutlandt.

Evanlyn shook her head doubtfully. For a moment, she said nothing. Then she realised that Will was right. Once the thaw was well and truly under way, they would have to leave whether she felt he was strong enough to travel or not.

'Anyway,' she said, at length, 'we have a few weeks yet. The thaw's only just started and who knows? We may even get another cold snap.'

It was possible, she thought. Perhaps not probable, but at least it was possible. Will nodded agreement.

'There's always that,' he said.

The silence fell over them once more like a blanket. Abruptly, Evanlyn stood, dusting off her breeches. 'I'll go and check the snares,' she said and when Will began to rise to accompany her, she stopped him.

'You stay here,' she said gently. 'From now on, you're going to have to conserve your strength as much as possible.'

Will hesitated, then nodded. He recognised that she was right.

She collected the hessian sack they used as a game bag and slung it over her shoulder. Then, with a small smile in his direction, the girl headed off into the trees.

Feeling useless and dispirited, Will slowly began to gather up the wooden platters they had used for their meal. All he was good for, he thought bitterly, was washing up.

The snare line had moved further and further from the cabin over the past three weeks. As small animals, rabbits, squirrels and the occasional snow hare had fallen prey to the snares that Will had built, so the other animals in that area had become more wary. As a consequence, they had been compelled to move the snares into new locations every few days — each one a little further away from the cabin than the one before.

Evanlyn estimated that she had a good forty minutes' walking on the narrow uphill track before she would reach the first snare. Of course, if she'd been able to move straight to it, the walk would have been considerably shorter. But the track wound and wandered through the trees, more than doubling the distance she had to cover.

The signs of the thaw were all around her, now that she was aware of it. The snow no longer squeaked dryly underfoot as she walked. It was heavier, wetter and her steps sank deeply into it. The leather of her boots was already soaked from contact with the melting snow. The last time she had walked this way, she reflected, the snow had simply coated her boots as a fine, dry powder.

She also began to notice more activity among the wildlife in the area. Birds flitted through the trees in greater numbers than she'd previously seen, and she startled a rabbit on the track, sending it scurrying back into the protection of a snow-covered thicket of blackberries.

At least, she thought, all this extra activity might

increase the chances of finding some worthwhile game in the snares.

She saw the discreet sign that Will had cut into the bark of a pine and turned off the track to find the spot where she and Will had laid the first of the snares. She recalled how gratefully she had greeted his recovery from the warmweed drug. Her own survival skills were negligible and Will had provided welcome expertise in devising and setting snares to supplement their diet. It was all part of his training under Halt, he had told her.

She remembered now how, when he had mentioned the older Ranger's name, his eyes had misted for a few moments and his voice had choked slightly. Not for the first time, the two young people felt very, very far from home.

As she pushed her way through the snow-laden bushes, becoming wetter and wetter in the process, she felt a surge of pleasure. The first snare in the line held the body of a small ground-foraging bird. They had caught a few of these previously and she knew the bird's flesh made excellent eating. About the size of a small chicken, it had carelessly poked its neck through the wire noose of the snare, then become entangled. Evanlyn smiled grimly as she thought how once she might have objected to the cruelty of the bird's death. Now, all she felt was a sense of satisfaction as she realised that they would eat well today.

Amazing how an empty belly could change your perspective, she thought, removing the noose from the bird's neck and stuffing the small carcass in her makeshift game bag. She reset the snare, sprinkling a few seeds of corn on the ground beyond it, then rose to her feet, frowning in annoyance as she realised that the melting snow had left two wet patches on her knees as she'd crouched.

She sensed, rather than heard, the movement in the trees behind her and began to turn.

Before she could move, she felt an iron grip around her throat, and, as she gasped in fright, a fur-gloved hand, smelling vilely of smoke, sweat and dirt, clapped over her mouth and nose, cutting off her cry for help.

ABOUT THE AUTHOR

John Flanagan's Ranger's Apprentice and Brotherband adventure series have sold more than eight million copies worldwide. His books are available in more than one hundred countries, are regularly on the *New York Times* bestseller list, and have had multiple award shortlistings and wins in Australia and overseas. John, a former television and advertising writer, lives with his wife in a Sydney beachside suburb. He is currently writing more Brotherband books and several prequels to the Ranger's Apprentice series.

A SPECIAL Q & A WITH JOHN FLANAGAN:

Are there parallels with everyday life or do you deliberately choose to make a new imaginary world? For example; wars in The Burning Bridge *— could the Skandian mercenaries be associated with Viking raids?*

I've intentionally created an imaginary world, but physically, it's pretty much parallel to the real one. In terms of history, it's vastly different. I didn't want to be constrained by real historical events or even the geo-political situation in medieval Europe. I didn't see a parallel between the Skandian mercenaries in Book 2 and Viking raids on England. I simply needed a force of 'enemies' who weren't as black-hearted or as evil as Morgarath and his inhuman Wargal soldiers. The Skandians were a convenient answer.

Do you see yourself as strictly a fantasy writer, or do you feel that you could branch out easily into something quite different, like non-fiction?

I'm not interested in writing non-fiction. I see myself as a fiction writer. But I'm not exclusively a fantasy writer. I've had two adult crime/action novels published in Australia and the United States.

Do you remember the moment that Will Treaty was formed in your mind? Was he different to how he eventually appeared on the page?

I wish I could say yes. But the answer is no. These things develop over a long period. He was modelled on Michael, my son. Originally, he had blonde hair, as Michael had when he was fifteen. But the model we chose for the cover photo was dark haired, so I changed that.

Do you have any tips for readers who would like to become writers?

When you have an idea for story, don't just jump in and start writing. Plan it completely. Know where it goes and how it ends. Keep the plan beside you as you write.

Is your office tidy?

I regret to tell you it's an absolute shambles. Paper everywhere, torn out crossword puzzles from the daily paper (I'm trying to do cryptics again), guitars on stands in all directions. I also have a very untidy shelf unit covered in sound gear, microphones, my eight-track recorder, guitar paraphernalia and two guitar amplifiers. From time to time, I find contracts on my desk that I should have signed and returned. I always tell my agent that I did sign them and he must have lost them. I think he's beginning to doubt my word . . . I have an in-tray and an out-tray but I haven't looked to see what's in them for some weeks.